STUCK

BEN YOUNG

For Lauren,
because without you,
I would have no voice

PARTONE

No Return

From: *Passing Through, Thoughts on Death and Dying* by Lucille Claremont, RN (p. 4).

"Several Weeks Prior to Death":

The first physical signs tend to be gradual, beginning around one to two weeks before clinical death. These changes are systemic and affect several of the body's natural functions, which become less necessary.

The respiratory and circulatory systems experience erratic changes in rhythm and efficiency, presenting as altered breathing patterns, coughing, and disruptions in circulation, particularly in the extremities. Initial changes are subtle, often difficult for the untrained observer to perceive.

These symptoms are unpredictable, coming and going rapidly. However, once they have presented as described above, it is a certainty that permanent failure of the vital organs is approaching.

CHAPTER ONE

On the worst day of his life so far, John Camden was both fired from his job writing parking tickets and started dying. He noticed one of these occurrences. A single, dry cough escaped his throat as he walked out of his now ex-manager's office. That's how death began patiently tapping him on the shoulder.

John stomped toward the exit of the Hallstown University Parking Authority, the echoes of his footfalls making the building appear more empty than it should for the time of day. At the door, he dodged a short line of people clutching yellow envelopes, clipping past someone as they entered from outside, seeing no faces. He only wanted to talk to one person. Everyone else was a blur.

Outside, John approached a parked car and opened the passenger side door. Sat. Left the door open. He glimpsed his own face reflected in the window. At twenty-six, his hairline was already receding, the closest brown strands to his brow farther back than they had been a few months ago. His green eyes, shadowed with the ghost of young ambition, set atop sleep bags the color of a late sunset crescendo.

"I got fired," he said to his friend Robbie. A statement of guilt, like he expected admonishment. Like he was Robbie's screw-up younger brother, though they were just two weeks apart in age. Usually, John was comfortable with this, it brought relief from the pressures of others' expectations of him. Now it made him sheepish.

"You what?" Robbie asked.

John regarded him in the rear-view mirror. In contrast to his own, Robbie's hair was not fading at all. There were no bags under his eyes, their color an intriguing mix of brown flecked in silver-blue. Within those eyes, Robbie's ambition was alive and well.

"Fired. I got fired," John said, again fawning at his thin reflection. He noticed a smudge from his fingerprint on the outside of the passenger window. It was the only sign of imperfection in Robbie's car, which he kept pristine. Hospital-clean. Expensive. He wanted it to look the part, always, especially on the outside.

John got out of the car and stood next to it, wiping the smudge away with his shirtsleeve. He wanted to avoid Robbie's face, which was a stark difference from their usual dynamic. He wasn't often uncomfortable talking to Robbie, except when admitting failure. Dirtying his car was compounding that effect. It made talking to Robbie much more like talking to everyone else. Robbie was a singular presence in John's life, the only person John expected to be comfortable around. That dynamic had formed within minutes of their meeting, and it was something John had yet to find with anyone else.

"What the hell for?" Robbie asked.

John sat down; the window wiped clean. Mostly. He pulled the door closed, using only his pinky finger this time.

He wished for his own car back, which was stolen a few days ago. John's confidence lessened every time he had to accept help from Robbie, rides home from work included. With his income cut off, he expected more of this. He settled into the seat.

"That's the best part," John said, avoiding Robbie's eyes by examining the floor of the car. "I don't even know. I don't get it."

"Well, what did that asshole say?" Robbie put on the turn signal.

"Some generic crap about ongoing problems with my performance. I think you were right, that new director had it out for me since she started. She thinks I don't issue enough."

"So, it's about a fucking quota."

John thought this streak of colorful language was out of vindication, not anger. Robbie was enthusiastic by nature, but could be calm and reassuring at the same time. John saw these as traits he lacked himself and had grown used to seeking them from Robbie. His sheepishness lifted.

"Yeah, I think it is." John clicked his seatbelt as Robbie pulled into traffic.

"And you're too nice for their quota."

"You think?"

They both laughed, John's colored with a slight nervousness balanced by Robbie's deeper, slower tone. John's fingers were suddenly cold. He reached to turn down the car's air conditioner, but it wasn't on.

"This is good," Robbie said, turning the car at an intersection.

"How do you figure that?"

"Because it's forced change. It'll shake things up."

Robbie's headstrong positivity fueled John. He reached over, patted Robbie on the shoulder, and said, "Thanks."

"It's going to work out, you'll see."

John wasn't surprised by this reaction from Robbie. For one, Robbie wasn't the type to worry. Plus, he had urged John on several occasions to make changes in his life, saying that things shouldn't always be comfortable, and it was time to move on. John liked that job, though. Liked knowing what to expect every day. Lately, Robbie kept asserting that nothing significant had happened to John for years. John wasn't quite sure where that was coming from, but it was getting frustrating. And he didn't like being frustrated with Robbie. He needed him too much.

But Robbie wasn't wrong. John knew he was stagnating. Reflecting on Robbie's words, his mind wandered to the first time Robbie had mentioned "shaking things up," around the time they had first met.

They had known each other since childhood, same hometown and elementary school, but hadn't become friends until about four years ago. Robbie got a job at the university not long after John, and they bonded right away, starting with shop talk but uncovering common interests quickly. Not surface things. They had found real common ground, personality dimensions often kept deep below. They shared a goofy-wicked sense of humor, for one, often joking about what kind of noises you can make to startle people in the grocery store line (they never followed through on this), or how to convince Henry Rollins to run for president. Such topics would lead to lengthy, passionate debates that usually ended when the one on the losing end pulled in a stranger for backup and then they were both forced to be polite.

It helped that they were both enrolled for their second year at the time, both having moved a few hours from home after high school to stretch. Neither knew anyone in Hallstown, what to study, or where they were going in the grand scope. Robbie handled all this uncertainty much better than John did, however.

John would fret over homework and follow a self-imposed curfew before big tests, while Robbie played video games until the sun rose. John saved his money and paid his bills a few days early, but Robbie somehow appeared to have both more fun and more cash.

Sometimes, Robbie was all but addicted to chaos; often his impulses bore sweet fruit. John got jealous at times, though Robbie was aware and careful not to twist that particular knife.

"I don't want you to take this the wrong way," Robbie said, breaking the brief silence, "but you know when I quit that place, it was about the best decision I ever made."

"Yeah, I get that. But I'm not you, you know?"

Robbie seemed not to hear this. "Shaking things up. Sometimes it's just what you need."

Robbie never had the discipline for school. He stopped attending within a few months of them working together, showing no regard for the costs, then delivered his less-than-formal resignation to the HUPA, in the form of a lump of his own feces stuffed inside a citation envelope and placed under the wiper of the basketball coach's roadster. When John asked what he had against the coach, Robbie had replied, *I didn't know whose car it was, but the fucker parked in a fire lane.*

"I keep telling you because you can learn from it," Robbie said now. "I got out of that shit job and that shit school. Look what happened."

John knew the story well and wasn't pleased to be reminded today. He sensed Robbie's good intentions, but was too vulnerable. Robbie started his own business and never looked back. At least, that was his version. John's version was that he had tripped moving backwards and fell ass-first into that great cosmic cruising lane. John was happy for him, but never expected his own luck to match.

"Robbie, you sell energy drinks to gas stations," John said. He meant this to sound jovial, a good-natured jab to lighten the mood. It didn't. It came out like a cheap shot.

John's fingers were now turning blue, and there was a cold sweat clinging to his palms and forehead. The act of talking about leaving his perpetual comfort was enough to make him uncomfortable. And this uncharacteristic defensiveness and vulnerability with Robbie wasn't helping. John sensed himself acting that way, but was struggling to control it.

"Pays the bills, doesn't it?" Robbie patted the pristine leather steering wheel of his pristine silver Alfa Romeo. He gave no indication that John's barb had landed. "All I'm saying is that you need to take risks, man. You can't be safe and comfortable and bored your whole life. Who wants that?"

"I do," John said. "I do."

"I know you do," Robbie said in a neutral tone.

Getting fired from that job was like losing his favorite threadbare T-shirt. John needed the structure; he needed the purpose. Such as they were. John liked his rut. He hoped to change the subject.

Robbie made a different decision and pressed it further. "You think you do, but you'll find out different someday."

"Tell that to Scott, dude."

John's younger brother had been the risk-taker of their splintered family, and it earned him a lonely demise. He had died in a cave-in while working as a coal miner somewhere in West Virginia. "You talk to him about 'shaking things up.' I'd rather stay put." His voice was rising, which deterred Robbie now, as it tended to.

"Hey, okay. Just trying to spin this."

"I know what you're 'trying to.'"

"Look, I'm sorry you got fired. I am."

"Thanks for the ride, Robbie."

The conversation ended there, to John's relief.

Soon the car stopped in front of John's building. As John opened the door, he noticed a couple walking on the sidewalk, a young girl between them, each holding her hand. She was jumping, and with each jump they pulled up, holding her in the air for a few seconds, laughing. As if triggered by that scene, a tightening sensation dropped onto him like thick, form-fitting ice. His joints locked in unison. He couldn't move his arms or legs. Tried to turn his head and failed. He toppled back into the seat, all seized up like one giant knot, his muscles coarse as rope. He lay sideways, trying to scream, breathing rapidly but otherwise paralyzed.

Robbie was saying something, but he couldn't hear, saw his mouth moving in the periphery. Then John's eyes failed, as his muscles had already. He saw only a gray curtain.

And he couldn't move at all. His heart was racing and his lungs fought to take in long, whooping swallows of air without getting enough. A cold settled into his limbs like the ambient moisture around him had flash-frozen.

Then it ended.

His vision seeped back through the gray. Numbness trickled out of his arms and legs, they relaxed. It lasted a few seconds, but seemed far longer.

He found his control returning and screamed, a harsh and truncated sound. His breathing evened out.

"Hey," Robbie said, "you okay?"

"Wha—" John found breath, but no words.

"What just happened?"

"I... I d-don't know."

"Looked like you were hyperventilating. What was that?"

"Felt," John panted, out of breath, "like I was trapped." It was the best word he had.

"Trapped? What does that mean?"

"I mean, that's what it was like. I couldn't move." His heart was still beating fast but slowing down, along with his breathing. He coughed a few times and thought about his brother Scott dying alone in a tunnel. *Is that how he felt?* John wondered.

"You sure you're okay?" Robbie asked, putting his hand on John's forearm.

I don't remember answering yes *to that question.* He may have seen a smile play around Robbie's eyes then, but dismissed it. Clearly, his senses were off.

"I'm good." He placed a finger on his wrist to make sure his pulse slowed. He'd experienced nothing like that before. It was a vivid dream, dropped clean out of the sky while awake. It had come over him as broad and undeniable as a sneeze, his whole body seizing up, and then it passed.

"You should lie down. You're probably just tired."

"No, I don't think that's it. At all. I'm fine now."

"So it was like a vision? Weird."

"No, not like that. I mean, I couldn't *see* anything. It wasn't my eyes." Still holding a finger to the pulse in his wrist, John noticed a few beats out of synch before the rhythm returned and slowed.

"Well, it wasn't a few minutes either. Only a few seconds."

"Seemed longer." There was a note of pleading in John's voice. His face was flushed, feverish, but still with that cold sweat. *Please don't let me be getting sick too.*

"No, it was quick. Must have been intense, huh?"

Robbie sounded more interested than concerned, and John pined for someone to console him. Robbie wouldn't do that. It was not in his nature.

"You're telling me," John said, stepping back from the car. His need to be alone grew. He'd had enough trouble for one afternoon. "See you tomorrow, Robbie."

"Yeah, tomorrow."

John closed the door, and Robbie rolled down the window in a hurry, catching John as he turned away.

"Hey. Come over for dinner."

"Tonight?" John noticed that the flop sweat had left, and his fingers weren't cold anymore.

"Yeah, tonight. Mags would be glad to see you."

"Another time," John said, followed by a short fit of wispy coughs. "Been a bad day."

"Nah." Robbie had decided on John's behalf. "I'll pick you up. You'll tell her about the getting fired thing. She'll listen. We'll all eat." A list of instructions. "And you ask her about the whole vision thing—"

"No." John cut him short. "I don't want to tell her. It was nothing. Let's keep that quiet, okay?"

"Sure, whatever. Just trying to help."

"I know what you're 'trying to,' Robbie."

"Well, you're welcome too."

John was silent a few seconds, weary a few after.

"Pick you up around seven," Robbie said.

John coughed the entire way to his door, plying his fingers in and out to warm them as he realized the cold sweat was back, coating his forehead.

Definition of unknown origin:

Odic force: a vital life energy that exists in all manner of flora and fauna, most predominantly in humans, comprising the combined electricity, heat, and magnetism of living things and which at times manifests as a surrounding field or aura.

***

From: *Astral Projection and Tabloid Mentalities, a Pragmatic Interpretation of Paranormal Psychologies* by Dr. Arthur McGuire, PhD (p. 9).

Though the concept of the aura is a household term, a large section of the general population is less familiar with its parent force. This is most often referred to as the Odic force— after the Norse god, Odin—so named by Baron Carl von Reichenbach in the mid-nineteenth century, an era not well known for its levels of enlightenment.

Reichenbach proposed all living things emanated a combination of electricity, heat, and magnetism, which is accurate enough. However, he further claimed this force could have either positive or negative flux and even that sensitive individuals could "see" it surrounding another person, provided certain conditions were present. Those conditions included total darkness, high psychic sensitivity and a character or emotional state strong enough to cause a fluctuation in the Odic force.

To those intensive criteria, this author would add one additional: the convenient absence of an objective third-party observer.

Auras are alleged to exist in various colors corresponding to the mood and/or character of the person projecting them. It is further alleged the shade of these colors can vary, implying different aspects of a certain characteristic, emotion, or personality. For example: red auras are associated with adventurousness when lighter/more pastel, or anger when darker/more opaque. Blue, with intuitiveness in lighter forms or neglectfulness when darker.

To claim living things contain such elemental energies is not inherently radical, but suggesting these energies combine to form something visible to the naked human eye is ludicrous. This is further demonstrated by the adoption of the Odic force, in various iterations, by popular fictional tales from the Star Wars films to the Harry Potter novels, or any number of other stories with elements of magic, hypnotism, or the manifestation of visible auras.

The Odic force is firmly dismissed by all educated members of the scientific community, but remains in use as a ploy for financial gain. For example, a brief internet search will provide an endless list of frauds offering their "aura cleansing services" for a fee to gullible idiots.

Pure lunacy.

I urge anyone considering these types of services to opt instead for a thorough colon cleansing. This medically approved procedure will produce the same results as an aura cleansing. This includes both the figurative and literal output of the procedure.

CHAPTER TWO

I wonder if the handcuffs will be cold? Lucy Claremont thought from behind her brick wall of apathy. It had taken four years to build that wall, and its protection was of some comfort. The driver's door of the police cruiser opened. She knew this from sound, not sight. It had stopped close behind her, all lights pointing, and she didn't have the will to squint enough to filter it to a useful amount.

Her vision swooned, colors mixing in the reflection cast on her windshield.

When I see it happening on a screen, I always imagine them being cold, she thought, listening to the clicks of boot heels as the officer approached. She moved to roll down the window, not noticing it was already down, even though she heard him walking outside.

"Evening, ma'am," the officer said. He stooped over and shone his light into the front seat, then the back.

"Hi," Lucy said.

"Anyone else with you tonight?"

"Nope, it's just me," she said, except it came out more like *shust meh*. She heard the slurring and accepted it. Wall of apathy doing its duty.

"License and registration, please."

She fumbled in the glove compartment, grabbed an envelope, passed it through the open window. Then handed her entire wallet to him, rather than removing her license from it.

"How much you had to drink tonight?" He shifted his attention to her documents. And her whole wallet.

"A few."

I'm probably not measuring the same way you are, though; she left that part out. In the ranks of alcoholics, Lucy had long since graduated to the status of full-bottles-per-sitting.

"Mm-hm." He pointed his light toward her face, studied it a moment, then looked to her driver's license, and back again. At the license one last time.

Now *he recognizes me*. Most of the Hallstown PD still remembered the name Lucy Claremont, even if they hadn't worked on her case. *Let's see how the pity changes his attitude toward protocol.* Even in its liquor-sogged state, her brain was functioning at a higher level than she'd prefer. Or maybe the booze was wearing off. A bad time to come down. Or up, whichever your perspective.

"Do you know why I pulled you over, Mrs. Claremont?"

"Miss. Not married. I could venture a guess." She thought of flirting, knowing if he arrested her, she would face her longest period of sobriety in months. She must look a mess. Hadn't showered in days (or was it weeks?), her clothes filthy, long hair greasy and disheveled as if occupied by birds. She knew the dazed quality of her glassy eyes. There was probably dirt on her face, or food, but she hadn't checked today. Or the day before. Perhaps longer. Mirrors and self-disdain were not friends.

"Let's keep an eye on that tone, ma'am."

Well, maybe this one won't dismiss me because I'm wounded. I might be in trouble this time. Maybe he won't treat me like a victim.

She was too familiar with feeling like a trapped rabbit. It was intolerable, and she craved something to turn her around.

A dead end.

An inescapable decision point. To stop her driving in aimless circles nightly, like a would-be bridge jumper. A coward.

She wasn't capable of forcing this decision upon herself, as she had accepted some time ago. It had to come from somewhere else. Somewhere hard. She needed out. No more unanswered cries.

"I'm sorry, officer."

"We've had reports of a suspicious vehicle driving in circles around the cemetery here." He motioned toward the decorative iron gate a few dozen feet ahead, on the side of the road where her passenger would get out. If she had a passenger.

"Yeah, I guess that's me," she said, preferring his description. Suspicious was better than pitiful.

She checked his face and saw the disapproving look she hoped for. And a little something else? A flicker of blueish light. Probably a trick of the beam coming from the streetlamp behind him.

"Step out, please."

She complied, stumbling as he led her to the front of his cruiser and asked her to place her hands on its hood.

He treated her like every other drunk driver, which was good. And she failed his tests, which was bad. The handcuffs came out. She braced herself in case they were cold.

They weren't. But her surprise was fleeting because a sensation came that outshined the temperature of the metal when it connected with her skin. Almost came, at least.

It had happened one other time she could remember. Long since dismissed and now quite foggy in memory. Ephemeral, even. She remembered *when,* but not *what.* Now, it was only a drop of rain landing at her neck's base, between the first and second vertebrae. Only rain and not that fierce wash of sensation she nearly recalled, faint as a previous night's dream fading by the afternoon. Relief came then, and nothing else.

The officer read her rights, his words clunking past the rim of her awareness, like logs floating downriver in shallow water. She'd prefer a normal hangover like other drunks, but was in line for much worse.

I'm definitely sobering up, she thought, as he ushered her into the backseat. It was a significant problem, but still not worth leaving her brick wall sanctuary to avoid. She cared, but not enough to act. Her lot in life: burdened with emotional responsibility yet devoid of the conviction to act. In jail, she would sober and deal with that until she could drown herself again in another night of mental numbness and emotional sloughing. Wash herself back behind that brick wall, constructed with care and intent.

While they drove to the police station, she caught him sneaking looks into the backseat. Her infamy among the small town's law enforcement was intact, that was clear. She didn't remember this officer being involved with the search for her missing daughter, but that wouldn't stop him from hearing the gossip.

And while she was stealing glances at him stealing glances at her, she caught several more wisps of that blue light floating out around his head. Caught them and refused to acknowledge them. *Trick of the light,* she told herself.

"What's your name?" she asked him, trying to distract from the strange glints of light she was already pretending she didn't see.

"Henderson, ma'am. We'll be there soon. Sit tight for me."

"And you recognize me? My name, at least."

"Well, yes." He failed to hide all his discomfort, but he answered anyway. "Yes, I recognize the name."

Lucy admired his straightforward answers and wondered if it would've been easier had he been around to help find Anna. If he would've been one person to give her the truth, no matter what, as soon as he knew it.

"It's okay. I'm glad you're not trying to pretend otherwise. That's what most people do."

"Ma'am?"

"Pretend they don't recognize me. My grief tends to be hard to watch."

"It's no excuse for driving around a cemetery at night, tripping-over drunk. Is there someone you'd like to call?"

She considered the question as her admiration of him grew. "No. I have no one to call." It was funny in that tragic way that an impartial person would probably label dark humor.

Who am I going to inform of my arrest? Only daughter? An irony. I'm too scared to go visit her, which is part of the reason I'm in handcuffs right now. Ex-husband? Couldn't if I wanted to. Not that I'd want his help. Parents? Both gone too. Family? Just one brother and I don't even know where he lives. Friends? The last one I talked to was at the hospital four years ago. I can't face that again. God? I know he doesn't give a shit. God stopped listening years ago.

The officer drove, and Lucy inched toward dreaded sobriety. She tried to ignore the flecks of blue light emanating from him in the front seat. Another test she had failed, and this one in repetition.

Further back than she cared to consider, she had sensed things she first didn't, then couldn't, now *wouldn't* understand. Since her daughter died, only washing them away in high-octane liquor helped. At one point, while seeking her nursing degree, she had mentioned something about these foreign sensations to a college psychology professor. When she did, fumbling for description, she used a word he had objected to. Strongly.

That word was *aura*. That professor was condescending and furious, and the words he had returned (in repetition) in the loud conversation that followed were *idiot* and *lunacy*. Wounded by his reaction, she never again mentioned it. To anyone.

A traffic light turned red ahead of them and Officer Henderson snuck another look at the damaged thing in his backseat, whose daughter's disappearance and death were the most tragic crime in a small town's recent memory. Which made it akin to the blockbuster movie of the century. All the buzz. The water cooler go-to. The instant classic. She was the center of the gossip universe. Her tragedy would echo without end, perpetuated by people too bored to turn away.

Her story had painted the town on a national map, in her only daughter's blood. And Officer Henderson remembered it.

He may not let it fog his judgment, but he damn sure remembers it.

She longed for a bottle as the cemetery she circled every night grew more distant and her head continued its crawl toward agonizing clarity. Some extra part of her brain, one that shouldn't be there, was climbing out of its cage.

As they approached the police station, Henderson was talking to her, and she wasn't listening. She was watching blue lines dance, and she was fighting off the memories of the few times she'd sensed these things she couldn't name. And the one time she had tried to tell someone else about them.

The car stopped, and Officer Henderson escorted her inside. He led her to a cell. She sat on the thin mattress, trapped and alone, emotionally, mentally, physically.

Lucy Claremont had stopped praying soon after the murder of her daughter. She had stopped hoping after that, then stopped wishing. She hadn't attempted these in years. The bars clanged home and now she tried to do all of them again.

Please, let this be the bottom.

From: *Passing Through, Thoughts on Death and Dying* by Lucille Claremont, RN (p. 26).

"Eating":

Eating is a necessary part of living. It is how we keep our physical body alive. Food is our body's form of sustenance, so it is typically a cause for concern when eating stops. However, when the body is preparing to die, eating becomes less necessary.

When someone is nearing death, eating habits will alter, beginning with subtle changes to preference of flavor, texture, consistency, and/or temperature of food, followed by a decrease in frequency and size of meals.

Eventually, they will have a limited appetite and may refuse to eat. This is natural because the energy derived from eating is no longer needed. The body will not remain alive much longer; therefore, its cells and tissues do not require a steady supply of nutrients.

Lack of appetite is one of the most reliable symptoms of an impending death. When a body is preparing to die, it requires different energy for sustenance. Living requires food for energy, but dying requires a spiritual energy that food will not provide.

Chapter Three

John had another trapped vision after Robbie left. Its onset as sudden, but more overwhelming. When it hit with an abruptness striking him like a fist, he was standing. When it snapped shut, and he returned to himself, he had fallen, curled on the floor of his kitchen. The discolored tile cooling his fevered face on one side, for several minutes he watched his rapid breathing fog the surface before sitting up.

In the vision, he had seen only gray, a fog thick as cloth covering his entire field of sight. He was immobile from head to toe. He went numb below the neck, as if all the nerves in his spine had severed.

It lasted several seconds, then ended like a TV being turned off.

Some composure regained, he stood. Braced himself with a palm, slick with sweat, on the countertop to his right. Weathered a coughing fit. Talked to himself.

"What the hell is happening?" he asked. No one answered.

The light outside his kitchen window faded as he stood still, thinking. He thought about his job, the last structure holding him. The plank in his gallows.

He thought about his life with no job, car, or direction. He thought about his thoughts, and why they were circular. Much focus on little substance. Much effort but no progress.

He thought about Robbie, his only remaining connection to the world. Thought about Robbie's wife, Margaret (Mags to friends), whom John had met first. How he had lost her to Robbie, and this made him ping-pong between hoping to see her tonight and hoping not to. Between wanting to talk to her and not wanting to. They were equally perilous.

He did not think about his health, but his heart beat in and out of rhythm and his toes were cold inside his shoes.

Later, John walked to Robbie's house—a few streets away, yet a different world. As he walked, he sensed the inclining condition of the buildings. The siding covered in paint flaking like molting snakeskin gave way to elegant brickwork. Two-step concrete stoops were replaced by wooden wraparound porches. Dandelion patches faded to lush, manicured yards. It should be more gradual a change, and he only noticed its suddenness because he was walking. It was not divided physically, but the separation was clear. He knew when he reached the other side.

The right side. Where Robbie and Mags lived in their newly wedded bliss while he sold toxic liquids to jerk-offs and she hung on his every word. Where she had chosen the wrong guy and Robbie didn't realize how lucky that made him. Where bravado and disregard earned the spoils and there was no room for caution. Or stagnation.

John walked into Robbie's world for a meal and found he had no appetite. None. He decided not to tell Robbie about today's second episode in his kitchen.

Robbie's car was the only one in the driveway. Mags was not home. John balanced himself between disappointment and relief. This was a learned skill.

Their house was like something Robbie had conjured from thin air. Unique from the others around, a picturesque, two-story Tudor, complete with half-timbering and a rotunda entrance that led to a spiral staircase. Fifty years older than the rest, with all the extra character that allowed. Mags was awed immediately, giving John all the details while he had helped them move in.

He smelled food cooking from the porch, but his lack of appetite stayed, settling into his stomach like a weary dog finding a blanket, winding around then falling. Not like a weight, but occupying the space, preventing its use. He was not nauseous or uncomfortable. But there was no hunger.

He rang the doorbell. Robbie shouted for him to come in. In the kitchen, Robbie sat and motioned John toward the table, across from him. There was a place set for John, surely Mags' doing. Food on the table in ceramic dishes. The lids were on, he couldn't see what they contained. His stomach made no protest when he ignored them. John sat, looking across the table at Robbie, whose plate had only a few bits of leftover food. He was twiddling with his cell phone.

"Where's Mags?" John asked.

"Picking up a few things. Back soon," Robbie said, keeping his eyes fixed on the phone screen. "She wanted you to eat something."

"Oh, I already ate," John said. A lie.

"She made that chicken you like."

"I'm good."

"Here," Robbie said, spooning some of the meat onto a plate and handing John a fork.

Backed into a corner, pressured by Robbie's standoffish apathy and not wanting to offend Mags, John took a bite. When Robbie stood and turned around, John spit it into a napkin. It was his favorite meal, but she must have changed the recipe. The bite was wrong, the texture foreign. Gritty, with little flavor.

Luckily, Robbie didn't notice that John stopped eating after that first trial.

"It happened again," John said, abandoning his decision to keep it to himself, to distract Robbie from his eating. Lack of, rather.

"What did?"

"The thing, the... vision. Like you said before." That word was more distasteful than the food.

"What caused it this time?" Robbie met John's eyes for the first time since he arrived.

"I don't know. Didn't know then either."

"That's messed up, man. You have to do something. I'll bet it will keep happening until you figure out where it's coming from."

"Think it's related to my job?"

"Yeah, maybe. I guess it started around the same time, right?"

"The exact same time, yeah."

"So, it's a psychosomatic thing."

"You think? Like... that I'm causing them myself?"

"You liked that job, right?"

"I did, yeah."

"Plus the whole car thing."

"Right. That too."

"So, I'm sorry if this sounds harsh, but your shit's kind of falling apart over there. Right?"

"I wouldn't put it that way."

"That job was all you had left, wasn't it?"

John didn't appreciate this stacking of his disappointments. Robbie wasn't prone to coddling, but it also wasn't like him to amplify John's guilt this way. Robbie's tone implied this line of questioning was leading somewhere. It had a point, but John didn't know what.

"I mean, I liked it but it was just a job."

"Oh, I agree with that. A pointless job. Now you're out, you have this opportunity."

"What are you talking about? The only opportunity I see is me living on the streets. Can't even sleep in my car."

"Okay, but still. Look at it. Lose your car, lose your job, of course that would cause you to panic."

John's tongue fought behind clenched teeth.

"So, it's kind of logical that this panic would build up and start, like, manifesting itself somehow. See?"

"I question your use of the word 'logical.'"

"John, it's a sign, man."

"Sign of what?"

"That it's time, man."

When Robbie got worked up, he called everyone "man". Mags included. And if he called someone "bro", it meant he was on his way to dominating a conversation, a sign of his transformation into a steam engine of will. A character flaw to some, but John had typically seen through that to the confidence behind it, relying on that often to augment his own.

John felt them headed for an argument, rare in their time as friends. And he did not intend to lose. *I've got far more at stake here. Don't I?*

"Time for what?"

"To shake things up, man. To shake the shit out of shit."

"And how do I do that?"

"Lemme think. When you have these… visions—"

"Don't call it that."

"—it's like you're trapped, right?"

John didn't answer, tired of Robbie's cross-examination routine and wanting to leave. Between the lack of appetite and Mags being gone and now this crap from Robbie, he wished he had stayed home. He coughed twice.

"So *that's* what you're afraid of. Getting trapped."

Robbie's growing excitement was mirrored in John's growing insult.

"And if you're afraid of being trapped…" Robbie turned to John, smiling in realization. Epiphany. Revelation. He put his hands on the table and leaned toward where John was sitting with his arms crossed. John's heart fluttered and his face was covered in clammy flop sweat.

"Let's get you trapped," Robbie said.

John did not know what point he expected Robbie to make, but certainly not that one.

"What? Are you listening to yourself right now?"

"I mean it, man. It's your subconscious telling you to do something about your situation."

"What situation?"

"Your subconscious can do weird shit when it wants to get your attention. Believe me, some very, very weird shit. If you're afraid of being trapped, to where you're having these vis—"

"Don't call them that."

"—ions, that's a signal you have to deal with it right out. Squash that shit. Only way, man."

"You're my fucking shrink now?"

"Hey, woah, I'm just trying to—"

"I know what you're 'trying to,' and I don't like it." John stood to leave, fearing Robbie would keep pressing and needing to escape before the actual idea came out of him. He didn't make it far.

Robbie gave voice to John's fear, letting his revelation into the air around them, unwelcome as an oil spill.

"Let's go caving!"

"No."

"It'll work, you know."

"No."

"I'm telling you, man."

"I said no. I'm not going."

"John, calm down. Sit down." Robbie pulled a chair back from the table, motioning toward it, coaxing.

"Tell Mags thanks for the food."

John walked toward the kitchen door and Robbie followed.

"Let's talk here, John, man. Let's just—"

"I'm not. No. You're fucking crazy. I'm not going. That's the craziest shit you've ever said, and I've had a terrible enough week. I don't need this right now."

"Hey, don't get all defensive. I'm only trying to—"

"I. Know. What you're 'trying to,' okay? I get it. It's not helping. You're not helping. I won't follow you into some fucking hole in the fucking ground because you think it's fucking aversion therapy. That's idiotic."

Robbie gave John a wounded look, which he'd never done before. John relented but didn't speak.

They had moved to the front hallway. John raced toward the door. Robbie grabbed his shoulder to stop him and John pulled away.

"All right, all right. Bad idea. I'm sorry," Robbie said. John couldn't remember him apologizing before, either.

"I'm going home, I'll talk to you later."

"Yeah, okay. I'm worried about you, is all."

John turned to look at Robbie. They made brief eye contact. John gave a small nod before spinning back toward the door.

"John, I take it back. It was a stupid idea. Really."

"It's okay, bro," John said. *Dammit, now he's got me doing it too.* "I'm sorry I blew up. Lot of pressure, you know?"

"I know. Believe me, I know."

"I'll talk to you tomorrow, okay?"

"Yeah. We're good, right?"

"We're good, yeah. We're good."

Robbie walked away. John opened the door, stepped into the brisk evening air, then went backward, into the hallway. He saw a row of hooks beside the door. One held Robbie's key ring. A second was empty. The third held only a ribbon, the kind used to tie up hair in a ponytail. It was rose red, eight inches long. John grabbed and stuffed it into his pocket, reflexively. Like covering a sneeze.

Robbie had gone upstairs. John was glad for that.

John walked home with Mags' hair ribbon in his pocket. He never ate dinner. He ate nothing at all and had trouble sleeping. Lying in the dark, he had a more severe episode of feeling trapped. This third time more of his senses joined, all except sight. Pressure came over his whole body as though paralyzed in a vacuum. He smelled something that reminded him of the air after a brief and needed summer downpour. Tasted dry cotton. Heard a distant beeping.

When he emerged, he came back to himself lying on the bathroom floor this time, and was clutching Mags' hair ribbon and coughing. His fingers were blue but his knuckles were white as exposed bone.

Definition of unknown origin:

Extrasensory Perception (ESP), also referred to as a "sixth sense" or "precognition": A general term used to describe any supernatural ability to receive and interpret information using the faculties of the mind rather than the physical senses.

***

From: *Astral Projection and Tabloid Mentalities, a Pragmatic Interpretation of Paranormal Psychologies* by Dr. Arthur McGuire, PhD (p. 4).

The parapsychological community often relies on the generic and ill-defined term "Extrasensory Perception" (ESP) to fill in large holes in their purported theories and methodology which should instead be addressed using the comprehensive scientific method. Frankly, this is pure lunacy. This broad concept of receiving stimuli without use of the physiological receptors of sensation is both fanciful and convenient when leveraged in a rational scientific discussion.

Besides being a catch-all for unexplained psychological phenomena, ESP becomes an oft-used and frustratingly effective fallback argument for parapsychologists and like-minded idiots, because most of the world's populace is familiar with ESP, and a believer is always present when its existence is denied. Those who argue on behalf of ESP can only win debates through strength of numbers and blind faith, never through rationality.

Though descriptions of clairvoyance and paranormal intuition have been present in literature for a minimum of two hundred years, the term ESP was not developed until the 1930s. During that time, the well-known researcher J.B. Rhine and his wife became known as the first parapsychologists. With a commendable-though-misguided focus on recording empirical evidence, Rhine devoted his time toward experimentation and meticulously exploring and defining terms, including what he and his wife came to call "Extrasensory Perception."

Most famously, Rhine conducted ESP experiments by employing a set of cards, each depicting one of five basic symbols: square, circle, cross, star, or waved lines. Now known as "ESP cards" (originally Zener cards), this experiment involved having one person, the "sender," concentrate on one of the card's images so that a second person, the "receiver," can discern which of the five symbols was displayed, without use of their traditional senses. On the rare occasion when the second person "received" the correct card image, they would attribute this to their natural clairvoyance with a complete disregard of the inherent twenty percent statistical chance of *any* guess being correct.

To call this an experiment is both an idiotic farce and an affront to legitimate researchers everywhere.

This procedure appeared in the 1984 film *Ghostbusters* in a less-than-glamorous depiction of Rhine's original concept, which hardly stands as a monolithic achievement in any field of scientific research. Even more disappointing, perhaps, is that the fictional Dr. Peter Venkman has made a more widespread contribution to advancing the human race than has the concept of Rhine's Extrasensory Perception.

CHAPTER FOUR

Lucy was alone in her cell for hours, sobering quickly. Dreaded clarity was cresting like the sun. Rays of light revealed how weak her emotional shield was. How tenuous her grasp on sanity. How fragile her sanctuary.

This time, she had nowhere to run from it. No bottom-shelf bourbon to dowse her singing nerves with.

She had spent years surrounded by death, palliative care as a career. Her most frequent companions in life were the dying and death itself. But for years, it had worked that way. She had kept her life separate from her dying patients'.

She had wept with them, yes. Consoled their families, wrestled with sorrow for their tragedy. But there was always a separation. A gap. She maintained a great and wide chasm between life and death. She watched over these tortured souls from a safe, elevated plateau on the far side. Empathy was her telescope, her greatest gift as a nurse. And the abilities she possessed but couldn't control enabled her (at times) to have greater understanding, to form stronger connections. To see and know things others couldn't. To give true comfort, and claim small victories.

Then Lucy learned you can only spy on death for so long, before it notices you.

Death found its way across the gap, claiming her Anna, and that had changed everything. It climbed from that impassable chasm and came for her in a rage. It was no longer a respectable professional adversary but a ruthless personal demon. Death had taken part of her with it. Or maybe it took all of her that mattered.

After the death of her eleven-year-old daughter, her only child, Lucy's brain became septic, poisoned. Turned on her like infected tonsils or a breast with a tumor. It was destroying her. Before, she couldn't will it to turn on, it acted on its own. After, she couldn't shut it off. Her brain became an agent of death.

Phantom images, impossible voices, unexplained sensations. A constant showcase of the impossible. A promenade of the terrible. It had become a boisterous bully and the only switch she had found to stifle it was alcohol. Evan Williams Kentucky Straight was her standby, at twelve dollars a bottle. When her structured payments were tight, she went to Old Crow. Maker's Mark was a rare treat—it burned a little more on the way down, scorching shut her runaway neurons. When she drank Maker's, she imagined her stomach turning the same angry red as the wax seal on the bottle.

When she was drunk, her mind was silent. Tolerable.

She'd been following that formula for four years. Now she was alone in a locked cell with her fractured consciousness stirring in its cave, and not a bottle in sight. Death's agent was stalking her from inside again, and she was defenseless.

Within an hour, she sensed a low buzzing inside her skull. Like a swarm of insects crawling in a tight ball. This was familiar. It first happened while she watched the small coffin drop from sight on a clear fall afternoon. When death had forced her down. It seemed her anchor to reality had followed that coffin into the earth.

In the second hour of her police-enforced detox, those buzzing brain-insects stopped crawling over each other in circles, one at a time, to strike out on their own. Lines of bees drilling around her head looking for fuel for their hive. Theirs was not an angry buzz, but a productive one. Alarming, warning her of the flood approaching.

Incoherent voices came to her. Fragments of words, disjointed and not spoken but sensed. She pressed her hands over her ears anyway.

Flashes of events that may have already happened, may have yet to happen, or most likely mere delusions caused by a break from reality. She saw a three-car pileup, a woman falling down concrete stairs, an armed robbery in a convenience store. Vivid images all, but existing in her mind. She closed her eyes anyway.

And wept.

For her lost Anna, for her fading sanity.

"You okay in there?" a uniformed officer asked her. He paused for an answer, then went back to his computer monitor.

She knew what he was reading, even locked in her cell in silence. It found its way to the buzzing hive in her head.

An article described a man trapped in a cave nearby. He survived miraculously after days alone and without food. She saw the headline, the typesetting as clear as a billboard. It came to her through a vision separate from her eyes.

Harrowing Ordeal Ends, Missing Hallstown Man
Found Alive After Four Days Trapped in Cave

How awful, she thought, demanding herself not to think about it further. *Such a torturous experience, almost medieval. Like being confined to an iron maiden then released.*

To redirect herself, she thought of the professor who dismissed her as a "lunatic" after one mention of these sensations in her mind. She had asked him, with trepidation, was it possible to see a person's energy? Their aura? He answered with a barrage of insults, and she never asked another person. Even though she had similar experiences, again and again.

In that damn cemetery, she watched her reason for living drop from sight, and the thing in her skull, that knew things it shouldn't, had ignited from candle flame to bonfire. Had been consuming her since.

She made herself change the headline to prove its fabrication, saw a new version and knew she had projected this one, not received it.

Local Woman Found Hanged in Cell
After Minor Traffic Offense

She lay down on the cot and pulled the coiled sheet around her neck. Enough to feel it, but not more.

Time drew out and Lucy's brain buzzed louder by the minute.

Chapter Five

A few minutes before 5 AM, according to the plain wall clock behind the booking desk, two officers (who may have also recognized Lucy's name) carried in an unconscious woman. She hung from one officer's shoulder as if he'd saved her from a burning building.

"This should keep you from running around on the interstate, throwing things at cars," the carrying officer said, while dapples of green light waved from his forehead.

They set her, prone, on the other cot and left. She was wrapped in a stained and fraying blanket and snoring, her face covered. Lucy saw shoes protruding, worn to the end of their function, one sole near falling off, as the snores inside the blanket expanded and contracted.

Lucy noticed tiny wisps of gold and silver snaking out from the blanket, blending with the surrounding air, then disappearing. She tried to ignore them, shaking her head from side to side until everything was blurry. The blanket stirred. An odor of stale urine filled the cell.

She wished for a drink. Any drink. The Old Crow would do fine. Or drain cleaner.

The woman pulled the blanket from her face, using fingers coated in grime and knotted with arthritis. Her cheeks and chin were covered in dozens of layers of foundation makeup, thick and doughy as a pancake, too dark to blend with her skin, which was a marble of powdery white and red blotches on her uncoated forehead. Hair slick and full of knots, making it resemble the type collected in shower drains. Lips chapped under a sediment of doll-red lipstick. The smell grew stronger.

In the presence of a vagrant, an apparently homeless woman, Lucy recalled her former life's work. The care of the wretched, the dying, the helpless. Every aspect of the woman denoted her lost-soul status, unable to care for herself and awash in a stream of suffering with a swift current and no buoy.

She opened her eyes. They were blue, bright as a hawk's. She fixed them on Lucy's and spoke as wisps of gold light left her crown.

"You've got it too, then," the woman said.

In those flint-lined eyes, Lucy recognized something she had seen in her own, at the times when her brain was most alive in its oppressive, uncontrollable activity. Its inexplicable reception. A glimmer of more than intelligence, something otherworldly.

Lucy startled, her breath caught.

"It's time for the rest to clear their garbage out." The woman sat up and her volume increased. "The garbage in the streets and the garbage in their minds. It's all got to go."

Lucy scolded herself. She was so desperate to recognize that part of herself in another that she had projected it. Manufactured it. Her cellmate was not clairvoyant. She was plain crazy. That was a part of herself that Lucy recognized, but not the one she longed to see reflected. Instead, it was a future part, a later version.

Herself, farther down the path.

Lucy lay down and rolled toward the wall. The vagrant woman continued her diatribe; Lucy listened to as few words as she was able. With nothing else to distract her, she still caught some of it. And each unavoidable word excited her mental hive; the buzzing fed off this woman's speech.

Crazy begets crazy.

"So quick to dismiss, Lucy?"

Lucy shot around. "What did you say?"

The woman smiled and gave no answer. Only mouthed words that had no meaning. Her insanity dribbled out with no sound.

"Do I know you?" Lucy asked.

No answer, but she glared at Lucy across the holding cell.

Lucy searched her face, this piss-covered woman who was an omen of her own future, a "Do Not Enter" sign given human form. She was a raving, syphilitic vagrant. Lucy studied the caked-on foundation, frantic twirls of hair, layers of rotting clothing, the musty smell of her own waste. Her entire appearance showed a complete lack of credibility.

Except the eyes. Her eyes held a different story.

Lucy closed her own eyes after a few seconds and rubbed them with the heels of her palms.

The woman spoke again and Lucy bolted upright as if shot, her jaw falling open.

"Not the bottom yet. Not yet, no. But it's near."

Lucy had no response.

Officer Henderson opened the cell door.

"Miss Claremont?" he said. "Time to go."

Lucy's mouth was still open. The woman was not smiling anymore, but her stare was piercing. Lucy broke from it with effort, moved to the cell door. As Henderson escorted Lucy out, the woman gave one more line of would-be prophecy. Before she did, Lucy's brain fell silent for the first time in years, and she knew it was this woman's doing.

"When you get there, you come find me."

Henderson shook his head, led Lucy outside.

In the post-dawn light, the buzzing roared back like a burst faucet.

From: *Passing Through, Thoughts on Death and Dying* by Lucille Claremont, RN (p. 65).

"Retraction":

When a person nears death, they become less strongly tied to this world, to their physical body and to those they will leave behind. In the progression toward death, the things that anchor them to this world give way, to release their hold on the spirit.

One of the critical internal processes to occur as these ties come loose is that of understanding death. Once a dying person has put death and their own mortality into perspective, their next task is to obtain a true comprehension of what it is to die.

It is important to note that this understanding can be completely internalized, and it is not necessary to share with others. A dying person may even retract or become despondent from loved ones or caregivers.

Retraction, or withdrawal, occurs during this stage because the dying person is retreating inside themselves as they prepare for what is next. This is an entirely solitary process. They may long for solitude.

However, if a person is unaware or in denial of their own terminality, they cannot achieve this understanding of death, or to complete the internal steps needed to prepare for it. They are facing spiritual bankruptcy.

This may cause extreme mental distress. A person unable to accept their own imminent death may experience hostility toward those around them, without understanding its origin. This is due to a competition between their need to process the events of their life in isolation, and their denial or failure to acknowledge their own fading mortality.

To face death unprepared, unable to understand it, or to die without sorting through one's life first—each of these is nothing short of terrifying.

CHAPTER SIX

A few days later, John returned home from a fruitless job search to find his furniture stacked by the curb outside his apartment. A pink notice taped to the front door told the rest. There was a clause in his lease stating he needed to notify the owner within twenty-four hours of losing his job. And if he didn't, well...

How did they know I got fired? It's only been two days.

Robbie was there before John finished reading the eviction notice.

"That doesn't look good," Robbie said, as he stepped out of his car. John heard a smirk in his voice, but denied it. Robbie was his friend. Robbie cared about him. Surely, he did not find it amusing that John's life was crumbling all around him, breaking like glass.

John had no desire to talk about it, even with Robbie. He ripped the note off the door and tried his key. It wouldn't turn. They had changed the locks.

John couldn't breathe or move. Suddenly he was in a vacuum beneath a mountain of dirt, the Mariana trench, a crater on the moon. The air pressed from his lungs as if he were a giant tube of toothpaste, in one large whoosh of life leaving him. He saw only an impenetrable granite-hued cloud. Felt pressure over every inch of his body, cradled in an unseen vice of stone or steel or earth. No movement possible.

He sipped in a breath, as if through a tiny straw pinched in his lips; this iteration of his own entombment was lasting far longer than the others. His lungs burned with the stolen air. Phantom wads of cotton filled his mouth as if the liquid inside had evaporated in an instant.

The pressure coating him was shocking, cold, then faded into numbness. Every part below his neck grew numb—his limbs, fingers, toes, genitals, his back and sides and chest. None of it felt attached anymore, like parts of him were floating away and only his head remained. And again there was a distant beeping.

He heard a voice. A woman's voice, familiar, but whose? His mother? No. Sister? No. Mags? Certainly not. Someone from childhood? A teacher?

Everything fell away, and he crashed back to a body he had not left.

His senses returned, slowly. John had no concept of how long he had been incoherent but feared that it was drastically longer with each occurrence. The first thing he noticed was Robbie bracing him up, and holding his hand.

Neither spoke.

Soon he and Robbie were sitting on the curb like childhood friends after a bike ride, John's arms wrapped around his knees, his head resting on them sideways, looking at his belongings in the grass.

John took solace in how he and Robbie could sit in silence. He was glad to not be alone, and also not have to speak.

The pile of his stuff in the grass wasn't *some* of his possessions. It was everything. It was all of himself discarded roadside. All there. Everything he owned fit into a space totaling less than a small dumpster. Less than a tiny storage pod.

As he looked at the meager stack of furniture and clothing, he found words worth speaking.

"When you put it all together like that, my life looks so hollow. So... two-dimensional."

"What do you mean?" Robbie asked.

"There's nothing to it, I mean."

"They're only things, John."

"Easy for you to say. How much of your stuff fits in an F-150? Because all of mine fits."

"So what?"

"Robbie, don't you see how bad this is? I have nothing left. You could erase it with a single match."

Robbie pondered this, as if running an experiment in his mind. A few minutes passed before he spoke.

"John, did I ever tell you how I used to be terrified of public speaking?"

"What? No. Never."

"Yeah. I can tell you don't believe me, but it's true. Right up until we started hanging out, actually. That's around the time I'd say I got over it, finally."

"Robbie, come on."

"No, I'm serious. I mean, I guess it sounds convenient if I step back and watch us talking right now. I've never mentioned it before, and it probably doesn't jibe with how you see me. But for real, it was a problem. Big problem. Like, even if I was talking to more than a few people at once, in a meeting or something. I hated being the center of attention like that. I'd just about go braindead and forget everything I wanted to say. It was kind of pathetic. I was already thinking about quitting school, and I knew if I was going to have any kind of success without more education that I'd have to be able to persuade people."

"Well, that at least I know is true."

"Yeah, see?"

John nodded.

"So, I started thinking about how to deal with this problem. And not just to cope with it, because that would be the same as avoiding it. Same as not dealing with it. I knew the only way out was through. I started looking for opportunities to dive right into that discomfort, until I got more used to it."

"Robbie, I see where you're headed, okay?"

"Just… just hear me out. That's all I'm asking."

John nodded.

"I tried starting small and looked into coaching a youth sports team. Signed up to coach basketball at the Y."

"Do you even know the rules?"

"No, but I figured that didn't matter much. Wasn't the point. Anyway, that didn't help because talking to a group of kids wasn't the same. You know? It was like taking a bath to get over a fear of drowning. There was no danger, no stakes. So I signed up to start reading stuff in church."

"Robbie, come on. Just stop. You're not even baptized or whatever."

"They didn't know that, John. And it helped me, okay. That's my point. Believe me or don't, but it happened. I just dove in. After a few times I was less afraid. That fueled me. I knew I was making progress, so I wanted to amp it up. Go further. Deeper. I took that public speaking class, the semester before we met. I didn't have to do it, either. I wanted to."

"You told me you hated that class, Robbie."

"Well, sure, I did. I hated every class. But in a weird way I also loved it. Especially toward the end. I was so damn used to it, John. It felt good, and halfway through I was even looking forward to these speeches. My final speech, I didn't even prepare anything. I just got up there and talked like I'm talking now. It just flowed out like a conversation. It was... natural. And amazing. Like I had climbed a mountain and saw the world different."

"Robbie, please."

"I know, I know. I'm not asking you to agree. Just think about it some more, okay? The only way out is through. I really believe that."

"Fine, I'll think about that more if it shuts you up."

"I don't know why you're getting hostile, John. I just want to help."

"I get that, alright? I don't mean to be a dick but you're needling me about something crazy when I have real problems to deal with. Immediate problems."

"These panic attacks aren't a real problem?"

"I have nowhere to live, Robbie."

"You have a place to live."

John noted he didn't have to ask, Robbie barely needed to offer. The outward decision was not necessary.

Within days, his life had become so bleak he was moving in with Robbie without it being mentioned aloud in any detail.

They loaded what of his belongings fit into Robbie's tiny sports car. It took less than an hour to move every piece from the curb to Robbie's garage.

CHAPTER SEVEN

When they pulled in with the last load, John noticed Mags' car absent again. He asked where she was, and added this to the list of questions he'd take back if given a second chance. But not because he knew the answer. Because of how the answer wrung his heart in knots.

"She left, John," Robbie said, his tone implying more information withheld than shared.

"Left where?"

"Her sister's. I think."

John followed Robbie into the house, almost shouting after him as the door closed.

"You *think*? That mean you don't know?"

"Why so interested, John? She's not here."

"I wanted to say 'Hi.' Haven't seen her in a while."

"She didn't tell me where she was going. Left in a big huff and I didn't ask. So, if I'm guessing, she went to her sister's house for a while."

"Did you get in a fight?"

"Yeah. Yeah, we did."

"What about?"

"I think you know the answer." Robbie's voice had turned chilled, short. John was taken aback, expecting another argument and taking note of how different Robbie was just then. Accusatory, in the eyes. John stayed in the doorway, as if planning an escape.

"Why would I know that? I wasn't here."

"We fought about you, John."

"Me? Why? What about me?"

"She wasn't too happy with you."

"What did I do?"

"She was coming home when you stormed out the other night—"

Oh, is it because I stole her ribbon? John thought. *Does she know that? Did she see me?*

"—and said she called after you but you ignored her."

"No, I didn't. I didn't even see her."

"She said there's no way you could've missed her. Then she came in and asked why you ate nothing, and I told her you had taken one bite and spit it out."

John was getting angry. There was a clamor of untruth behind each of Robbie's answers. The whole situation felt... orchestrated.

"Why would you say that?"

"Because it's true, that's why. So she got all mad, and I was defending you. Told her about you getting fired and all that. Anyway, I don't know what got into her, but she started trashing you. Pretty bad too. It was ruthless."

"She did what?"

"Yeah, she was laying into you."

It was clear Robbie was lying, but John didn't understand why. It was as if Robbie was campaigning for his loyalty, or using him as a scapegoat when he had wanted Mags to leave. Perhaps both.

"So, I stood up for you, buddy. I had to, you know? I couldn't stand by and let her talk like that."

"What did you say to her?"

"I don't want to repeat it. I don't really remember."

Well, which is it? John thought, unconvinced.

"She packed a bag and left. Didn't tell me anything."

"Are you okay?"

"Yeah, why?"

"Why? Because she left you. I mean, she took off like that. Are you okay? She's never done that, it must have been bad."

"I'm good, yeah. It's been coming for a while. Didn't I tell you?"

"Tell me what?"

"That things were kind of... rocky. For a few weeks now."

Robbie's recent indifference to John's misfortunes had been surprising, troublesome, even hurtful. His lack of emotion toward his own problem was more shocking. They stood in the kitchen, exchanging glances like two people eyeing a crime scene and guessing which clues the other had noticed.

Robbie went back to unloading boxes of John's clothing.

"Rocky? Hey, I'm sorry. I'm sorry she left, and that it was about me."

Robbie offered little consolation to this plea for forgiveness. Moved away from the boxes and into the kitchen.

"Hungry?" he asked, then foraged in the refrigerator.

John was not. He had eaten very little for the past few days, not enough food to be labeled a "meal" since before he'd lost his job.

John wished to go wherever Mags had gone. He wanted comfort, and unlike most previous times of hardship, he wanted it to come from someone other than Robbie. This new, sometimes indifferent version of his friend, at least. He found himself wondering how much of this shift in Robbie's behavior was real, and how much he was projecting because of his own issues.

"No," John said, deciding it best to pull away and be alone. "Not hungry. I'm going to go to bed, that okay?" He faked a yawn.

Robbie was shuffling things around in the fridge, and held his hand backward, forming an "O" with thumb and forefinger. He didn't turn around.

John went upstairs, dropped a garbage bag filled with clothes on the floor of the guest bedroom. He didn't change clothes, even leaving his shoes on. He lay in bed tossing and turning all night with short-ness-of-breath fits and his fingers and toes formed of ice, what sleep he got filled with dreams of being trapped, not unlike those recent waking episodes. In these dreams, he was not alone. Someone else was there with him this time, in the tunnel or under the mound or wherever he kept imagining himself suffocating and immobile.

Mags was trapped with him. And she was hurt.

Chapter Eight

In the early morning, before the sun, John rose and went downstairs. He walked out to the large back porch and sat in a wrought-iron chair under the stars. Robbie came out shortly after him as if he'd been waiting, watching.

John still didn't want to talk to Robbie, but had no choice. Tied to the tracks on the railroad trestle that was his best friend. And a loud noise was approaching.

"Nice night," Robbie said. "I like when it's this calm out. Makes me wonder if there's a storm coming." He sat in the chair next to John, clapping him on the shoulder. "You know how nature likes to keep things balanced."

John nodded, hoping it would keep him on the sidelines of this patter. He begged himself not to pull away from Robbie's arm. After a few seconds, Robbie removed his hand. John sighed, scolding himself for being so withdrawn when Robbie was trying to help. His heart raced, and another episode or attack loomed, descending on him like an airliner falling from the sky.

"If it's calm here, that must mean it's raging somewhere else, you know?" Robbie said. "And probably on its way here."

"What am I gonna do, Robbie?"

"I already told you what to do, buddy. You're afraid of something, you face it head-on."

"Not about that. About everything else. I can't stay with you forever. Everything fell apart so fast; I don't even get how that happened."

"That's what I mean, though. That's your problem right there. You're looking backwards and it's terrifying you. 'How did it' and 'why did it' and 'woe is me,' and it's breaking you apart to be stuck on all that. You see? You're stuck, man."

John didn't see at all but wouldn't let himself question any further. He knew Robbie was poised to mow him down with a grand lecture, and hadn't the will to divert it. He would let it wash over him like he was a tree standing downriver from a rupturing dam and hope to anchor until it passed.

Robbie brought the floodwaters.

"That's what's causing these visions you're having. You know? It's self-induced. Not on purpose, but you're causing it and only *you* can stop it. You're fixated on this idea that everything is happening *to* you, that you're being forced into this trap, and that scares the shit out of you. You can't accept that it's on you to turn that around. So, you keep asking, 'What am I gonna do, what am I gonna do?' and the answer is clear. You have to move forward. To push through it. To stop blaming everyone and everything else and playing a victim of circumstance. Stop looking back and crying, John. Turn around and move forward. That's how you start fixing everything."

Robbie paused. Both were silent as they pored over everything from opposing sides of a major pending decision. Robbie added one more point.

"Aren't you sick to fucking death of being trapped here all the time, John? I sure am."

Those last words stood out, ill-fitting or misplaced. He was the one having these episodes, whose life was falling away. What could be trapping Robbie? Did he resent John? Was he somehow holding Robbie back?

He didn't have long to consider it though. He was interrupted by Mags' voice in his head: *"The only way out is through."* That one statement convinced him; it had less to do with Robbie's impassioned speech about holding himself hostage.

"Let's do it," John said.

Robbie turned toward him as if the words were a gunshot.

"Did you... That mean what I think?"

John nodded. "Let's do that... cave... thing."

Even as he voiced his agreement, John wondered if Robbie was right, if he understood something that John himself didn't. He did so not because Robbie's supreme confidence assured his safety (it didn't), or because his words had been compelling (they weren't), but for a different reason. Because saying it brought relief. At once, his hands weren't cold. There was no clammy sweat. His heart beat with a renewed strength, measured and even. The threat of another attack lifted away like a stage curtain.

The first rays of sun rolled toward them, cutting through the trees.

Robbie's reaction was not proportionate, and it was much louder. He shouted as if he were about to backflip into the yard. A smile flashed across his face, teeth showing, soon contrasted by a look of deep concern.

"Don't tell Mags, though. Deal?" Robbie said.

"Oh. Why not?"

"You know her, she'd fret too much and we would probably scrap the whole thing."

Why is he hiding this from her? Why does it seem like he was trying to get rid of her? Like he's got all these secrets from her?

Then, a more troubling thought came.

Is he keeping anything from me?

Robbie was miles ahead of him already, almost outrunning himself as he laid out plans for this adventure underground.

"Got work to do," he said, walking back inside. "Research. Find the right one. Need equipment."

"Wait, you don't have equipment?" John said. The earlier relief had left already, replaced by a renewed desire to leave Robbie and go find Mags.

Regret was already eating at him, like a school of tiny fish pricking his feet. But there was no stopping Robbie now.

Definition of unknown origin:

Precognition, derived from the Latin *prae (before)* + *cognitio (acquiring knowledge)*, also known as *future sight*: A form of extra-sensory perception characterized by the reception of information related to a future event. This reception of information is unrelated to any current stimuli or available sensory input and generally experienced in the form of emotion(s).

***

From: *Astral Projection and Tabloid Mentalities, a Pragmatic Interpretation of Paranormal Psychologies* by Dr. Arthur McGuire, PhD (p. 29).

To the caliber of mind willing to accept the existence of ESP, it is not a far leap to also accept all the different forms that this unsubstantiated concept may take, including precognition.

This term, most illogically, refers to an inexplicable awareness of events which have not yet occurred, sometimes in great detail. All information derived from a precognitive event would, of course, be obtained through mental clairvoyance alone and could not be rationalized by any surrounding events or circumstances.

A meager amount of research into precognition yields multiple theoretical explanations for this phenomenon, each more comical than the last.

Precognition has been attributed to everything from the tenuous concept of "exceptional subliminal awareness"—wherein an overdeveloped cortex absorbs and interprets far more data than average—to the ridiculous notion of time-traveling particles (aptly named *psitrons*) moving backwards in time to make contact with the brain of an observer.

Particles traveling backward in time? A further example of the utter lunacy inherent in the attempted study of all things paranormal.

The irony of these propositions lies in each of their benefactors attempting to use scientific principles to explain occurrences inherently defiant of the most basic of those same principles. That being: Cause and Effect.

Take note; it is scientifically impossible for the effect to occur at a time before its cause. Still, there exists a widespread acceptance of precognition. I ask, what does this imply about the state of our collected intelligence?

Despite this level of popular recognition, the scientific community does not acknowledge the existence of precognition nor any other form of ESP that may have spilled from histories' most unfettered imaginations.

Imagination is a thing best contained within the entertainment industry, thus maintaining the purity of scientific research.

Chapter Nine

L ucy's brain was humming with a ferocity on pace with the spreading sunlight. But this did nothing to interfere with her senses. Her eyes saw the sidewalk fine. As she walked away from the sheriff's office, they picked out the cracks and spots of blackened chewing gum. Her ears heard as normal. While she stood waiting for the city bus to come, they relayed the too-loud music from a passing car. The slight breeze slid past, touching her skin, perhaps in search of someone more appreciative.

But she was experiencing much more. A flash-image of falling glass from a broken window, a phantom voice crying for help before cutting off, an urgent prayer that should have been silent but arrived in her head, a strange sourceless heat on one of her forearms.

Her driver's license now suspended, she possessed only the clothes on her back and an empty wallet. Officer Henderson left change for her to catch a ride home, had written out the bus route for her in scrawled blue ink, and accounted for the two transfers needed.

Her fingers traced the details of the coins' engraved surfaces, but another part of her brain was sending its own maddening input. Her eyes still received the sun's light coming off the surfaces around her—wooden bus stop bench, glass car windshield, green blades of grass—yet she still had glimpses of other objects.

She saw white sheets. Saw beige tile flooring, flecked with maroon. These images came in flashes, projected on top, inside, around the physical world, like spliced frames in a film reel. The buzzing in her head was like static pouring from an enormous speaker, yet she could still hear traffic nearby.

The bus arrived, she stepped on and dropped her fare into the top of the slotted pedestal next to the driver. He looked at her with a mix of self-concern and trepidation.

"Morning," the driver said with a kind smile, his thin hair lit like a bulb in the early morning light.

She heard him clearly, over or around or through the static of her imaginary speaker. She may have responded to him.

Lucy sat toward the middle of the bus, looking out the window. In it, she saw a hospital room, herself reflected to appear like she was too large and seated next to the high-set wheeled bed, its sheets white as sun-bleached bone.

The mirage was complete. In full detail. Glass jar of cotton swabs on a counter. White cabinets with plain silver pulls. Biohazard container hung on one wall. IV pole. Heart rate monitor with an active display. It was the perfect illusion.

Lucy was seeing a room from the hospice wing she had once worked in. A building where she had not set foot for years. She thought this hallucination was a memory.

It wasn't. The curtains didn't match her memory. When she worked there, a petition was circling to change out the dated, orange-and-yellow draperies. In this bus-window tableau, the curtains were a plain and tasteful navy blue. Traffic-worn hardwood replaced with clean, polished tile. Somewhere in that room was a beeping sound, or sounds, and as she tuned in to them, the picture became more defined. Less transparent.

Though she didn't notice at first, the roaring inside her head slowed.

With these details she realized this wasn't a scene she'd witnessed before. The bonfire or hive or static mess inside her brain was showing her something that hadn't happened yet. Something that was *going to* happen.

Lucy knew this because she saw someone else enter the room. It was a male security guard she had worked with. His name was Rick, and he was the only person there she had spoken to since losing her nursing license.

Rick peeked in, to his shoulders, searched from side to side. Then he left.

There was someone in the bed, she noticed next, still as a mannequin. Or a corpse.

Lucy thought back to the newspaper headline she had "read" from inside the cell.

The bus stopped short, the driver sounding the horn. It broke Lucy's concentration, and she looked away from the window. The driver shouted a few choice words and drove on.

She turned back to the window; the images were gone, except the bed. It stood alone, somewhere outside as if projected in a field.

One hand raised, under the sheet. She saw the fingers, curled from atrophy and loss of muscle. The hand pointed at her.

She screamed, an abrupt, sharp sound, and dashed toward the front of the bus as it was arriving at a stop. The doors swung open, and Lucy went down the three stairs in a quick leap. She ran.

It wasn't her stop, Henderson and his thoughtful instructions and extra change were quite forgotten.

CHAPTER TEN

Lucy didn't run far. After a few hundred feet, she saw the gates.

She'd fled from the bus when it stopped by the cemetery where Henderson arrested her a few hours ago. Anna's cemetery.

The same cemetery she circled in a nightly ritual of shame and weakness.

Still looking for the bottom, she crossed the gates and floated through the grounds, a sleepwalker in broad daylight with extra-special consciousness to guide her.

Anna's headstone was elegant in a minimalistic way. Amidst a row of oversized, statuesque, even boastful monuments, the stone Lucy had chosen to mark her daughter's resting place projected an underwhelming grace. It told Lucy that this stone would last for eons longer than those around it, with their fragile outcroppings, sculpted to frailty, ill-prepared to weather the endless storms and shifting pressures of this world.

All qualities Anna had in life. Her grave marker was a deep, hematite gray with white marbling. It shone in the early morning light, casting an omnidirectional brightness that would be difficult to absorb, were it not so magnetic. It was a fitting stone.

The engraved dates seared into Lucy's self with the most opposite of memories. And so little time between them.

The grass was wet with the time of morning, a slight chill in the air as it moved restless through the rows like the breaths of the interred, all moaning for her attention.

The buzzing in her head straightened into a beacon, pointing wildly from one direction to the next. So much to pique its interest here. She ignored it as best she could and kneeled in the grass, dew seeping into her jeans.

The stark image of an occupied hospital bed set in a grove of trees held its place, in the back of a field of vision not connected to her eyes.

She placed a hand on Anna's gravestone. The image of the bed pulsed, and she understood, or was told, what it meant.

Someone was calling her back, whoever was in that bed. They were dying and needed her help. They were shouting for her, in a way that touched neither their vocal chords nor her eardrums. Out of desperation, anguish. Terror.

Someone at death's door was calling for her help. But it was a call she refused to answer.

Leave me alone! she shouted back. *I can't take any more death, I can't. Find someone else. Please.*

The image of the bed faded. Lucy exhaled, her shoulders dropping.

A pair of cardinals, male and female, flew in and landed on a headstone nearby, two rows to Lucy's left. Grateful for the minor distraction, she watched them for a moment. Their landing stone was much older than Anna's, adorned with a large Celtic cross made of marble. Mold trickled down its side like seeping green blood. The male cardinal faced her direction, his feathers red as the heart of a flame. The female alighted, and he followed.

They landed fifty feet farther away, in a mature, white-barked birch tree, and her knees buckled. In a way she did not understand, that tree's image recalled her past patients, as if they were together on the other side, hurling themselves at her for attention. Except it wasn't coming from the past.

It was a sign of something in her future. Something that had yet to happen. A call for help from whomever she had seen lying in a hospital bed, reflected in the bus's window, and now projected farther away in the cemetery.

Lucy knew she didn't have the strength to answer this call. Death had taken too much of her already. She was hollowed. Her life had been a struggle with no value, one she could end. She lacked the strength to return to that place and face it again; the dying patients would always call for her help and she would always hear them because she had a unique, unseverable link.

It was unbearable.

With folded legs covered by the short shadow of her daughter's headstone, listening to the song of a cardinal in that bleached-white tree nearby, some para-gland part of her brain singing an unwanted song of impending events, Lucy made a decision.

She would give death what it wanted.

If it would not leave her be, if it would keep pulling at her through every waking moment, she would give in to it. There was no other choice left.

She began to walk home. It was several miles and would take her over an hour.

When she got there, she would grab the two bottles she had stowed under her kitchen sink, on another black day when she knew this decision point was coming.

She was going home to surrender to death, in the comfort of her lost daughter's bed, with the help of some Old Crow and a handful (or two) of stolen Halcion sleeping pills.

From: *Passing Through, Thoughts on Death and Dying* by Lucille Claremont, RN (p. 48).

"Sleeping":

As the dying body continues to shut down and organ function slows, sleeping increases, often accompanied by a growing sense of disorientation. At this stage, the processes of the brain are altering similar to other vital organs. The brain is typically the last organ to cease functioning before a death by natural causes.

A person within days of death will have difficulty remaining awake or lucid although they can be awakened with some effort. This is a sign of passing through, leaving this world.

They will become confused easily and regularly. This includes talking about past places and experiences, or about people and events unknown to others. It is also common for them to have encounters with others who have died before them.

As the amount of sleep increases, it will also become more restless as the body is less able to recharge itself. As death nears, it is common to see agitated movement of the limbs during sleep, sometimes becoming convulsions.

Their concentration is shifting from this world as they prepare to die. They are becoming more detached from this plane of existence as they prepare to enter the next.

This detachment is often very difficult for others to perceive or understand.

Chapter Eleven

By the third day after John moved in, Robbie claimed he had learned enough about caving to keep them alive. John remained unconvinced but unable to mount a successful protest. When he tried, Robbie wouldn't hear it through his excited fog.

"Look at all this cool shit," Robbie said, turning over a duffle bag (tags still on) to reveal his payload of newly purchased gear on the oak kitchen table. John's reaction to the spread of rope, carabiners, flashlights, and assorted metal objects was that it made the table look larger. Already, Robbie showed his eyes were bigger than his aptitude.

It was evening, and Robbie had insisted on leaving the windows open rather than running the air conditioner. Outside was mild and pleasant, so John hadn't protested this, yet the air in the house was stagnant, oppressive. The strange humidity was making him feverish, sapping his will to argue.

John feared another episode, but was spared for the moment.

"That's it?" John said.

Robbie made a disappointed face, a mime without the grease paint.

"What do you mean, 'that's it?' How much do you think it takes?"

"Robbie, this is dangerous stuff."

"What? No, it's not. We're mostly walking around down there. What's the worst that can happen?"

"We die. That's not bad enough?"

"We'll be fine, dude. Trust me. Besides, there are worse things than dying."

John found that statement more believable than he would have a week ago. Robbie repacked the bag. It didn't take long. He slung it over his shoulder, feigning extra weight.

"We'll leave in a few hours, okay?"

"Sure, whatever you say."

"You better pack, is what I say."

John went upstairs and as he ascended he glanced at a picture of the three of them, hanging on a wall to his left. Taken the day Robbie and Mags had moved into this house. John and Robbie were carrying a brown leather sofa, on opposite ends, while Mags lay across it, her head propped and a feigned look of exhaustion on her face. Robbie's smile was much bigger than John's.

John didn't remember this picture being taken, but his thoughts strayed back to the events leading to Robbie and Mags meeting. John had met her at work and asked her out almost immediately (to his own surprise)—another reason he was distraught over being fired, having wanted that connection to be permanent. He got her number but hesitated to call for a few days. Then Robbie's parents both died and he grew lonely and depressed. John decided to set him up with Mags, to see if meeting her would help him cope. It did. Since then it seemed John was the only one looking back.

One step up, the next picture on the wall was a solo shot of Mags. A different tone than the couch-moving picture. It had a seriousness to it, almost somber.

She hated the picture, but Robbie had insisted on hanging it despite her protests, and John agreed with him. A simple shot of her sitting on a beach, taken by her younger sister who had an eye for composition. Her knees were bent, chin resting on her crossed arms as she leaned forward. Her clothing, mostly white save for a few thin vertical stripes of soft blue on her pants, appeared loose and comfortable. The infant sunbeams lay across her face, bringing life to her long blonde hair, tied into a ponytail. The corner of her mouth turned upward into an inkling of a smile.

John had studied that picture dozens of times.

Robbie didn't seem to care where Mags had gone, though he hadn't heard from her in days. John thought of little else. A seed of resentment toward Robbie grew. He was actively avoiding Robbie, his days becoming a constant blend of sleep, wishing he hadn't agreed to go caving, concern for a woman who seemed to mean more to him than her own husband, mourning the loss of his home, job, and car, and the self-hatred that came with all the above.

Plus more sleep. He couldn't get enough, or was getting too much—either way, his chronic fatigue was leading him to suspect illness as the cause. A mental illness, or some psychosomatic response which Robbie claimed as the source of his episodes.

He threw some clothes in a borrowed backpack, wanting only to climb into bed. Instead, he went back downstairs.

As he passed the photo of Mags, he slid his hand across its frame.

Robbie met him at the bottom of the steps, grinning wide as if summoning John to the stage from a game show audience. Robbie's eagerness, which in the past John found contagious, was draining him like a tapeworm. He now saw Robbie as a parasite and yearned for escape from this symbiotic relationship they'd created.

"Ready?" Robbie asked, moving toward the garage without leaving time for an answer.

John was ready only to run, find Mags. Then run farther.

Instead, he followed.

Chapter Twelve

Minutes later, they rolled from the driveway into the night. John was fighting to stay awake in the passenger seat before Robbie made it to the first stop sign.

"How far is it?" John asked around a stifled yawn, not wanting to talk but trying to keep awake.

"Not far," Robbie said. "Few hours."

Robbie drove. John drifted into an awkward and disjointed sleep. His dreams were the same painted canvas as his episodes of being trapped, though less intense, but again Mags was somewhere near him. Invisible but audible. She was hurt and calling for his help.

While he struggled in his dream-vision to find her, John's hands twitched inside Robbie's car.

As Robbie led him ever closer toward an unknown abyss, some lightless chasm carved deep into the Kentucky rock by a thousand years of underground water flow, John slipped further away. While the full moon cast down its light like judgment, and the spinning wheels of Robbie's car threw the miles carelessly behind them, John slept.

Halfway through the drive, the tremors in his limbs grew more pronounced. Movements more frequent, lasting longer and building in intensity.

In the trapped state within his dream he saw other people reaching toward him, trying to dig, to free him. Their faces came one at a time, and as each new face arrived, the prior changed to a blank oval in his periphery, becoming department store mannequins, walking in a line until they faded.

They were speaking to him and he couldn't hear, something clogged his ears. Or they weren't making sounds. His parents were there, followed by his older sister Kathy, who had taken up with a biker and moved west.

His younger brother Scott came next, the only face showing an expression. A look of abject terror was twisting his plain features (he and John had heard many times that they looked enough alike to be mistaken for twins, despite the four years that separated them). John imagined his brother's face looked like this when he realized he would die soon, breathing his last, trapped in a tunnel that had spent years turning his lungs a cancerous black before falling around him like a natural coffin.

This receiving line of the dead faded, and it was he and Scott staring at each other. Unlike the others, John heard him.

"Almost too late, Johnnie." Scott was the only person who called him that. "You're running out of time, and you still haven't noticed what's happening. You have to hurry."

Then Scott was pulling back, like a marionette yanked behind a curtain after the show, arms and legs hanging forward as he shrank into some impossible distance.

John was shaking, shaking, shaking.

No, he was *being shaken*. The dream drifted away like smoke leaving a chimney in an upward trail.

He opened his eyes to a squint, coming to enough to discover it was Robbie shaking him. He didn't remember where he was. He looked around the inside of Robbie's car and saw only darkness outside.

"John!" Robbie shouted. "Wake up, Johnnie, wake up."

"Wh-what's going on?" John asked, his awareness clouded like a mental cataract had formed.

"You were really out there. Took me a while to get you up, I was starting to worry a little."

"Up?"

"Yeah, up. You were asleep."

It hadn't *felt* like sleep any more than his episodes of being trapped had. Seemed more like he was pulled out of his body, transplanted somewhere else, some*time* else, even. His energy was drained, not recharged.

"You were out right away. But when you started mumbling and spazzing around, that's when I thought I'd better wake you up. You were dreaming about something bad."

"I was talking?""Not really talking, I only caught a few words. You were dreaming about your dead brother, weren't you?" Robbie's tone was disapproving.

"Yeah, he was there."

"What for? You're still scared, aren't you?"

"Of course I'm scared, Robbie. I'm fucking terrified. I told you I didn't want to do this, and it was your idea and you haven't convinced me you're ready for it either."

"Woah, slow down. If you didn't want to—"

"No, I didn't want to. When did I say I *wanted* to?"

"You told me 'let's go,' didn't you? You said that. That kind of gives the impression you're into it."

"I gave in because I was desperate. But I've never stopped being scared, and I never thought it was a good idea. I don't want to do it anymore."

"Too late, John," Robbie said, putting the car in park and opening his door. "We're here. Time to face your fears."

Definition of unknown origin:

Psychometry, derived from the Greek *psukhe (spirit, soul) + metron (measure)*, also known as *psychoscopy*: A form of extrasensory perception characterized by the ability to divine accurate information regarding the unknown history of an object by making direct physical contact with that object.

***

From: *Astral Projection and Tabloid Mentalities, a Pragmatic Interpretation of Paranormal Psychologies* by Dr. Arthur McGuire, PhD (p. 17).

Another such unconventional practice is psychometrics. Literally interpreted as "measuring the soul," this involves a supposed ability to divine specific facts through the tactile exploration of an inanimate object. Usually involving the personal possessions of deceased individuals, particularly metal objects such as jewelry or trinkets, a psychically sensitive individual (or "medium") is, in theory, able to sense and describe past events or experiences involving the object in question. This would, of course, include instances or details that the medium was not aware of before handling the object; thus the process comprises a "psychic reading" of the object's residual aura or spiritual energy (see also Odic Force).

Joseph Rhodes Buchanan introduced psychometry in 1842, proposing that all things give off an observable and measurable "emanation." Buchanan made further claims that psychometry would have far-reaching implications for all scientific disciplines, employing such amusing terminology as "mental fossils." Through this, he equated the application of his theories to the study of ancient human history in much the same way that a geologist uses mineral fossils to study the ancient history of the Earth.

As though there is any rational connection between an archaeologist studying the fossilized remnants of an ancient society and a boastful lunatic holding a necklace while rolling their eyes back.

In his discourse, presumptuously entitled *Manual of Psychometry: the Dawn of a New Civilization*, Buchanan detailed his claims toward the value of knowledge that such studies would provide and how that knowledge would lead to an "enlightenment of humanity."

This author, for one, is still awaiting the enlightenment which the regular practice of psychometry will afford us.

In its modern form, psychometry exists as a mere pseudoscience based on cold-reading the eager members of a susceptible audience and is most commonly employed at psychic exhibitions or trade events for profit.

Throughout the myriad psychological and medical journals published since its inception more than a century and a half ago, there exist zero credible documented occurrences of psychometry. Though I would argue that Buchanan's concept serves one reliable function: parting fools from their money.

Chapter Thirteen

Lucy walked home from the cemetery, hoping the entire way for rain, if only to have a novel sensation, to distract from the grinding miasma of her sober and fractured mind.

No rain came.

Her house was too big for a woman alone, and she made little effort at upkeep. She had lived there with her boyfriend, Chris, who eventually willed it to her. She wasn't much for upkeep, assigning higher priority to tasks like drinking to quiet her raging extra-consciousness, hiding from memories, denying all the deaths around her that held no meaning, and taking the occasional shower, time permitting. But she had also never considered leaving it. The upstairs shrine to Anna was not mobile and she dared not part with that. Or set foot in it.

She could pay for cleaning services, at least a few times a year, or even for a painter or window cleanings or landscaping or anything (in place of liquor). The expense was not the obstacle. Chris's life insurance had been sizable, high six figures, and he changed her to the beneficiary alongside drafting the will. The state of disrepair would have been a problem if she lived on a street where anyone gave a damn. She'd found it wasn't much of a problem to live in squalor and never cut the grass when the next house was a half mile away and her only visitors were stray cats. At least it was tolerable to a degree she had not yet reached.

She despised herself for taking the insurance payout, but the money had been helpful when she got caught drinking at work, sneaking sips of neat vodka from a Styrofoam cup she'd grabbed from the cafeteria in the main building at Mercy Medical West. That day she'd lost not only her job and her nursing license, but also the last of her self-worth. Still, she wondered how no one caught her sooner. She'd been doing it for weeks.

When she made it to the house, she charged through the door, unlocked and covered in curls of flaking white paint, and moved straight toward the kitchen sink. One solitary and final action was in her future.

The kitchen floor was a minefield of plastic TV dinner trays (bits of food and sauce dried to dark sludge), glass empties (bottom shelf bourbons but also a few Southern Comfort and Grey Goose and even a Margaritaville to show her sense of adventure), and discarded clothes, all sprinkled with used and wadded tissues like a strange indoor hurricane was followed by a stranger hailstorm.

She flipped the under-sink cabinet open, finding her emergency kit of Old Crow and pills. She picked both up.

Lucy Claremont had reached the bottom, at last. Arrived at the point of no return.

She walked upstairs.

Standing outside Anna's room, Lucy took a generous pull from the bottle in her hand, reveling in the familiar but brief sensation of calm it gave. She pushed the door open slowly.

The walls in her late daughter's room were each painted a different color, all pastels, green, blue, yellow, purple, but not pink. (*"Eeeww, no, Mom. I don't want a pink room. How girly."*) The purple wall was the barest since Lucy had ripped down the W.C. Fields poster Chris gave to Anna. It was the only change she made to the room. One small corner of that poster still held to the wall, a slice of the comedian's chin showing, reminding Lucy she could never cleanly separate Anna from her father.

On her dresser sat a small music box from their trip to the ultra-touristy Dinosaur City near Mammoth Cave National Park, covered in a volume of dust that took years to build up or might come from Pompeii-scale preservation.

She intended that trip as a reward for Anna, but it was a gift to them both. In second grade, Anna entered a city-wide spelling bee, her own idea. She was a natural, taking to the contest like a small Olympian. The day before the final, Lucy found her sobbing and had to coax out the reason. Anna was not usually guarded, and it cracked Lucy's heart.

A boy from another school had made fun of Anna's pronunciation, saying she had a "dumb hick accent." Anna, bruised, didn't want to continue. Lucy wanted to thrash the little shit and reminded herself he was likely just a bitter loser. In one of her proudest mom-moments, Lucy had crafted a meandering speech about "staying open even when you get hurt, because it makes you stronger," or something in that vein. Anna won that spelling bee and the trophy still stood proud and gleaming next to her dinosaur music box.

A tear broke free and ran down Lucy's right cheek as she continued to scan the room.

Anna's corner bookshelf held an endearing mix of authors and titles that obscured both the age and gender of their owner. Beverly Cleary and several of *The Boxcar Children* series sandwiching a worn copy of *The Collected Works of H. G. Wells*. Bruce Coville leaned on a volume of Sylvia Plath poems. Lucy once brought home a copy of *The Giver* she picked up in the drugstore on the way home, and it became Anna's favorite. The copy on the shelf was her third, each prior read until the spines gave and pages fell out and only then would Anna part with them, provided the outgoing copy crossed paths with a new one.

Another time it had been *Little Women* that went in the shopping basket, Lucy's favorite, which to her disappointment suffered the opposite fate of The Giver. *"Don't know where it is, Mom. I must have left it on the bus yesterday."*

She lobbed the Old Crow bottle toward the small bed. It flipped end-over-end, twice, landing with a muffled *slosh*. Still holding her pills, she walked to the window and looked at the backyard. Saw the rusted swing set that enamored Anna for only one month before she decided she would rather spend her summer evenings using her telescope or driving an RC Jeep around the front yard while supplying the sound effects from the stoop.

Lucy always believed passersby would interpret Anna's divergent personality as precocious. To Lucy, the correct adjective for it was *aspiring*. Anna would hope, push, and experiment until she found exactly what and how she wanted to be defined. Not the reverse, like other children her age. Lucy had loved watching her child turn the adolescent experience upside-down that way. It was something she was incapable of herself, and it brought her pride beyond measure.

Set on the windowsill, Lucy noticed a piece of Anna's jewelry. She took another swig of bourbon and the scraping and humming and grinding in her head quieted. Almost gone, distilled to a single point of tremor like the idling of a finely tuned car engine.

She was looking at the last birthday present she ever gave her daughter, on her eleventh birthday. Two months before her death.

It was a gift Lucy took pride in, clever in its simplicity and its strong-but-subtle meaning. Anna loved it. *Had* loved it. The police let Lucy keep it once she identified the body, a cold blue alien in the shape of her baby, on a metal shelf in a basement morgue on the same hospital campus where Lucy tried to usher so many patients to their own death.

Tried to ease their *passing through*, a term of her own design.

She did not remember bringing that bracelet home. Nor did she remember leaving it on the windowsill. A ten-inch length of aluminum ball chain she purchased at a hobby store, enough to wrap a little girl's wrist twice. Affixed to that chain with small chrome rings were three pads from antique typewriter keys. Her initials AEC, Anna Elise Claremont.

When she opened it, Anna asked what the keys were, where they had come from. And when Lucy explained, Anna was silent for a few seconds while Lucy worried that her gift had fallen on its face. To confirm her acceptance, Anna said in a no-nonsense, no-arguing tone, "Well, now I need a typewriter."

That day Lucy had smiled until her cheeks hurt.

But there was no typewriter. Anna was gone too soon after.

Lucy picked up the bracelet in her left hand, the bottle of Halcion in her right.

Then something happened.

It was a sensation she remembered from childhood. She once found a brass key lying on the sidewalk, coming home from school when she was near Anna's age. She picked that key up and learned it belonged to a woman who lived four houses from her parents who had died of cancer the previous month. These pieces of information were accessible enough to anyone willing to ask, but Lucy learned with them a few additional points, simply by rolling her fingers around that key.

Lucy learned what that key opened (a small wooden jewelry box, full of mementos from her favorite occasions with her husband, waiting for the perfect day far later in life to share it with him), where she had hidden it from him (tucked behind a loose rock, part of a wall built around her raised garden in their backyard; she even used the key to scrawl a heart shape on the front of the rock as a marker), and that she'd not told him about it before the tumor in her brain stole her from him.

That perfect day, that far-later life, it never came.

Lucy learned all this through a staggering rush of sensations. Not only sights or sounds, but complete events, coming fully formed to her, with the force of ocean waves. One after another. But not her own, they were someone else's, and Lucy was experiencing the feelings those events made, delivered directly into her consciousness, like memories of things she had never seen or heard or done. But they became part of her.

Lucy saw the two of them together, this woman and her husband, holding hands in a park, holding each other in a ski lodge, him proposing on a starry night in a city Lucy did not recognize. Her placing a dried flower from that park day into a wooden jewelry box, her ski lift pass, ticket stub from the opera (*Otello*) they had seen the night he proposed. All stowed safely in the locked box, her message in a bottle that she hadn't the chance to cast into the water.

It took Lucy nearly an hour to explain this to him, the man whose wife's key she had found. *How could she know these things?* he had asked. *Is this some cruel joke?* But Lucy persisted until he had at least taken the key from her.

She mentioned the ticket stub, and that was the detail that convinced him. After a pause, his reaction switched to an immense gratitude, he hugged her, then apologized for hugging her, and disappeared into his house.

Lucy had moved around to the side of the house, peeking through two slats of the wooden privacy fence at an angle, to see him racing toward a rock wall in the far corner of their large backyard.

The gift Lucy had given him that day, watching that man find his lost wife's hidden treasures, drove her to a life's work of bringing peace to the dying, helping her patients and those they left behind to claim victory over death.

To die well.

Lucy chased that moment for thirteen years, but had not recaptured it.

She had come close a few times, only to fall short again. But she kept trying until death took notice and fought back.

After struggling with her own understanding of what happened when she touched that key, Lucy settled on a term to describe it, or at least where it started. She called it a "blink."

Last night, when the handcuffs first touched her wrists, she thought it was coming. Then, it hadn't. Now it did.

When she picked up Anna's type-key bracelet, a focused chill found the base of her neck, spreading over the back of her skull, in all directions, like frozen fingers tracing her scalp.

She shirked her shoulders in reflex, all back muscles tensing as one. Hair on both arms rising to attention.

Then, as if those cold fingers had flipped a switch somewhere, came a long rush of sound like a waterfall and she was not in her body anymore but spinning free in that water as it rushed over a cliff, casting her toward a pool of sensory input below. Soon she crashed into the pool, the water hitting her like concrete from all sides, and everything went white and silent.

After an immeasurable time, Lucy heard a heartbeat, and breathing. They should be hers, based on the proximity of the sound, but they belonged to someone else.

A person like her, but also not like her.

They belonged to Anna. Lucy was experiencing her daughter's final days.

She soon recognized things she had heard from the police, along with what she'd read in reports and articles and the countless news stories she watched.

She had blocked some of it out over the last four years; she knew these details already, but it was entirely different to get this way.

Lucy now experienced it from Anna's perspective. Everything the police had once told her. With the bracelet in her hand, she saw Anna's final moments playing out, as if Lucy had lived them herself and was now unlocking the memory rather than acting as a spectator.

For a short eternity, she was Anna, through a gauntlet of sensations and emotions. Surprise, joy, running, sadness, fear, jumping, cold water, longing, confusion. And finally, happiness. Then a loud noise that could only be a close-range gunshot.

The world flashed red. Went dark. Lucy felt Anna's breathing and heartbeat cease.

It was over, the "blink" ended there. There was a re-emerging sensation, then a sudden lessening of density in the air, like she was rising from the bottom of a swimming pool, and cresting the surface.

She was back in Anna's room.

Lucy looked from the pill bottle in her left hand to the bracelet in the right. Her eyes were shrouded in tears and woe. And back again, again. Then again. Her indecisiveness came as a surprise as she stood at the bottom, up against the point of no return.

From *Passing Through, Thoughts on Death and Dying* by Lucille Claremont, RN (p. 88).

"Meeting Death":

Facing death is a highly individualized experience as are the human responses to doing so. This makes it difficult to predict. The experience not only varies drastically from one person to another, but it also represents a new and incomparable experience for the individual undergoing it.

It is simply not possible to be certain how each of us will react upon meeting death. There are, however, common factors that can affect this experience, and these factors can be analyzed and considered with moderate reliability when present.

The strongest and most prevalent among these factors is fear.

Fear is a driving force behind many behaviors throughout one's lifespan and continues to guide through the process of dying. This fear can stem from a large variety of sources, including: separation from what is familiar, consequences for actions taken during life, the destination of one's soul or perhaps fear of what or who awaits us there. The common thread behind these possibilities is that a fear of the unknown largely guides the way we approach death during our last days and hours.

The second such factor influencing a person's death is the concept of closure. It is both unsettling and undesirable to leave behind "unfinished business." When a person who is dying nears the end, any perceived lack of closure will affect their response to dying. Events not complete, decisions not made with finality, questions unanswered, plans made but not followed; these items, when present in the consciousness of someone preparing to pass through, will most likely result in a strong urge to resist death. A person seeking closure for events in their life will struggle against the natural progression of dying, and therefore cannot achieve the desired sense of peace. The only way to attain peace in death is to rectify "unfinished business." Again, it is difficult to observe or attempt to understand how this resistance to death manifests.

The living cannot tell how a dying person, sensing a lack of closure in this world, will fight death. It is possible for this struggle against death to have a physical impact on the person's body while resistance takes place on a subconscious or spiritual level. A spiritual fight can take a physical toll in extreme cases.

Along with all other aspects of preparing for death, only those close to death can see or experience this.

Resisting death is an entirely solitary experience.

Chapter Fourteen

"It's late," John said, looking through the windshield at darkness and the vague suggestion of distant trees. An outline of forest sealed them in without shape.

Robbie's door opened, the dome light spilling around John like he was in a police interrogation room.

Robbie stood outside the car and stretched his arms upward. He surveyed, looking from side to side, then reached back in and snaked his arm between the seats, into the back of the car. He grabbed a map and held it to the dome light.

"Ah," he said, taking a step toward the car's hood and pointing. "That way."

"You mean you don't know where it is?"

"That's what you just heard? It's that way, John. I had to make sure."

"How did you find this place?" John asked, getting out of the car himself, doing his own bit of surveying.

The moon was large, a few days shy of full, obscured by thick clouds and delivering only enough light to tease his eyes. John was certain only of the distant tree line (defined like an impressionist painting seen up close), the gravel road that brought them, and a rolling hill hundreds of feet beyond, rising far enough to imply the Earth may abruptly end on the other side.

The clearing was a fishbowl.

"Friend of mine," Robbie answered. "Said it's unexplored, so I knew this was the one. It's perfect, isn't it?" John couldn't see him in the faint light of the covered moon, but he heard Robbie's game-show-host smile. Robbie opened the car's small trunk and took out his duffle bag and a few bottles of water.

"Unexplored? Why the hell is that perfect?"

"It's more of a challenge. Higher stakes. Plus, nobody knows about it and the guy who owns the property won't even notice us here."

"Fuck, Robbie, when you string all that together, it kinda sounds like we're screwed if something bad happens. Did you at least tell Mags we were coming here? Or your sister?"

"Hmm? Yeah, we'll be fine. She knows where we are."

"Which one?"

"Which what?"

"Which one of them did you tell?"

"I told them both, okay? Stop worrying so much and trust me."

Robbie was fussing with the map, held under a flashlight he had produced. John knew he needed to press Robbie harder for information, there were things he was trying to hide that John needed. If he was going to trust Robbie with his life, he deserved all the information. Then he'd decide if it was worth going any farther.

Before he spoke, the moon rolled from behind the clouds, as if on Robbie's cue, giving a farther view of the landscape.

They both saw the cave's mouth. John found the term "mouth" quite apt. When Robbie first suggested it back home, John imagined the type of cave bears would shelter in, a stable and perhaps welcoming archway in a hillside. Somewhere the light could reach. What he saw, in strong contrast to that more-digestible version, looked like the ground itself yawning upward. John guessed the mouth to be about forty feet in diameter, larger than most rooms. It was on a gentle slope, the opposite rim higher than the edge closest to them.

To enter it, rather than the even-footed walk he expected, meant going straight down.

"Is that it?" John asked. He swallowed hard, coughed a few times, and his lungs contracted. His face flushed while his fingers were frigid. And he was dog-tired.

"That's it."

"That's not a cave. More like a well."

Robbie held up a length of heavy rope, wound into a figure-eight, for John to see, then threw it to him underhand.

"That's what this is for. It's called rappelling. You're gonna love it."

"It's certainly *repelling*."

"Say what?"

"I said, did you learn that in a book this week?"

"No. Magazine article."

"Oh. That's much better." Robbie shut the car doors and walked toward the hole, a second length of rope in his hand.

John followed.

Robbie saw it first, and though he tried, he couldn't hide all of his reaction from John.

Past the cave's mouth, at a distance that in the moonlight could have been fifty feet or a thousand, was a white tree. It stood alone, taller than a house, a stark outline against the amorphous backdrop of the forest that grew farther past it, like a sentry before the impenetrable barrier, there to warn them.

"Looks like a good place for a cemetery," Robbie said.

John agreed; it looked out of place in this landscape. Its trunk was a column of peeling tissue paper with solid white beneath like dead skin flaking from bone, marred by a few large black spots like cancer. Its branches were bare, despite it being summer, without making it appear dead. He had never seen such a tree.

Another episode came. The quickest, over in an instant like a slap, it was also the strongest. Again, John heard his brother Scott's voice.

"Have to hurry, Johnnie. That's it there. Point of No Return."

John lost his balance and fell, but Robbie was there to catch him by the arm. He pulled John back upright though John's knees suggested it wouldn't last. And he knew he wouldn't make it. He didn't have the strength to face this. He needed to leave.

John ran away like death was chasing him.

Chapter Fifteen

R obbie was right behind him, yelling. John passed the car, not slowing. But Robbie was faster.

Still yelling, he brought John down with an arm wrapped around his legs. They fell hard, onto the gravel. A dozen scrapes came alive on John's skin like burns.

"John!" Robbie yelled. "Stop!"

"What the fuck? Get off me!" John said, pushing, kicking, trying to get up.

Robbie held tight.

"Stop. Where are you going?"

"I'm going. I'm out of here."

"You can't go, okay?"

"I'm going. I can and I am. I'm going. This isn't safe, Robbie. You're not ready for this and it's not safe. Someone will get hurt."

"It's safe, trust me."

"Stop telling me to trust you. I-I don't, I can't. You say that but you're obviously not telling me everything. So, no. I can't trust you."

Robbie stood. John stayed seated in the gravel, hands on his bent knees and looking straight ahead. At the tree. Not at Robbie.

"What? What are you talking about? I'm not keeping anything from you."

"You are. Don't do this shit."

"I'm not. What's gotten into you? Why are you so mad?""Why are we here, Robbie? Really? Tell me why we're really here, or I'm gone."

"Where you gonna go? You don't know where we are."

"That's more true than you realize."

"I get you're scared, okay? I'm scared too."

"You don't seem scared."

"Well, I am. You want me to scream? Run? I won't. That's you, not me."

"Why are we here? Tell me now or I'm leaving. I'll fucking thumb a ride if I have to."

Robbie turned away. "I need this, okay? We're here for me."

"Why make it about me, then?"

"I knew you wouldn't go for it otherwise, that's why."

"What is this about, though? What are you trying to get out of it?"

"I need something else, man. Christ, you're going to make me spell the whole thing out, aren't you?"

"Yes, damn it. If I'm going in there with you, I deserve to know the whole story. And if you need help, that's one thing, but in case you forgot, I've got plenty of my own shit to deal with right now."

"Mags left me, for one."

"Yeah, but you didn't seem too concerned about it."

"Of course I'm concerned, John."

"You should be going after her, then. Not dicking around in the woods."

"We're not in the woods. It's a farm. And I can't go after her."

"Why not?"

"I don't know where she ended up, that's why."

"Call her then."

"Not that easy, John. You know that."

"Robbie, I know a whole fuck-lot less than you seem to think I do. What does that even mean? Just call her."

"I can't call her."

"Then make some guesses and start calling around. Do something, man." John pointed past where they were standing, toward the mouth of the cave. "She's not in *there*, that's for damn sure. How is that going to help?"

"It's something we have to do."

"We? Why we?"

"We're stuck in this rut together, that's why." Robbie was crying and it struck John like a plunge into cold water. He had never seen Robbie cry. "I have to do this, and I can't do it alone. I don't expect you to understand, I never did. That's why I tried convincing you to do this for your own sake. But the truth, actual truth, is I have to prove something before I get her back. To myself, but I honestly think it will help us both."

"I don't know, Robbie. It's not safe."

"But it is, I've got it all figured out. You just have to trust me, okay? Trust me for tonight and by this time tomorrow we'll be done and it'll get better."

John was still sitting on the ground. Robbie reached a hand toward him.

"Trust me. Please."

John said nothing but took his hand, putting his trust not in Robbie's plan, but at least in their friendship, and for the moment, in Robbie's intentions.

Robbie shouldered his bag and handed John a small flashlight. They walked past the car. Approached the gaping hole that waited to welcome them into the earth like a pre-made grave.

Robbie pushed a metal stake into the ground, a few dozen feet from the hole, slipped the rope through it, tied it in a quick but sophisticated knot.

"See?" he said, pointing at the knot. He threw the rest of the rope into the pit.

"How far down is it?"

"Not far. About thirty feet. I'll go first, if you'll promise not to ditch me."

I'm not sure that helps, John thought. A silent minute passed.

"Well?" Robbie said.

"I'm not going anywhere," John said. The truth of it stung.

Robbie pulled some kind of nylon waist harness out of the bag, slipped it on and clipped the rope to it. He handed another rig to John, told him to put it on. John did.

Then Robbie was holding the rope and lowering himself ass-first into the hole. When he was down, he called up: "Your turn!"

Definition of unknown origin:

Premonition, derived from the Latin *prae* (before) + *monere* (to warn): a type of precognition, often described as a paranormal sense of warning regarding a future event. Premonitions are usually unwelcome and may cause varying degrees of anxiety. The resulting sensation may be perceived as numerous types of sensory input with a correlation between intensity and the degree of danger involved.

***

From: *Astral Projection and Tabloid Mentalities, a Pragmatic Interpretation of Paranormal Psychologies* by Dr. Arthur McGuire, PhD (p. 46).

We could describe precognition as not only a single form of ESP but a dense category all its own. We could further develop this category by exploring one of the more commonly cited instances of precognition, that being premonitions.

Essentially, this is a precognition with a decidedly negative or foreboding tone, warning of impending disaster—a warning received strictly in the mental and/or emotional arenas, and which cannot be explained rationally by any information available through traditional vehicles.

Premonitions are referenced daily throughout most cultures (both historic and modern), thus lending a false credibility to another unsubstantiated and unproven form of parapsychology. In addition, premonitions appear to be one of the more "researched" arenas in parapsychology, though every published experiment reviewed by this author has yielded only two consistent products: questionable scientific technique and false claims of validity.

To mention the obvious, pure lunacy.

A typical example of these illaudable experiments are Ganzfeld hallucinations. This amounts to no more than an intentionally over-complicated form of sensory deprivation, aimed at producing the "Ganzfeld effect," which comes from eliminating any perceivable pattern of sensory input, thus theoretically allowing the psi-capable portion of a "receiver's" brain to become more active and allow for the paranormal reception of information.

Most published examples of Ganzfeld experiments disregard the absurd manner in which the effect is achieved.

The subject is first placed into a comfortable, relaxing environment that is more "conducive to precognitive activity." The sensory deprivation is then brought about through the simultaneous implementation of colored light bulbs, white noise and opaque objects placed over both eyes. With those bizarre and unrelated conditions in place, it would not take long for even the least psi-sensitive among us to experience strange cognitive occurrences. There is a strong possibility that an extended amount of time under such odd and unfamiliar circumstances, one would feel a sense of impending danger.

When following such idiotic logic as this, perhaps one could also achieve time travel by winding their watch the wrong way, while wearing their clothes backward, balancing a spoon on their nose, and reciting the lyrics of their favorite song in reverse.

The chances of successful time travel are equal to those of a Ganzfeld effect producing reliable data concerning the future.

Chapter Sixteen

Lucy did not take the sleeping pills on the morning she returned home after being arrested. Perhaps she'd not reached the bottom just yet. Or perhaps she decided by not deciding. She did, however, drink the entire bottle of Old Crow, then passed out.

When she awoke an indeterminate time later, head throbbing, the buzzing reasonably quiet but growing, she still clutched the bracelet she had gifted to her now-dead daughter.

Lucy sat up on Anna's bed, leaned forward, and cradled her head in her hands, her elbows on knees. She vomited, noting what came out was entirely liquid and asking herself in passing when she had last eaten. Her eyes were swollen, her tongue dead. None of this surprised her. Waking like this was familiar. Customary. The only difference, today, was place. She thought venturing into Anna's room, this in-house shrine, would help to force her hand. Press her irrevocably against rock bottom.

She was half right; it had been forceful. But it forced her into reconsidering suicide, just long enough to get blackout drunk again, instead of making a more permanent decision.

She was compelled to clean up the vomit. To fix something. To enhance. This gave her pause, and her pummeled brain explored, clumsily, what that implied. Surely, she did not care for the condition of the house. The problem then, must be something foul happening within Anna's room specifically. Part of her brain, a common and normal part, rather than the part that did inexplicable things, explored this. She did not want this place sullied. That meant, most likely, she still cared for something. One less brick in her wall of protective apathy. An absurd and unnecessary realization. Of course she still cared for something that had belonged to Anna. Her daughter was dead, but she never stopped loving her behind that wall. She just had not focused on that subtle and important difference for so long, which made realizing it *not* absurd, and very, very necessary. She could deny without end, but never forget.

Did that mean she was not ready to die? It had at least stalled her. Another brick gone.

The pills were still in the room somewhere, she knew. Thinking of them drove a similar reaction to seeing the vomit. Revulsion. A third brick falling out. She didn't want those vile life-stealing chemicals in here either. Lucy stood, wavering on her feet, vision swooning as she scanned for the small white bottle. She noticed the corner of a colorful piece of paper sticking out from under the bed. Her eyes watery and exhausted, she squinted for a better look, then stooped and picked it up.

A comic book. Or something like one.

When did Anna ever read comic books? she wondered. Lucy did not remember buying her any. Certainly not toward the end, after she and Chris had split. He owned a few, and she wanted to shed anything stained by him. Taking a closer look, Lucy noticed the roughness of the pages' surface, their uneven edges, then saw it was not bound along the side but rather stapled in the top left corner. She squinted, bringing the thing closer then farther from her field of vision, hoping to see it more clearly and wishing for her reading glasses, then realizing she hadn't needed those in months upon months.

It seemed homemade. When she held it near arm's length, the words at the top of the cover page were readable.

Lucy Lightfoot, Nurse Awesome!!

Lucy gasped. Her protective wall crumbled as if struck by an earthquake.

Its cover depicted a clumsily drawn female figure dressed in white, with a long blue cape and a hat with a red cross, standing hands-on-hips with a beaming smile.

Lucy flipped through the first two pages, scanning for context as her chest swelled. The plot was adorably simple, characters bordering on farce as one may expect from a child Anna's age, but this did not lessen the impact. She had been a hero to Anna.

Her knees buckled, and she dropped to them, taking care not to bend any pages in her clasping hands.

Unlike the other bits of information she'd found since entering her dead daughter's bedroom, the meaning behind this one was clear. Holding this tribute Anna had crafted, with the pure dialect and innocent style only possessed by the young, Lucy felt simultaneously held aloft by love and crushed by the weight of her failures. The more recent failures, those of denial, wallowing, hiding, and choosing hurt over healing again and again daily, for years. She had done the opposite of her motherly advice. She had closed herself up and stopped growing.

Lucy stood again, wobbling, looking in the mirror hung on the back of the bedroom door several feet away, drips of vomit on her shirt, eyes puffy and red, not turning away from her reflection this time. No more wall to hide behind. She took mental inventory of the realizations she was having, bracelet in one hand and the thin booklet in the other.

She still cared. Still desired better. And she saw how far she had let herself fall. She was able to look at herself once more, face what she saw, and not turn from it in cowardice.

What did that all mean, though? Had she truly known none of this until coming in here? If she still cared, did that apply to the kind of person she was? What would Anna think of what Lucy had become?

She had once been a hero to Anna. What would she be now?

What title would the comic book have today?

When she first walked in this room, she saw the end of a path with one option.

But, after living the events of Anna's death in first-person, then realizing she'd devolved into someone Anna would not be proud of, there was a firm tug at Lucy's resolve. Like a hand grabbing her from behind as she prepared to leap from a building top. There came a reason *not to*.

Lucy had drive, again. It was meek, but present. She wanted better.

To do better.

To *be* better.

In the cemetery, she had denied her calling because she wasn't sure she was strong enough. That no longer mattered. She had to be strong enough. For Anna.

CHAPTER SEVENTEEN

Oh God, where do I start? Lucy thought, wavering on the razor's edge that was her newfound resolve to make better choices. To fix herself.

Could she help the person she'd seen in that hospital-bed vision? Become a nurse again? Reclaim her unique position in front of death's door? She wanted to, had a desire, however tentative, to become someone her daughter would be proud of again. If or when they reunited, Lucy would not go with her head hung low.

An idea came and painted a smirk on her face.

She would charge, hold nothing back. That was how to begin again. She would return to the scene, march through the doors of the Mercy Medical West hospice wing as if she were engaging in an act of civil disobedience, and ask to come back. *No reason to be shy about it.*

The idea was terrible, yet part of her knew it would at least serve as a test of her wavering new resolve. If she failed to take those first steps, the journey was over before it began.

Her head was buzzing again beneath her hangover, thoughts straying back to the pills lying somewhere nearby.

Before her arm could betray her, she moved away from the bed and started downstairs, setting the homemade comic book gently on the comforter. She changed clothes to her last pair of clean-ish jeans, plain gray V-neck T-shirt, and the barely worn New Balance sneakers she had bought the day before Anna disappeared.

All these items were in a moving box in her closet. *Another emergency kit? Made ready in case of another decision point, like the pills under the kitchen sink?* She wanted that to be true.

She tucked Anna's bracelet into her front left pocket.

Her car now impounded, she would need to navigate through the spider's web of lines and forms and fees and scowls at the DMV to get it back. After she walked there, of course. Her true destination wasn't much farther of a walk.

It was early afternoon now. The walk would do her good. She could think about what to say and hopefully not detour to a QuikStop or pharmacy to buy a bottle.

Less hesitation would help, she told herself. *No more time to consider alternatives. That's the pit I've been wallowing in, and it's time to pull myself up.*

So, she walked. It was near seven miles, would take three hours. As she rounded the corner at the end of her street and headed west on Edwards Road toward the parkway, it may as well have been seven hundred. The distance strode out in front of her, dry when she wanted a drink, silent when she needed distraction from the noise in her skull.

She walked anyway. And thought of Anna.

After what seemed an hour but surely wasn't, grateful for the hum of rushing traffic from the nearby six-lane Thornton Parkway, she heard a noise.

It started as a shrill beeping, with rhythmic pauses, sounding like the synthesized call of a sea bird.

reeet... reeet... reeet... reeet

She looked around before realizing that it wasn't coming through her ears and that she recognized the sound. Its quality and frequency and timbre were familiar. Too familiar.

Life support equipment. To a seasoned hospice nurse, it was a common sound, recognizable as her own voice. It continued, steady at first, and strong enough to vibrate her organs inside her chest. Lucy tuned closer into that sound as she expected a change in its speed.

The beeping held its pace through the rest of the walk. As she made her way toward the Mercy Medical West campus, Lucy wondered what it meant. Why was she hearing it? It was as if a heart monitor were rolling down the sidewalk behind her as she walked.

Was it a warning? That seemed most likely. But was the beehive in her head feeding this information to her to prevent her doing something? Or prepare her for what was coming?

Was it telling her to turn around or to keep going?

Was it an omen? If so, a good one? Or a bad one?

She kept going, reminding herself of what lay behind her. There was death in either direction, but the way back was an impasse. Rock bottom. Liquor and pills and jail time. Continuing to circle the cemetery at night like a moth begging for the flame to burn its pain away.

Killing herself may be easier but at the same time it was a mountain unscalable. She again had not been able to go through with it, and now doubted that would change. She kept walking, and thought of her daughter's comic book. Held that image like Polaris while she forged shakily ahead.

As the cluster of medical buildings came into sight, the beeps grew far louder. They were still at the same steady pace, a speed that implied stable condition, but becoming so pronounced that it hurt. Each individual *reeet* punctured her left arm like a pin. She stopped walking, to see if that affected the beeping.

At first, nothing changed. Same sound, same intensity, same frequency. She took a few steps backward. Still no change.

She walked again, and that's when the beeping sped up. Were this an actual machine, supporting an actual patient's life, heard through her actual ears, that would mean only one thing. Their condition was deteriorating. At worst, respiratory or cardiac arrest. At best, some organ failure that may cause permanent damage.

Then she heard a voice, and the warning message soon became terribly clear. Barely noticeable, at first, rolling out of the cacophony that had become a regular part of her consciousness (when not muted with alcohol). As she strode nearer and nearer to her former self, the words became a little clearer. Then clearer still. A dozen more steps and she recognized the voice, if not the words.

Anna was speaking to her.

Lucy stopped; the voice stopped. The phantom beeping continued. She took two steps and heard it again. Clearer this time.

Mom, it said.

Lucy walked faster, realizing that the closer she came to the hospice wing, the clearer that voice became. It was an affirmation, telling her she was headed in the right direction, both geographically and morally.

Her tenuous resolve multiplied, as she strode across the sea of parking spaces, a swelling in her chest that was energizing. As she closed the distance from the outside world to the hospital, the empty parking spaces gave way to sparsely occupied ones, then to rows of cars like an unorganized auto mall. The medical buildings loomed on all sides, midday sun glinting through glass lobby atriums and off-gray steel support beams. Towers of red brick formed an unnatural canyon with a river of concrete at the bottom. All dressed up with professional landscaping on each corner that did little to hide the pain and tragedy within.

When she still worked here, spending hours upon hours inside one of those brick-and-steel nests of suffering, Lucy had either not noticed or ignored how bleak the space outside the hospital was.

Anna's voice was becoming louder than the cars speeding down the highway behind her, louder than the brain static that had debilitated her for years.

She approached the hospice wing, looking at the expanse of awning drawn across the driveway for transport vehicles, held by two brick columns like legs too far apart. In letters six feet tall on the front, it read Mercy Medical West Hospice.

She stopped short of the front doors, almost close enough for the sensors to signal them open. There was a small gathering of people at the reception desk, including someone she recognized: an officious, short man in a brown suit. Kent Johanssen, the Hospice Director.

He was talking with the family of a patient. She recalled how he acted involved, but only when the occasion struck him, when he found time for a break from the bean-counting.

It was a problem because he would recognize Lucy. And remember her trespassing warning. And enforce it without hearing a word she had to say.

What __do__ I have to say? she thought.

If she had any hope of speaking to someone who would listen, maybe one of her former co-workers, and planning out a legitimate path back, she would need to avoid him. She walked around the side of the building, past a small, manicured garden that was likely never noticed by anyone except the landscapers, making her way to one of the side exits on a path of paver stones dug into the lawn.

That was when Anna spoke to her, in full clarity.

You gotta help him, Mom, Anna said, her phantom voice pleading. *Help Robbie. Something bad is happening to him. He's all alone, and he needs you and there's not much time left. He's trapped, Mom. He's stuck and he can't move.*

CHAPTER EIGHTEEN

*R*obbie? Lucy thought, working to understand the cryptic message that her too-active mind delivered in her dead daughter's voice. *Is that someone I should know? Surely it's not him, not my Robbie? Is it?*

You're the only one that can help him, the voice added.

It couldn't be *her* Robbie. Her brother. The only Robbie she knew, but had last seen over twenty years ago, once he realized their mother wasn't coming back. As his car pulled out of the driveway of their childhood home, Lucy had watched for Robbie to wave. He didn't.

A clear lesson from their parents: people you attach to yourself are like anchors in a sea of blandness, and to shed their weight is liberation.

Momma, Robbie needs you, explained the voice that was impossibly Anna's. *He's in there and he needs you.*

"In there?" Lucy said aloud, pointing toward the emergency exit on the side of the building.

She peered in the nearest window and saw a familiar scene. Raised bed, IV pole, a bag of comfort meds piggybacked to the saline drip, white counters, white sheets, white cabinets. Items that should appear in a dying patient's room. She recognized the navy blue curtains, though they were new since her time here.

But she saw one exception. A large white tree trunk, dead center of the room. It grew up out of the linoleum floor and disappeared straight into the ceiling tiles.

When she looked behind her, outside, the window was not showing a scene inside the room, but reflecting one from outside. The same scene she had witnessed earlier, first on the bus and then in the cemetery, past Anna's grave.

She fixated on the bed, so displaced in the grove next to the hospice building. A ripple went through the whole of her illusion, making it appear as if projected on a screen made of fabric. The body under the sheets rose. The head, shrouded and unseen, lifted from the pillows.

One hand raised next, then the other, as if the person under the sheets was emulating Frankenstein's monster waking, brought back with a jolt of electricity. The sheet slid down, revealing the face beneath.

It was twisted, lifeless, an unmoving mask. The face of a dead man. His eyes trained on Lucy's, without blinking. The hand moved.

He pointed at Lucy. She recognized him then. She knew who Robbie was.

Chapter Nineteen

Robbie called up to John. "You coming or not?"

John stepped to the rim of the cave's mouth, a human morsel offered to the earth itself, shining his light down. It failed to reach the bottom, returning only an infinite darkness. His shoes gritted against the loose soil at the edge and his heart fluttered. An image of Mags came to him, the beach photo. He looked back at the car, knowing the keys were in Robbie's pocket. His fear was a presence all its own, as if there were a third person preparing to enter the cave with him.

John grabbed the rope as Robbie had, putting the mouth of the cave behind him, a massive wormhole plummeting into the abyss.

He moved a leg backward, standing with one foot on solid ground and the other dangling over everything unfamiliar below.

PART TWO

Going Deep

From *Passing Through, Thoughts on Death and Dying* by Lucille Claremont, RN (p. 103).

"Near-Death Experiences":

For those attempting to understand death from an outside perspective, it is helpful to consider the difference between the process of dying and a near-death experience (or NDE).

At a cursory glance, there appears much common ground between the two occurrences (NDE and dying); however, when scrutinized, the inherent differences become significant. Logically, a patient on an inevitable path toward death experiences a far different mental process than someone who comes close to but avoids dying.

The two are readily distinguished by examining certain notable traits. Most prominent is the amount of focus placed, by the patient, on sensory information. Someone who has an NDE will recall sights, sounds, smells, and touch sensations in detail.

In contrast, a patient nearing clinical death will describe (in lucid moments), how the experience felt, rather than what they sensed externally. This is because, when one brushes with death, the conscious mind remains the driver of how that experience gets interpreted. It translates sensory input until the spiritual energy has shifted. When that shift in spiritual energy occurs, the frontal lobe cedes control of information processing to deeper, more primitive areas of the brain, those responsible for understanding emotion. Therefore, through their last days, a dying patient will experience the common themes of the afterlife and their focus will be on the internal sensations.

A second observable difference is that someone having an NDE may describe a sensation of pulling or tugging that brings them back to their physical body. This sensation is often felt at the back of the head and considered a safety mechanism for the conscious brain, allowing it to anchor itself. This sensation is not associated with clinical death.

One additional consideration that should be given to NDEs is that most terminally ill patients will first experience these types of glances-with-death when at an advanced stage. An NDE can become a precursor to clinical death.

In most cases, an NDE where one witnesses their own physical death during an out-of-body state should be taken as a sign that the subconscious mind is attempting to wrest control from an unwilling conscious mind. This occurs when death is imminent but the patient has unresolved concerns of a critical nature.

Chapter Twenty

As John lowered himself into the cave, with the hesitance of a starving animal approaching an outstretched human hand offering food, he fought to keep himself from falling and from fixating on how similar this environment was to his episodes of being trapped.

It was as if Robbie had plucked a scene from his plagued subconscious and sculpted it in 3D from wet clay. Then convinced John to fall into it.

Falling was not quite the truth but also not far from it. He slipped in a few spots, but stayed careful. Twice he bumped an elbow into the wall, a third time his foot glanced off an unseen protrusion and his face clapped into the wall rudely. It was only by an involuntary death grip he kept his hands locked on the rope to prevent himself from plummeting the rest of the way into Robbie's lap.

No, had he fallen, Robbie wouldn't have caught him. Robbie was nowhere in sight when John's feet found the bottom (limited though it was as the moonlight was sending only its most stalwart fingers all the way down).

John turned in a tight, cautious circle, using his flashlight to search and finding it little more effective than the filtered light of the moon. His eyes returned nothing outside a ten-foot radius, like he was inside a chimney. The darkness was oppressive. And it was cold. The surrounding air in the chamber was much colder than outside, some three-dozen feet above him.

That's not right, is it? Isn't it supposed to be close to room temp down here?

He called out. "Robbie?" No answer. John had no intention of going farther alone. His lungs were tight and his skin feverish, despite the cold air. He wrestled with the instinct to escape back up the rope.

"Robbie!" Louder this time, hearing his own voice echoed back from some unseen tunnel or chamber or another hole that led deeper underground. Still no answer.

"I'm about to go, man. This shit doesn't fly."

Only his own echo again.

John grabbed the rope. "Here I go," he said, meaning to convince himself more than Robbie. His mind wormed toward some of the terrible outcomes waiting for him down here.

We could end up lost. Or fall and break something. Fall and break everything. Or something falls on me and breaks everything. The rope leading out snaps and we wait days for help before eating each other. Get trapped and suffocate like Scott.

John wanted to pull himself up. Regardless of what Robbie wanted or needed or said, he was done following. John grabbed the rope with both hands and lifted one foot into a hold about two feet off the base. He hoisted himself on that leg while pulling on the rope, then took a second step up, muscles straining already, far weaker than he expected.

He couldn't see the top, just black and a few stars, the same distance now as earlier, before they descended. Muscles in his arms burned. He'd climbed past his own height, not quite eight feet, judging by his limited depth perception.

His hands slid on the rope. No, the rope slid down from its fixed point up top. He was still, but the rope was moving.

Then he was falling.

Robbie was there, this time. John landed flat-footed and Robbie braced him to keep upright.

"It's over this way." Robbie pointed into the darkness, thick as curtain cloth. "I found the trail."

Two thoughts stuck like thorns as John aimed his flashlight at Robbie's back and returned to his pattern of following.

How could he get out if that short climb was so taxing? And had the entire rope fallen in when he dropped back down?

He hadn't the stomach to check the rope.

Robbie was already fading into a black so thick and nebulous it was like ink in water.

"Wait, Robbie. Isn't it supposed to be the same temperature in here all the time?"

"Yeah, that's right. Why?"

Robbie slowed, shining his light around in an arc, revealing the opening of a tunnel. Its ceiling low enough to require them both to duck.

"It's freezing in here, that's all. I thought the air temp stayed comfortable this far underground, no matter what season or temperature it is topside. Right?"

"Not in this part of the country," Robbie replied without hesitation, gliding into the tunnel like an apparition.

John hunched over to follow, barking an elbow on the opening.

"I remember reading somewhere that caves are always the same temperature. Because of being underground or something."

"Yeah, they stay the same temperature year-round, but that temperature can vary from cave to cave depending on what region of the country it's in. Around here they're usually colder. You should have worn long sleeves, buddy."

Robbie's gaze flitted left to right as he used his light to examine the tunnel ahead.

As John entered the tunnel himself, uneasy but determined to stay within arm's reach of Robbie, claustrophobia hummed throughout his body, pulsing out from his chest. He leaned ahead, tensing his shoulders as he moved farther away from the outside world and the open sky. The tunnel mouth swallowed him alive without moving, without sound. In his mind's eye he saw it draw up in a serrated malevolent smile as he passed through. He turned back, hoping to dispel that image and saw only impenetrable darkness outside the tunnel. The opening had vanished.

CHAPTER TWENTY-ONE

"You know, there's actually a word for the fear of caves," Robbie said. His voice echoed off the walls of the slim tunnel, making it seem like he could be moving in any direction. The trail from his flashlight flickered from around a curve like a lone candle. He could have been two feet ahead or twenty.

John reached out to the adjacent wall. The rock was solid, smooth, and cool. And a little wet. That was the extent of his courage to explore. He realized he was completely at Robbie's mercy.

"No shit," John said. "Claustrophobia. You're bringing that up right now?"

"No, that's not even it. I'm bringing it up because we came down here for a reason, in case you forgot. When you first told me about your little... episode, I dug around." The hint of a laugh lined Robbie's words like a picture frame.

"Did you, now? I thought we came here for you."

"Right, but we can kill two birds. Only trying to help, believe it or not. I'm concerned, so I looked into it. Anyway, claustrophobia isn't about any particular tight space. It could be an elevator, a closet, a small room, a car, or a—"

"Got it, okay. I got it," John said. *Don't say grave.*

"What you had sounded more specific. It didn't sound like it was just about the... the tightness. It was about what was outside that, causing that sensation of confinement. And then it hit me! It's about being trapped deep inside somewhere. With no hope of getting out. Sound right?"

"Sounds fucking awful, Robbie. Can you stop analyzing me and focus on keeping us alive down here?"

"Don't worry about that, we're fine." He stopped, turned to face John, and his flashlight blinked out, as if on cue. He tapped it twice; it came back on. "This is important, otherwise we're wasting our time. There *is* a term for fear of depths. Specific to that. Have you heard it before?"

"I'm not guessing, if that's what you're fishing for. Just fucking tell me."

"See, you're getting angry. This is good. You're uncomfortable and that means growth. Ready?"

"For Christ's sake, Robbie. Will you just—"

"Bathophobia."

"Bath."

"-ophobia."

"As in, fear of bathing?"

"No. Think Greek root. *Bathios* means depth."

"And?"

"And that means we have a diagnosis. Next step is the cure."

John turned his head from side to side, hunched over, waving his flashlight in theatrics dulled by the lack of performance space. "You're about the worst fucking doctor ever."

Robbie grinned. "How do we cure a fear of depths?"

"Robbie, really."

Robbie shone his flashlight (much stronger than John's) through an opening in the narrow tunnel ahead. Past that point, the cave opened again. John heard running water, maybe a waterfall. Saw a steep but passable (*Was it?*) declining grade beyond Robbie's feet, dropping out of sight quickly. Then oblivion.

Robbie answered his own question.

"We're going deep, buddy."

CHAPTER TWENTY-TWO

The climb down wasn't as bad as John expected. The rock had been carved into a shallow staircase, and if he turned his feet sideways, he could remain stable.

On the way, Robbie casually informed him a mere handful of people had set foot in this cave, less than ten, and even fewer had gone this far. And they were relying on a hand-drawn map.

John wondered again how difficult (avoiding any derivative of the word *possible*) resurfacing would be. If the rope was still there, to climb back out to his safe, comfortable, and predictable life outside. Then he remembered most of that was gone too. He felt desolate, like a small plant fighting for life between sidewalk cracks when the weedkiller came spraying.

As they reached the bottom, Robbie said, "We're headed for part of this cave system no one has ever been through. Completely unexplored."

John wished he had told someone where they were going. Anyone.

They were standing in a vast chamber compared to the tunnel they had stumbled through. The darkness was thicker than ever, preventing John from seeing any borders of this space, but he still sensed its size. The sound of the waterfall was no closer, for one. And they had descended at least forty or fifty feet, down the slick rocky staircase. It was much deeper than the drop when they first entered from the surface.

Robbie held his arms out, extended to each side, and breathed deep.

"Aaah. This is going to be great. I can feel it."

Unable to stop himself, John wondered why Robbie was so insistent, so excited, so comfortable with all of this. That led to more disconcerting thoughts, like he was pulling on a loose thread in his own safety net, one that barely held him in place as-is, above a pit of spikes.

Does he think I'll have some revelation down here? And what, become more like him? That makes less sense than ever, now that we're here. Am I here for backup, if something goes wrong? If he needed that, wouldn't he have told more people where we went? So they could find us?

The mental thread gave way in sharp lengths.

He said he told his sister and Mags, right? John thought, remembering how unconvinced he had been when Robbie had answered that. *What if he didn't tell them? What if he doesn't want anyone to find us?*

"Which way do we go?" John asked, not wanting to feed into Robbie's unnerving excitement, wanting instead to push through this outing as fast as possible. Get it over with, his only remaining control.

Robbie looked around, took a few steps, sending his light forward, redirected, looked further again. He repeated this a few times as John watched.

"Can you tell which way the waterfall is?" Robbie asked. He was feigning nonchalance, acting casual. And failing. "The tunnel is supposed to be behind it."

John listened, hearing the rushing water from no particular direction. "No, I can't. It's hard to tell in here, sounds like it's echoing in at least a couple places."

"We need to find it. That's where we go."

"You don't know where to go? What about the map?"

"I know the map, there's not much to it. But I'm not sure which direction we're facing."

"Didn't you bring a compass or something?"

"Compasses don't work in caves."

"They don't?"

"No, why would they?"

"It's all magnets, isn't it?"

"Yeah, there's no magnetic energy in caves. That's basic stuff, John."

"Doesn't sound right. The earth has a magnetic field, right? And we're *in* the earth."

"Common misconception."

"How do you know?"

"Because I read the fucking books, John. Did you?"

"No. This was always your show. Why are you getting all worked up?"

"You're questioning me, like you still don't trust me."

"Are we lost?"

"No. No, we're not lost, we just need to find the goddamn waterfall. I hear it, don't you?"

"Yeah, but—"

"So, we're not lost, we're close. I'll go this way"—Robbie pointed in the direction he was facing—"and you go that way. And we'll find it. That simple. Okay with you?"

"Yeah, fine. I trust you"—*no, I don't*—"so long as you don't get all pissed off and lose your cool."

"Go look over there and stop questioning me. All right?"

They split up. Walking in the opposite direction, John realized that threatening as this place was while Robbie feigned control, wandering alone was far worse.

It was slow going, his flashlight performing a little better without Robbie's around to trump its efforts (the irony of the metaphor did not escape him), but still he found it difficult to judge distance, to avoid the piles of loose rocks waiting to trip him, or the irregular outcroppings on both the walls and floor.

And ceiling. Without realizing how low it had become, John's forehead met with a stalactite. Had he been moving at a normal walking pace, it may have knocked him flat on his ass.

He rubbed his head and stopped to listen for the waterfall. It sounded the same equi-non-distance from where he had set off by himself. But, coming from his right. He faced left, and the sound moved behind him.

He turned back to look for Robbie and immediately regretted it. The flashlight found nothing in any direction he pointed it. Nothing except brown-gray rock that the sun would never touch.

"Robbie?"

"Yeah?" Robbie's voice was small but clear, as if coming through a telephone dropped on the floor. *Or he's trying to sound farther away than he really is? Is he testing me?*

"I think I found it. Sounds like it's this way."

"Okay, I got nothing over here so you're probably right, John. Stay put, I'll come with you."

John took a few more steps, checking his would-be sonar. His left foot came down on nothing. There was a cliff, he hadn't seen it, and now he was falling.

No, not falling. Not quite. His hand shot out, on reflex, and hit a rock wall with enough friction to catch him while his foot came back to solid ground.

Heart pounding in his ears, sudden coughing fit erupting, John leaned his face against the wall that had saved him from falling into that void not seen in time, grateful for the cool moisture on his sweaty skin.

He peered over the lip his foot had nearly missed, hand still held tight against the wall for balance. He directed his light along the edge and saw nothing but sheer drop-off as far as the light reached. He bent (hand leaving the wall, but only for a split-second), picked up a walnut-sized rock, dropped it straight down and waited. It made no sound. He crouched a few feet back from the edge.

Wondering how far this chasm went, John heard a scuffling sound behind him. Someone pushed him. This time he *was* falling.

CHAPTER TWENTY-THREE

It came from behind, two hands, one on each of his shoulders, glancing off after lending enough force to topple him from his crouch. As he leaned forward, air coming up from beyond the cliff brushing his cheeks, unable to stop himself from pitching over, he slapped both hands onto the ground behind him. He knew it wouldn't be enough but surprised himself by wrenching his torso clockwise far and fast enough to swap his hands as his feet fell over. The edge of the cliff pressed into his stomach as he tried to gain leverage with his arms.

He had stopped the fall but was now dangling like a human L-bracket. Legs hung over, both hands slipping, not registering his own screams, and somehow, seeing himself as if from several feet away. His body looked absurd, bent too sharply above the waist as if he were a book opened to the middle and placed spine-up on the edge of a counter.

As he watched himself struggle for a grip, the cold temperature in the cave gave way to a soothing, almost tropical warmth. He heard his own searing cries for help carried around the confines of the cave walls. The darkness in the cave lifted, light flooding in from an unseen source and displaying the full depth of the canyon his other, screaming, book-spine-bent self was sliding toward. There came a weightlessness as if he could propel himself through the air by waving his arms.

He saw himself let go. He saw himself fall, no less than three hundred feet, flipping head over feet twice before hitting the unyielding rock floor below in a crumpled mess of gore and clothing.

John hovered over his own shattered form and could do nothing more than take in the sight, the smell of his own blood and shit mixing, the sound his bones made as they shattered. Then came a pull, like there was a fishing line leading to the bottom of his neck, reeling him backward in small jerks. Back to his body.

It could only have been a second but in that second he saw himself landing crumpled and mangled on a cluster of loose rocks at the bottom, and then Robbie's hand grabbed his, pulling him upward with a force that yanked his shoulder away from its housing. He cried out in pain.

"I got you," Robbie said, crouched and straining to pull John up above the lip. "I got you."

John's feet found rock again, and he kicked himself up the rest of the way, landing on top of Robbie. They rolled to opposite sides, panting in a duel.

Neither spoke, at first.

"You okay?" Robbie asked, still catching his breath.

"No. Not okay." John pushed himself backward along the rough surface of the cave's floor. He was desperate for space but couldn't get himself up. He was panting and trembling all over.

"What happened?"

"Are... are you serious? You're fucking crazy."

"Me? What?"

"Pushed me."

"What are you... John? Who pushed you?" Robbie stood.

"Don't, okay. Just... don't."

"You think, what? You think *I* pushed you? Come on."

"Who else, Robbie? Who else? It's only us. I knew something was up with you."

"Fuck are you talking about John? I saved you and now you're going to talk this shit."

"What, then? I imagined it?"

"I don't know, but I sure as shit didn't push you. I've only ever looked out for you, John."

"You were right there when I fell."

"Yeah, surprised you're complaining about that. Seems fortunate for you."

"Robbie, I'm serious. I didn't imagine that."

"All right, whatever. For Christ's sake, John, why would I do that?"

"Why didn't you tell anyone we were coming here?"

Robbie seemed genuinely hurt. "What? Goddamn it. How many times do I... I'm trying to help you here. Help us both."

"See, you're not even denying it. No one knows we're here. I'll admit I'm not in the most rational state of mind lately, but you've got to help me understand why it seems like you're setting things up against me."

"John, how long have you known me?"

Too long was John's first answer to himself. The second was worse, uncertain. *About four years, right? How long had it been? When had they met?*

"Then what, Robbie? What's with all the secret shit and the half-truths and the changing your story?"

"Look, I know I'm not perfect, but you have to trust me. This is what's best. For both of us. I meant what I said about looking back and holding yourself hostage. That's no way to exist, John. I couldn't stand by and watch it happen anymore. We need this."

"That, see? That shit right there. What does that mean? You have to tell me everything. I'm not going any farther until you fill me in on the whole picture."

"Just a little farther, okay? There's something I want to show you first, and then I promise we'll talk about everything."

"No, Robbie. No, goddamn it. Here. Right here, right now. All on the table. Or I'm out."

"Out? Where are you gonna go?"

"Back."

"Back where? Up there? To what? To who? You got nothing up there, John. There's nothing for either of us. All that routine you've been hiding behind, it's gone. Your boss found out you had been taking back tickets when people complained. You got kicked out on the street. Mags is gone. It's all falling apart. Remember that?"

"And what's down here? A new life? You aiming for king of the goddamn mole people? What the fuck is wrong with you? I never should have listened to you," John said, before revisiting each item Robbie had listed. Something stood out but he couldn't quite place it.

"No, not a new life. A... change in perspective. Believe me here, man. I'm desperate, can't you see that?"

"Robbie, how does this play out? What's the endgame?"

"You'll see. Trust me, please?"

Then it hit John, harder than the jutting rock that had collided with his head.

"Wait. How did you know that, Robbie?"

"Know what, John? Quit stalling. The waterfall's this way."

"Why I got fired. I never told you about that."

"Yes, you did. You told me as soon as you got in the car."

"No, I remember that. I told you it happened, but I didn't tell you why. Hell, I never even told you I was doing that."

"Doing what?"

"Taking back people's tickets. Deleting them when they complained about it."

"Sure, you told me all about that."

"I don't think I did. When?"

"I don't remember when, John. But I didn't make it up. You must have told me and forgotten about it."

John let his suspicions lie for now. Robbie was walking again and taking all visibility with him. It surrounded him like a yellow bubble of precious oxygen and it was moving away. John, with no light source, rushed to catch up, stumbling over a curb of rock at his feet and keeping a safe distance from the cliff to his side.

"Hey, look, I'm sorry. I'm not dealing with this well. It's throwing me off and I guess I'm lashing out to cope."

"I get it," Robbie said, walking faster. His voice was a dial tone.

"Do you have another flashlight?"

"Yeah, here," Robbie said, pulling a small piece of plastic from his pocket and holding it in his hand, arm flexed backward. Still moving forward and not turning.

John took it, longing for a place and time where he needn't keep asking Robbie for help. Resolving to take back his independence. If he survived.

The small item in his hand seemed to John the single worst flashlight to bring into a place where it may mean the difference between life and death. It was attached to a key ring, two inches square, activated by a button that needed pressed continually.

Shouldn't light sources be the number one priority item to bring to an unexplored cave system? John thought. Robbie interrupted before he made it any further.

"Be careful with that one, it's the only other backup."

"You didn't bring any more? That's it?"

"I brought three. Everything I read said three sources of light."

"Yeah, but don't you think that means *per person?*"

"You should've brought one."

"I would've. You told me not to worry about bringing anything."

"I figured you'd bring a flashlight. And if I'd known you would lose one of mine, I sure would've packed another."

John recognized this behavior, otherwise it would've been more troublesome. A classic Robbie defense mechanism. And effective. In John's efforts to pull himself to Robbie's standards, a higher level of his own designation, it affected him when the guy shifted blame like that.

John suddenly thought Robbie didn't intend his shifty behavior and half-truths as a kind of willful deception. Instead, those were all the acts of a proud man brought low by poor circumstance. Robbie needed his help. And after all he had done for John, perhaps he was due this indulgence. There was something he needed to accomplish here, something Robbie needed to happen, and John would stay with him. For his friend's sake.

This realization brought him a respite from the weight of the past week, as they walked together without speaking, the waterfall growing louder with each step. John put the ineffective little light in his pocket and followed.

Definition of unknown origin:

Bio-psychokinetics (bio-PK): a form of psychokinetics (the use of mental energy to bring about effects in the physical realm), bio-PK deals specifically with the effects of mental energy on the biological systems of oneself or others. It is believed to be most commonly displayed as the exertion of control by one person over the body of another, such as lowering or raising heart rate or blood pressure, or otherwise influencing the body's autonomic functions, including breathing, contractions of smooth muscle, or blood flow.

***

From: *Astral Projection and Tabloid Mentalities, a Pragmatic Interpretation of Paranormal Psychologies* by Dr. Arthur McGuire, PhD (p. 144).

Though one of the lesser-known avenues of paranormal psychology, bio-psychokinetics (bio-PK) remains one of the more absurd speculatory abilities that fall outside true science.

Of some relation to other forms of psychokinetics, this term refers to a mental ability to influence biology (a true science). A person capable of asserting mental influence as bio-PK can allegedly raise or lower heart rate, blood flow, breathing, or other involuntary functions of the body by using mental energy alone.

From an accredited biological standpoint, the cellular makeup of such systems can only be activated, slowed, or otherwise altered by electrical energy. Without such energy, there is simply no possibility for changes to occur, and the body continues its activities as normal. Therefore, unless a "psychic" can somehow move electrical energy from their own cortex, through thin air, and into the organ tissue of another person, bio-PK remains pure fantasy (and lunacy).

Despite the relative obscurity of its title, bio-PK has still carved its meager place within many cultures. For example, it is widely believed that individuals living in secluded societies, through an extreme amount of discipline and meditation, can slow or even stop their own heartbeats. Depending on who is asked, these bio-PK masters may be Buddhist monks in China, Yogis in India, or lone (and charismatic) crackpots in any developed nation.

An outcome of little surprise, it is a far easier task to locate instances of bio-PK claims exposed as fraud than to find any respectable institute claiming to have proof of a controlled, verified demonstration of bio-PK. I shall save you the time of looking. There are none. Zero times has bio-PK been demonstrated or recorded under controlled experimental circumstances.

However, it can be of some entertainment value to read examples of the online editorials that claim to detail proof of bio-PK. As a note of precaution, if intending to read these, one should be prepared to overlook subsistent errors in spelling, punctuation, and grammar, as they have all been drafted by quasi-literate fools and never peer-reviewed.

It remains clear that the concept of "mind over matter" has earned no scientific merit and is better suited to remain a bumper sticker slogan propelling the motivational stylings of the feeble-minded.

***

Excerpt from an anonymous letter left in the Hallstown University office of Professor Arthur McGuire:

Dr. McGuire,

I doubt you know my name, you may not even recognize it in a list. I don't know that you'd be able to pick me out of a crowd, either. I understand and expect all of this. And I am certain that my words won't reach you emotionally, I don't expect this letter to change anything for you. Still, I am compelled to tell you the following, not for myself or your own benefit, but in the interest of others like me.

You have changed my life in a large way, one I may only be starting to understand. You're probably thinking: "Indeed, molding lives is my charge as an educator" (how I imagine you phrasing it). In that much, we agree.

What I need for you to understand, though, is how deeply your callousness can reach. How much positive growth you can undo with a single swipe of the tongue. How devastating a lone conversation with you can be.

You see, doctor, it is clear how much you appreciate your ability to have positive impacts on the students in your classes. And please know that I respect your intelligence and commitment to the field of psychology. These are valuable traits and should be appreciated. I fear, though, that you do not understand the full scope of responsibility you, like all teachers, possess.

The profession you have chosen comes with many burdens, and there is one you have lost sight of, or perhaps never considered at all. Speaking plainly, you can do more harm than good.

I now realize how much damage you have done to my faith, my understanding of the powers of the mind, and my ability to make healthy decisions. I came to you once, years ago, seeking help, and your response was insulting and tragic. It has taken the better part of my adult life to overcome your words and realize that the world does not exist in black and white, nor even shades of gray. It has all colors, and you are not all-knowing. Some things in our universe cannot be explained by science and for proof you need only look at the constant presence of belief in the paranormal. I believe that one day, perhaps a day that has already occurred, you will face irrefutable evidence of it. On that day, I implore you: open your eyes, open your mind.

Your students will reap the benefits.

I fear you have not or will not read this letter in its entirety, so I intend to keep it brief. In your own words, "brevity is king" (though, having read several of your publications, I see you don't practice what you preach).

Should I still have any of your attention, I hope you will remember these words if no others: please be aware of your darkness as much as your light, because their power is equal.

Sincerely,

A crushed former student

Chapter Twenty-Four

After realizing who he was, the "Robbie" her daughter's phantom voice was telling her to help, Lucy soon remembered more details about him. He looked like her brother, or at least how she remembered him. The dark hair, his almost-fresh-tanned complexion, a face built for a smile with subtle creases around the mouth. She wondered what color his eyes were. Her brother's were a deep, disarming green.

He had been admitted one week before Lucy was fired, and so she had not treated him long. But, in that week, both because he resembled her brother and because of the horrifying circumstances that brought him to her, Lucy felt connected with him. He was all but forgotten on the day Johannsen had stormed in, fueled by an anonymous tip, and told her she was lucky he was letting her leave without filing criminal charges.

With few details about Robbie left, she leaned toward what she had. The loudest part of it was: she had seen no one that close to death who hung on. He should have died long before they found him. By the laws of nature and medicine, he shouldn't have made it through the ambulance ride. To everyone's surprise, he clung to some tiny corner of life's fabric for an entire week, through procedure after procedure until he stabilized and the experts could help no more.

His resilience painted a clear picture to Lucy: he had a profound, uncanny desire to regain consciousness, and it was driven by some insatiable need. He was waiting; he had something important to accomplish before dying.

And Lucy knew she could aid him in that. Help him find whatever he was missing, or finish whatever he had started that kept him tethered to a broken and failing vessel.

He could have a good death, with her help. Now, he was all she had left. Her last shot at redemption.

She wondered again what happened to Robbie before he arrived first in the Emergency Room, then to a dozen or more Operating Rooms, before finally being turfed to Hospice because the combined expert medical opinion was that he couldn't be fixed.

How long was he alone like that? she asked herself, not for the first time. *It was so isolated there that it's hard to imagine how they found him in time. And the way he was beaten... I've seen patients attacked by animals that don't even compare. Who would do that to another person? What would drive someone to such a savage act? And what happened to the other person with him?*

Those answers would only be found if she reached him, helped him. Not by standing on the sidelines, glaring at illusions like a fool in a movie theater.

It was time to find that piece of herself, her drive, which she buried next to her child. Once it was strong enough she feared her small ability to make an impact. That concern had led to an idea, to compile the things she had learned. She would write a book, to help others deal with death, with dying, recognize its stages, know what to expect and how to cope. And by doing that, she may potentially help far more people. People she would never meet.

She had even started on the book. Chosen a title, made notes to herself after interactions with her patients. When she left, those notes stayed, settled, in a pile at the bottom of her locker.

Now, focus taken away from self-pity and self-destruction, she formed a plan. *I'll find that woman. The one from the sheriff's office, that's where I have to start. If Robbie is alive in there, somewhere, I'll have to do something I've never done. I'll have to... send. To project something, instead of only receiving.*

Her plan kept unfolding, like a road map rolled out on a tabletop.

Have to get inside the building. They won't let me in voluntarily, and I don't think I have time for the official channels back in. How much time do I have?

The beeping sound, having never left her, answered. Not long. Not long, at all.

She had a few days to save him. Probably less.

Chapter Twenty-Five

One step at a time, Lucy thought, now walking back through the hospital parking lot toward nowhere in particular. *How do I find that woman? She knew more about this. Didn't she?*

It was the first large problem in what promised to be a long list. Lucy didn't know where to look. As she approached the roaring stream of highway traffic, though, there came a mental *nudge,* something that changed her direction of thought.

Don't start with 'where?' That's the wrong question. Start with 'how?' As in, 'How do I find her?' or 'How do I help her find me?'

Send a signal, that's how. Sure, like it's no more difficult than making a phone call. Except try sending a phone call with a beeper, let alone a stubborn one with bad wiring.

She stared at the grassy spot where the mirage had been moments before, and tensed the muscles in her neck, raising her eyebrows, trying to sharpen the buzzing in her brain to a point, to use it like an antenna. Unfocused her eyes, then closed them.

It worked. After a few minutes, another *nudge*, bringing with it two flash images. The word *Scarlett (a name?)* transposed over a panoramic view of a bridge.

It was a strange sensation, receiving these images, and even the word *images* was not quite right. She had not seen them, so much as experienced them. It was a sensation of remembering something you had never seen. Even more, she was certain that someone had sent those to her.

More frightened by this mental-only transmission of quasi-images than anything since the phone call relaying her daughter's disappearance, Lucy found comfort in knowing more about who she was looking for, and where to go.

She recognized the bridge. She had crossed it every time she drove to Mercy Medical West. It was, more accurately, an overpass that crossed a highway on-ramp amid the largest interstate connection in Hallstown. When she had "seen" it, she noticed a cluster of tarps, mattresses, and bent shopping carts beneath one of the more secluded sections below the overpass. The woman she sought was right now in this homeless tent city.

It was not far. She'd arrive before sundown.

CHAPTER TWENTY-SIX

Lucy found the homeless encampment where she expected, first noticing the smell. Her once-held tolerance to the most offensive odors the human body emitted, in distended and irreparable conditions, had not been permanent.

A powerful mix of musty, rotting tangs cobbled together with the sharp, throat-swelling lowlights of feces. The ammonia-based reek of urine shed in large, regular quantities blended with burning rubber from a barrel fire tucked somewhere out of sight.

She allowed herself a moment to absorb the scene. It was like deciphering the tangled transit map of a foreign city. She became lost on approach.

She had arrived in a different world, a discordant landscape filled with the talismans and accoutrements of desperation. The claws and teeth used to cling to existence. The minimum of life essentials. Items deemed useless to the rest of society, reformed and repurposed. This description was applicable to the items (filled shopping carts and garbage bags, the mixed-material shelters of plastic and cardboard and cloth) as much as the persons collected in the overpass's shadow.

As she absorbed, revulsion turned to understanding with the timbre of an avalanche. Lucy relaxed, that tension of being lost releasing her. A defeated place, but not a dangerous place. She continued to take in what surrounded her. Mounds of vaguely human forms under blankets, desperate souls in need of comfort or solace or help of any kind. A circle of people, six of them, seated around a huge wooden spool that once held electrical wire, using it as a table to play a game of cards. She heard their voices carrying over the dense hum of vehicle traffic above them. A few turned toward her. The others kept to their game, and she walked past.

These were, in fact, her people. They accepted her presence, she was not intruding. They needed her, as much as those dying in their hospital beds. If not more so.

Then she saw a man, alone. Sickly thin, wearing too many layers for the temperature of this balmy spring afternoon. He walked hunched over from the severe contortion of his spine, feet shuffling, leaning on a folding drugstore cane that looked ready to crack under even his meager weight. A figure more tragic than gruesome if given enough consideration. Even in her darkest moments, consideration for the less fortunate was something Lucy possessed in stores.

"Excuse me?" she called to him. He kept his shuffling rhythm. "Sir." A little louder.

He stopped, pivoted to see her, moving more at the hips than the neck because of his deformed backbones.

"I'm looking for someone. Can you help me?" she asked and took a few tentative steps closer to him.

He stared back, blinking almost constantly. His sunken mouth moved around empty gums, white frenetic facial hair following in waves. His eyes were hollows, surrounded by a sea of wrinkles edged with grime. He wore a round-brimmed hat that had long since lost its original shape and color. He had no shoes. He replied one word, which sounded something like "fraged."

Lucy struggled for another way to pose her questions. "I... a woman. I'm looking for a woman and I think... I think she's here. Or was here. Have you seen any women nearby?" She was close enough now to place a hand on his shoulder, a thick dampness in the fraying cheesecloth-like material of his sweatshirt, a fading screen-printed mountain scene on its front.

The man said nothing further, spun his torso from her, in the manner of a crank on the front of an antique automobile, and shuffled away.

Discouraged, Lucy was about to approach the group of men at the spool-table when she heard a muffled *thud-thump* from behind her. It was clear, even above the steady highway background noise.

He had fallen. No, had dropped unconscious to the ground. She was still close and stooped down, trying to see his face. Blind instinct and training took over, wound together like electrical wires harnessed inside a machine. And she was a machine, a mindless whir of gears and motorized movements and a pattern of pre-programmed logic.

Airway clear, breathing shallow, circulation failing, she checked off the most critical elements of life in a calm state of automation.

She turned him on his back, and he switched to taking air in big gulping whoops. Or trying to, and perhaps not getting any in his lungs. The papery skin of his face was turning a pale shade of blue.

To the untrained observer it may have looked like he was choking. To Lucy, the problem was as clear as if she had a set of blueprints in front of her, outlining the circulatory layout of the human body.

Not a lack of respiration, a lack of perfusion. Air was getting into his lungs, but not much farther. His heart wasn't pumping. He was having a massive heart attack.

She began compressions, pumping his chest with a force that could break ribs, stopping after a few pushes. She pulled his sweatshirt over his head, the thick material catching on the bristles of hair covering his chin before coming loose like Velcro.

Underneath was a yellowed sleeveless T-shirt. She ripped that in two with her bare hands, the act made easier by its distressed condition. Her loosening his clothes had little effect, which she had feared.

If they were in the hospital, it would be a simple matter to give him some nitroglycerin or call for a crash cart.

She had neither. She wasn't in a hospital; she was in a desolate world of tarp tents and shopping cart possessions, where vagrants used trash as furniture and life eked by them like an indifferent river of sludge, the drone of traffic overhead creating a merciful buffer against the outside.

The card players had stopped, a few stood. One approached her.

"Stay back," she said, with the practiced calm of a first responder.

"Help him," the other man said. "You help Jerry. He never did no one no harm."

"I'm trying. Please, leave me space."

He stepped back in silent compliance.

The buzzing hive of her mind took center stage, and Lucy did something wholly new in response. She had typically tried to push it back, to contain that sound, that internal pressure, to force it into a bottle and close it up. On a few occasions she had tried to pull it forward, but neither of these methods was reliable. It did as it pleased.

Now she tried a third. When it surged forward on her, what she did was to welcome it, relaxing into it. She let it take over. A sense of power, of control slid over her like a drug-induced high. Everything went silent as if the world had turned to cotton.

Then she heard it, the uneven beating of his failing heart. *Th-thum... th-th-thum... ... th-thm... th-th-thum... ... th-thum... ... th-thum...*

As the troubled beating continued, she placed a hand on his chest, palm flat, fingers spread. She closed her eyes and saw everything.

Chapter Twenty-Seven

Lucy saw the meat of his heart, shriveled and aged. She saw its chambers, the arteries and veins pumping; she saw the flaps of ventricles moving as if by a breeze. But one was not moving—she saw the blood pooling back on one side, a fatal traffic jam of deep red elixir. She saw the clot causing it, wedging deeper against a thick layer of cholesterol like a net of yellowed cottage cheese.

Lucy saw the clot like it was something she could touch, like their connection was that intimate, as if the hand she had placed on the skin of his chest could move wraithlike into the cavity and aid her resuscitation efforts. She focused on the clot, pushing it, without understanding what she was doing but paying no notice to that.

Nothing happened, and precious seconds slipped by. She side-stepped her panic, thought about what would happen if she had the proper equipment and access and help.

The answer came to her. If this happened in a hospital, the defibrillator would jump-start his heart while the deadly clot would stay put. It waited like a spider at the edge of its web.

The real solution, the best way to save this man, was to dissipate the clot and clear the artery it blocked. And that would require surgery. But maybe she could do better. If she saw where the problem was, then she could focus there. Exert some physical influence. Perform the surgery without ever touching a blade.

To bring focus, she pictured the apparatus a heart surgeon would use.

Hand still in place, some ten seconds after she had ripped his shirt open, Lucy clenched her eyes further shut, pulling her focus away from anything outside, placing all her awareness on the mental image of an angioplasty bulb. A silicone tube or catheter, thin as pencil lead and tipped with a tiny balloon. She pictured it being inserted into his femoral artery, snaking its way up and around and through, arriving at the diseased artery causing his arrest.

Then, she was a gamer with a controller, pushing buttons in a frantic way, hoping to hit the right combination and watching as her efforts translated into action on another plane like magic.

Catheter in place, the balloon tip inflated, adding pressure inside the clogged artery and pushing the clot forward. It came loose like a wad of red bubbles swept into the strong current of a river and dissolved before it reached the adjacent chamber of the heart.

She pulled her hand from his chest and the sight of his insides, her unnatural camera probe into his chest cavity, flashed out, but not before she glimpsed the pooled blood flowing back through the reopened ventricle.

She saw his face again. He gasped, and it was a strong sound. She leaned back, wanting to give him room to breathe.

Breathe he did; they both did. And nothing else for several minutes.

There Lucy sat, watching the man she had grabbed from death's current come back to himself, both her hands on his chest, eyes reeling but probably not seeing anything, listening to her own breath and how fast her own heart had been going.

"You've never done that before," said a near-familiar voice behind her.

Lucy turned and recognized the face, the woman from the jail cell. Her frazzled carpet of hair was clumped and uneven. Foundation gobbed on so thick there may have not been skin beneath it but only muscle. Her piercing gray eyes.

"No. I've never done that."

From *Passing Through, Thoughts on Death and Dying* by Lucille Claremont, RN (p. 147).

"Mental Preparation":

Throughout the course of dying, a person's mind prepares itself for what is coming next, in much the same way their body prepares to die. The bulk of this preparation involves the long and complicated task of processing one's life.

As the physical needs change during the process of dying, so do emotional needs. This includes the need for contact with others, of which a change in communication is the most recognizable outward sign. The dying body no longer needs to derive energy from food, and likewise, the dying mind no longer requires words to communicate or interpret information. The desire to speak or to listen is lessened while nonverbal forms of communication become more emphasized and meaningful. Someone close to leaving their physical body relies more on gestures, touch, and facial expressions to telegraph their emotions to their loved ones.

As a person's time in the physical world ends, there comes a need for peace with the changes their passing through will bring. They need to meet death on their own terms, with a full understanding, to sort through their life's events and the state in which it is ending. This is a long and solemn road and comparable to climbing a steep hill, following a winding and unclear path, to gain an ultimate vantage point for the landscape of their life.

The external senses are distracting from this process, so it is performed most effectively under sensory deprivation; sleeping, in long periods of silence, or perhaps spending time in the dark, free of distractions.

This need to deprive the senses causes a difficult adjustment to both the person dying and anyone observing, but inside the consciousness of the dying individual, very important work is taking place.

Chapter Twenty-Eight

As they moved farther into the dark, John's respite, his reconsideration of Robbie's motives, evaporated like thin silk set on fire. He soon remembered what happened at the cliff, and with that came a renewed inquiry into Robbie's intentions.

He stumbled on the cave's uneven floor, following someone he no longer trusted, no defense against a lonely, unsolved death except for the key ring flashlight in his pocket. John wondered if Robbie meant for them both to leave this cave. Or, worse, if he meant for neither of them to.

As they approached the waterfall, several hundred feet or more below ground, John was sure of two things: he had not told Robbie any specifics about losing his job, and someone *had* pushed him.

The cave was no longer what frightened John.

The rush of the waterfall was getting closer. John wondered if it would be difficult to hear anything else soon, to speak and be heard, and he also knew Robbie might prefer that. John had infinite questions to voice, but Robbie wanted to hear none.

They searched for a tunnel nearby, which Robbie claimed was on the map. John realized he might run out of time to get answers. He considered what would happen when they found this tunnel Robbie sought.

"Help me find it," Robbie said. John was trying. He would prefer any way through. Any way out.

The extended time in the cave was causing a detachment in his brain, as if sanity shriveled without natural light, bombarded by the mocking echoes that the rock transformed all sound into. It was increasingly difficult to apply reason, to stop himself thinking impossible thoughts, like *I'm going to die down here*, or its more sinister cousin, *Robbie is going to kill me*.

These were driven by the growing suspicion that Robbie had gotten him fired.

The sound of the waterfall still distant but growing like an approaching train, John was fighting a divergent pair of urges, both clamoring for his focus and giving no quarter.

Get out, he told himself. *Now.*

Not until I hear Robbie admit it, he added in contention. *I want him to tell me.*

Wrestling with each imperative, he settled on an attempt at both, a decision which prompted him to drop whatever pretense remained and grab at it like a blind person seeking a life preserver.

"Why did you do it?" John asked. "Why did you get me fired?"

"We don't have time for this," Robbie replied, making no effort to deny or excuse. It confirmed John's suspicions, and a rage built in him like a blooming red flower. His voice became a steel rod.

"We do. It's all that matters."

"Good. You're making progress, that's good." Robbie moved his light around the floors and walls, searching.

John's teeth ground together like tank treads.

Robbie had pushed him, hadn't he? John was stumbling toward a crime scene, one Robbie had orchestrated and that would be invisible to the world. Eventually, Robbie would try again.

It was insane, though. Not possible. They had been friends for years, but John was fighting part of himself to keep up-slope of a place where some perceived murderous intent guided Robbie's actions.

He's scared too. He's your friend, and this is something he thinks he has to do. You don't have to understand it. You have to help him, and convincing yourself that he's planning to murder you? That's not helping anyone.

Look at the facts, though. No one knows we're here. He can do what he wants. I have nothing to defend myself with. Plus, why is he being so secretive?

Because he's ashamed. Trust him and you'll see.

John didn't know which of these arguments he believed.

"Are you sure it's here?"

"No," Robbie said, sloughing his backpack from his shoulders and charging toward John across the uneven rock floor, flashlight blaring at John's eyes and coupling with the sounds of the waterfall to leave him blind and deaf if only for a moment. "No, I'm not sure," Robbie said, shouting every word over the rushing water nearby. "I'm not, okay?"

"What? We're lost?"

"Yes. All right? That what you want me to say?"

"No... shit. No, I don't *want* you to say that. But if it's the truth don't fucking hide it."

"There's supposed to be a tunnel right here, somewhere. But I don't see it, do you?"

"Let's go back."

"We can't."

"Why the fuck not?"

"Because we're not done down here."

"Done what? What are you trying to do? What are you so determined to show me down here?"

"I'm trying to save you, goddamn it. Save *us*."

"Robbie, that doesn't make any sense. I was fine until you dragged me down here. We both were. Let's get out, okay? Where's the map? Let me see it."

"There is no map, John."

"What? Did you drop it somewhere?"

"I don't have a map. There is no map. No one has ever been here."

It didn't make sense. John knew he was lying again. Or omitting something, at least.

"How did you know where to go? The tunnel? The waterfall?" John said, realizing he no longer needed to raise his voice to be heard. The water had stopped. *How is that possible?*

"No tunnel, no waterfall. There's nothing down here."

"What? Robbie, you're not making any sense."

Robbie turned away. John's mind reeled at what was happening, trying to grasp hold of anything solid about where they were, what was happening. Why was it still so cold? And what happened to the waterfall? He had heard the sound, unmistakable, until a moment ago.

"Okay, I guess this is it then," Robbie said, dropping his hands to his sides. A preternatural glow covered his face, seeming to come from somewhere other than the bright rivulets kicked backward from the flashlight he held. "Now that we're finally here, I just want to get it over with. Be done." He tilted his head, pondering these words as if they were not his own.

"Robbie, you've got to help me here."

"That's all I'm trying to do, whether or not you see that."

"Not what I meant. You have to level with me. Please."

"Okay, let's get everything in the open."

John held his silence like a game show contestant waiting to see if his answer was correct. Wondering what his prize would be. His heartbeat was becoming erratic, making him weak and flushed. He coughed twice, a third time.

"First off, I have to say it wasn't easy to get you here. I hope you'll soon appreciate how big of an undertaking that was, considering we had no alternative."

"Alternative to what?"

"I had to bring things to a point, but it was further than I expected, and took a hell of a lot more patience. You know that's not my strength, either."

John's stomach burned like lava. "What? Tell me what the fuck you're talking about or I'm gone. I can't deal with any more of your slippery nonsense."

"Facts, then. When I stole your car, that was supposed to be the jumpstart you needed."

"You? Stole it?"

"But it didn't... motivate you like it should have. I thought if you lost something important, it would shock you, shake things loose, and you'd remember. But I was wrong. I underestimated how much was holding you in place. You were dug in so damn deep, John. I hope you can see that now. Can you?"

"I still have no idea what we're doing here. What any of this means. Why we can't talk about this somewhere else? Somewhere safe." He pointed behind himself, unsure if his arm was aiming for the outside world. "Out there. Not in here."

"Had to be in here, John."

"Why is that?"

"You'll see. We're getting closer now."

"To what, Robbie? Closer to what?"

"The truth. All of it."

"There's no truth in here, except what you brought in, and that could've come out anywhere if you'd let it."

"No, you had to see. You'll have to feel it before you can go back. In here I can force that connection because you just keep ignoring it. I'm no shrink, as you're probably reminding yourself, but I knew a few things all along. Telling you wouldn't help; I had to show it to you, John. Grab you by the ears and shove your face right into the thick of it. Doing it wrong would cause more harm than good, and we'd never be free."

"'The thick of it'? That's what you call this?" John held his arms out in the cave, an all-encompassing gesture.

"It took so much to get you here. Your car being stolen didn't do it, so I thought about what else might shock you out of your... ignorance. What else might open your eyes."

"You got me fired."

"Yeah. I knew part of you was still awake, squirming to get out and understand. I tipped them off with enough detail to make it stick, and they got rid of you. No car, no job. You should have wondered what else was out there. To feel how much you were wasting away, how pointless it all had become. But it still wasn't enough. You were still blind. So..."

John knew what was coming.

"Go ahead," Robbie said, coaxing.

"You told my landlord."

"Another anonymous tip. Did you remember that in the lease, John?"

John didn't. He would have read before signing, he always did. He should remember something like that. Why didn't he?

"And who helped when your back was to the wall?"

"What about the episodes I've been having, then? The visions, how do you explain those? You have crazy mental powers or something? Did you drug me?"

"Don't be a moron. That little wrinkle was all you. But it was convenient, I'll say."

"Convenient?"

"It was for me, yes. Even if I *could* make you have those, I couldn't have picked better times. It was like I would ask myself if I was going too far, making it too painful, should I just let you piss the rest of your life away in blissful ignorance. Then *bam*"—he clapped his hands—"you'd have a mind-numbing terror show about being trapped somewhere. It was like you were telling me to keep pushing you. I knew I was right. And it gave me an idea." Robbie walked a few steps away, his back to John, leaving John in a darkness so deep it was throbbing.

"You think I was telling you to bring me down here?"

"You don't? Maybe you're starting to understand, John. But if you think I'm wrong about that, we still have work to do."

"I've had enough," John said, fumbling in his pocket for the tiny key ring light. He pulled it out, pressed the button, and walked away.

"You can't go back, John. There is no way out. Point of No Return, remember?"

John saw the white tree again, as if Robbie had broadcast it onto the rock. The image weakened his knees and churned his stomach. He pocketed the light, back pocket this time. He wanted to take a run at Robbie and shut him up.

Robbie beat him to it, leaping like a predator at John's back and wrapping an arm around his throat. John thrashed his arms over the top of his head, making contact with Robbie's face and ears but not enough to break free. He tried striking low, but found no leverage, leaving him to slap at Robbie's legs while Robbie pushed him forward like a child afraid of water about to be thrown into the deep end.

"I can't let you leave," Robbie said. "Not when we're so close, buddy." He kept shoving, one arm locked around John's throat tight enough to restrict his breathing, the other arm now grasping John's right elbow, stopping half the flailing, twisting the arm and pinning it behind his back. John's feet stuck out in front of him like a bifurcated snow plow, slipping on the slick rocky floor, resetting and slipping again. His body jerked with a few record-skipping jostles for every step Robbie took, forcing him toward the nearest cave wall.

John tried to scream through his pinched pipes but what came out was a squeak like his mouth was the opening of a balloon stretched wide and pinched not quite shut. Still swinging his one free arm behind him, he glanced ineffective blows across Robbie's left earlobe.

"Almost there," Robbie said, no strain in his voice, like he could push John straight up the wall this way, maybe across the ceiling, while John was fighting for his life.

And losing.

Definition of unknown origin:

Telepathy, from the Greek *tele* (distant) + *pathos* (feeling or experience): a psychological phenomenon in which thoughts or mental perceptions are shared or transferred from one person's mind to another. This transfer of thoughts is believed to employ pure psionic energy, meaning it takes place devoid of physical contact and is an entirely mental process. Such energy is also reputed to be among the most powerful forces in the universe.

***

From: *Astral Projection and Tabloid Mentalities, a Pragmatic Interpretation of Paranormal Psychologies* by Dr. Arthur McGuire, PhD (p. 264).

Telepathy, though revered as perhaps the most powerful form of parapsychological ability, is one of the most fantastic and implausible mental abilities ever conceived. As popular, if not more so, than some of its ESP-related counterparts throughout popular culture, telepathy is a household term in the modern world. However, the public has a very different understanding of the term than did its earliest sponsors.

The term "telepathy" was introduced during the late nineteenth century, with credit for its first usage often given to Frederic Myers, who was also the founder of the short-lived and clumsily named "Society for Psychical Research."

Whereas the more current version of telepathy, propagated in movies and on television, deals with "reading" or even controlling the thoughts of others, Myers's version is more closely related to symptoms of mental disorder. Early accounts of the phenomenon resemble descriptions of delusions or the insertion of foreign (sometimes alien) thoughts, both often experienced by the schizophrenic or dangerously psychotic.

While I can't imagine a world where any of the previously reviewed forms of parapsychology function (i.e., ESP or precognition), as these abilities rely on the concept of information entering the cerebral cortex without first passing through any known physiological receptors, it is infinitely more absurd to believe that information travels directly from one mind to another. There is no scientific basis for such a transfer to take place; the most well-controlled experiments substantiated no occurrences of telepathy throughout the eleven decades since its inception.

Should one find enough interest, or perhaps amusement, in the research of telepathy-related experiments and what little documentation of their results is available, one would find a positive correlation between claims of telepathy and a later diagnosis of some debilitating mental disorder. The two are inseparable.

Esteemed reader, I need not repeat myself but do so out of a desire to underscore the central truth of this entire publication:

The belief in or study of parapsychology is a breeding ground for lunacy.

***

Online news item from the *Hallstown Gazette*, March 24, 2007:

"Tragedy at Barrett Riverfront Park"

Disaster struck out of a clear blue sky today as dozens were enjoying the first spring-like weekend in an area park. One week after its ribbon-cutting, Barrett Riverfront Park is already being heralded as a sign of the strength of the recovery underway in historic downtown Hallstown.

This morning, as temperatures were forecast to crest the seventy-degree mark for the first time of the season, the park filled early with the sights and sounds of children at the playground, friendly games of catch, dogs running across the lawn, barbecues, and other gatherings.

But the idyllic scene was soon brought to ruin when a plane fell from the sky, crashing into a picnic shelter, killing three people, including the pilot. A few minutes later, the plane's fuel tank exploded, killing one more and wounding at least six others.

The plane, a single-propeller Piper PA28 Cherokee, was registered to local business owner Ronald Barnhart. The picnic shelter had been in use by members of the Gall family. Mr. Barnhart, 57, was alone in the aircraft and died on impact. The cause of the crash is under investigation, but it is believed that Mr. Barnhart suffered a medical emergency shortly after taking off from the nearby Stratton Air Field.

Three others were pronounced dead at the scene, including one additional victim killed by the explosion that followed, while the six injured have been transported to several hospitals for treatment. Authorities have released no other names.

Further details remain sparse as authorities are still on-scene and the investigation is in early stages; however, we were able to obtain an exclusive interview with several eyewitnesses who claim to have seen an unidentified woman attempting to revive a young boy before the first emergency vehicles arrived.

Witnesses state the boy was lying motionless approximately twenty feet from the wreckage and appeared to have been thrown clear by the force of the impact. The woman was seen approaching the damaged picnic shelter, then stopped when she encountered the boy.

"I thought she might be his mom," one witness said. "She was holding his head with both her hands and neither of them was moving. I got closer and realized they didn't look much alike, though."

A second witness stated the boy "had blood all over his head, on the side. His eyes were open, but he wasn't moving. I didn't know what she was doing, it was so fast, but she was looking in his eyes for a minute, then the plane exploded and she was screaming. I've never heard such a scream."

Within minutes of the explosion, several ambulances had arrived to transport the injured for treatment. The young boy was taken to St. Catherine Hospital. He is in critical condition, but no further details are available.

The woman was in an ambulance en route to University Hospital when she allegedly jumped from the rear doors at a stoplight and fled. Her whereabouts and identity remain unknown.

CHAPTER TWENTY-NINE

"In is much easier, right?" said the vagrant woman, whose name Lucy still assumed was Scarlett. She walked away, and Lucy turned from the man with his shirt ripped open. He made no effort to stand but his breathing was coming in more even slips, eyes closed as he succumbed to the full-body weakness that follows a massive heart attack. He was weak, but alive. Lucy didn't have her cell phone, so she sent one of the other men to find help and get an ambulance.

Lucy shifted her attention toward the woman as she walked away, though not in an evasive manner. More like she was leading. She carried two large canvas bags, the reusable kind for groceries, and pulled their straps over her head as she moved away, setting them on the ground. Lucy saw inside one as it tipped over. It held crumpled sheets of lined paper, filled with scribbles in both English letters and symbols she didn't recognize, flowing into and out of each other as if used in the same sentences indiscriminately. Aside from those crumpled pages, her bag contained only a few clumps of clothing and what were likely slips of discarded cellophane packaging, as if she had spent the morning collecting debris from the roadside. She wore an ankle-length brown skirt over sandaled feet, and layers of sweaters and scarves, all dirty and discolored, melding into muted grays and browns with age and dirt.

"I-I don't..." Lucy responded but was stopped when she recalled how unsettling their first encounter had been. The woman's presence was jarring, more than just her piercing eyes. Lucy felt pierced in other ways, just being near her again. It was like she was probing Lucy's mind, but in a manner stealthy enough to avoid detection. To others there may be nothing perceptible to it, but Lucy, in her beehive of para-mental activity, sensed it in some small way.

"Did you... did you contact me?" Lucy asked, remembering the *nudge* while trying to picture where to go next.

"See?" the woman replied. "In is easier. So I did, yes." She sat in a rotting plaid orange-brown recliner and pulled crumpled pages from one canvas bag, unfolding them with deliberate care, taking her time to flatten and smooth each one, placing them in a stack on her lap. As she did, her mouth formed words with no sound. Lucy soon realized that she was counting as she stacked the pages. At each interval of ten she moved pages from her lap into another empty bag, then took a rock from a pile at her side and placed it on top. It struck Lucy as ritualistic nonsense, making her want to leave. She had sunk so low as to be asking for help using psychic powers from a woman who was at least mildly schizophrenic.

And she was passing silent judgment on this other person, dismissing her as mentally ill despite Lucy's own obvious mental health concerns of late: a suicidal addict condemning a harmless outcast.

Lucy wanted to leave, but she stayed. She did so hoping to regain some self-respect, some dignity, some purpose. For Anna.

The woman kept to her disciplined ritual of unfolding, stacking, counting, moving, starting over. "In has always been easier. But you see now, you can send it out too." She stopped pulling papers out, sending her eyes deep into Lucy's as if seeing below the surface.

"I... I'm not sure how I—"

"Of course. Not sure. That's why you're here. Of course."

"Are you... is your name... Scarlett?" Lucy asked.

"How much time you want to waste like this?"

"Waste? I'm not sure what I'm even doing here."

"You need help. I know. Help sending. Yes?" She dropped her gaze and returned to her paper shuffling exercise.

"I don't—"

"Don't understand, no? But you do. You understand fine, just not comfortable with it. Afraid. You're afraid you'll end up like this." She swept an arm around not only toward the expanse of poverty and grime and debris, but also including herself. "Like me. Right? You think, if you keep trying to use it, if you embrace it, you end up crazy bridge lady."

"I'm sorry if I—"

"You're not here to make me feel better. I don't need it. You need from me, not the other way around. We ready to start yet? Or do you need time to reconsider? Back out? May not look like it, but I have other things to do today."

"You do?"

"So do you. He's not with us much longer. And he needs your help."

"He? Robbie?"

"Okay, yes. You want to help him? He's now your spirit salve, yes? To help him will help you tenfold, you think?"

"I do, I guess. Or I'm starting to think that."

"Good, that's good. I agree, you could help, guide him through, and even get what you want for yourself."

Lucy stood up straighter.

"But you won't," Scarlett said.

"I won't? Why?"

"Not ready. I think you knew that. You're not ready for something like that, it's much deeper than you realize and you've just now attempted to send for the first time."

"But... but that worked. I did it." Lucy looked over at the man, coming to his feet in the shadow of the mammoth highway above them. She heard a siren, hoped it was approaching.

"That was nothing. You will see when you try bigger. It was good, but not a challenge. It's okay, though. Okay. That's why you came here. You're not ready yet, but you can get ready. If you hurry. You can be made ready."

"How? Will you help me?"

"I just said, we have to hurry. No time for these stupid questions. Here." She reached out, handing Lucy one sheet from the stack of pages on her lap. "Take this. Keep it close."

Lucy unfolded one side to find out what it contained.

"No," Scarlett interrupted her. "Don't need it yet, but hold it. This too." She handed Lucy a black ballpoint pen, the kind found in every hotel room.

Lucy pocketed the page and pen.

With an obedience built in, Lucy desired to please this woman. Perhaps it was the urgency of the task before her, or a reaction to the sense of authority implied by her firm and deliberate instructions. Or fear of what Scarlett might be capable of.

Or maybe she's asserting control over me.

Scarlett stopped her bizarre page-organizing routine and looked at Lucy. Straight on, passing undeniable knowledge. She said nothing, but she told something.

"Can you... hear... what I'm think—" Lucy asked.

"I told you, no time for stupid questions. You want help? I need trust. Okay? You ready yet?"

"Yes," Lucy said. And she was.

CHAPTER THIRTY

"You have a car, yes?" Scarlett asked.

"Yes," Lucy answered. "Well, I did."

"So we start there. Good." Scarlett stood, the decaying foam of the recliner maintaining her form in a permanent mold. She moved to its side, motioning with one hand for Lucy to follow.

They walked out of the shadow of the humming underpass, starting up a cement-lined drainage track and continued up to the unkempt grass beyond it, then climbed a large, debris-strewn hill. Lucy gave a passing thought to the litter she saw, useless even for the people living below to see value. She was feeling a kinship to scraps of roadside trash.

They stopped when the whirling traffic on a highway on-ramp was visible. It was near afternoon rush hour, and the stream of cars was thickening as they monitored it. All the normal people were leaving work, having served some daily purpose, providing for loved ones, now heading home to their living, breathing children. Lucy reminded herself again of the paths that lay both behind and in front, her shoulders slumped.

The ramp canted toward them, like the view spectators of an auto race may get: a clear shot of the cars as they moved over the concrete surface, gaining in speed and sound.

Scarlett pointed toward it and said, "This is you now."

"I don't—"

"Ssshh. It's much easier if you listen first. That's the first thing to learn. How to listen. And not just to hear."

Lucy was silent.

"More to it than that. But at least you're trying now. Only one way to go, see. In. You let them in, but nothing goes out. See?"

Lucy nodded.

"See this image. Keep it." Scarlett pivoted, moving only her upper body. Her feet stood firm, grounding her. She pointed to a different section of the highway.

"You want to be like that."

Lucy followed the line of her arm to see a full stretch of highway, four lanes with traffic moving in both directions. She watched with moored intent, thinking about the symbol Scarlett was presenting, yearning to reach a deeper understanding, force herself to absorb more.

The cars moved at speed, sunlight firing off their windshields and shimmering off the paint on their bumpers and doors and hoods. It was already difficult to see details, but she strained for them. There were dozens in each lane. Lucy tried to pick one and focus, and then lost track of it in the constant stream. She repeated this four times. It was like trying to watch one particular fish in a school moving downstream in murky, sun-mirrored water. Still, she pushed herself, hoping to catch the attention of someone in one of those cars, to take something, grab a piece of information from one of them. Any of them. She pushed harder, working to focus her unseen antenna as she had outside the hospice building earlier. But they were fast, too fast. And slippery.

She swooned, stumbling over. Scarlett caught her, one-armed, her hand grasping Lucy up under the armpit.

"That was good," Scarlett said. "You did that on your own. You learned something there. Can't be done too fast. You try too hard and you hurt yourself. See?"

"Yes," Lucy said, standing upright again.

"You want to be like that, fast. But you can't. It's too big that way, you will stretch too far and tear." At that, she tapped a finger on her own forehead. "And when you tear, there's no un-tearing."

Scarlett turned again, still keeping her feet in place, moving her upper body in a half-circle the other direction, pointing again.

"You need to be like that."

Again, Lucy followed Scarlett's direction. Some distance away, past the steady purr of the relentless highway traffic, was a two-lane county road. They were high enough that Lucy saw far, perhaps a mile, lined by telephone poles and power cables, as the road wound lazily through fields and past several farmhouses.

"See this image," Scarlett said. "Keep it. That is the goal."

Lucy nodded. "That's it."

"That," Scarlett said, motioning back toward the highway with her head, "you don't have time for. But that," head nodding toward the smaller two-lane road, "we can do. See this image. See it deep, see it with the part you need to learn. Learn how to use. Keep it there, hold it. You understand?"

"Yes, I do. I think I do."

"You do, yes."

Lucy's pulse quickened at that. She watched one car, a small four-door navy blue sedan, make its way down that road, moving from right to left in her field of vision. The driver controlled its speed with deliberation, matching the winding and curving in the path ahead, careful in its navigation.

"Good," Scarlett said. "Important, yes."

The car slowed at a sharp bend, another approaching head-on. A large pickup truck, so loud Lucy heard its modified or damaged exhaust system from their vantage a few hundred yards away. Black smoke billowed from an unseen pipe below its bed. It was not slowing as it neared the upcoming curve.

"Ah," Scarlett said. "Now watch. Very dangerous."

The truck was weaving between both lanes, too fast to keep to its own side. The driver of the blue sedan must have heard or seen it in barely enough time to avoid it. The sedan swerved to the side, careening and bouncing into a ditch, its horn sounding twice in rapid succession. *Bee-beeeep,* a sound that carried to where Lucy and Scarlett were observing a scant few seconds later. When it arrived, the truck had already whirred by unabated, appearing to thunder past the stopped car, made a few jerking strides back to its own lane, and hammered down the straightaway beyond it, soon disappearing first in sight, then in sound.

"You see that?" Scarlett asked, smiling for the first time Lucy had seen, creating cracks in her too-thick makeup, especially around her eyes. "That's a great image for you. Useful. You have to be careful sending. The blue car, that was sending. The big scary truck? Something receiving. You can't always control the *in*. You can be ready for the truck, but you can't drive it. You can control the *out*. Learn to drive the blue car. Do you understand? That is how it works."

"I... I think so." Lucy said. The analogy was clear abstractly, but she was a student of medicine, of science. Had been, at least. The transition to something practical, something *useful*, meant effort. But she understood the image, and that may give her enough of a focal point to ground herself at the time she needed to most. She had a small failsafe.

"You can put up signs, sure," Scarlett said. "Can get very good, with enough dedication. You can even rearrange the road, move the curves around, make them sharper or smooth them. All this, all possible. But it doesn't mean the traffic has to obey them."

"How do I learn the *out*, though? How do I open to both directions?"

"It can be done, yes. I can help. Takes much practice. In time, you could learn to do things you've only seen in fantasies. But it's dangerous. Tricky, you see? With the trucks coming in, you are vulnerable. Opening up? Not so hard. But opening up and avoiding the wrecks? Much trickier. Much, much more dangerous."

Chapter Thirty-One

They strayed to a wooded area, well past the camp and their highway viewing spot, and Scarlett tried to show Lucy how to develop her second lane. It was a slow, frustrating, draining process, and the sun set before Lucy had seen anything she considered progress. In the dark, Scarlett gathered sticks and built a small fire with the practiced efficiency of an outdoorsman. She was a survivor. Lucy saw she was learning from someone who knew well from pain, loss, daunting obstacles. These things had taken their toll on Scarlett, yet she overcame. Trundled on. Rose each day with purpose. She could always build a fire for herself, regardless of how dark the night ahead.

Scarlett explained the low light of the small fire was helpful; too much would be distracting. When it was too bright, she explained, even a tightly shut eye allowed disruptions to such an intense process.

With the fire lit, making small pops and casting a dim glow in a circle, she told Lucy to sit. The ground was damp, making it harder to focus. Moisture seeped through the seat of Lucy's pants and made her buttocks cold. But, Scarlett explained, unlike sight, this was not distracting, and could even be useful.

"The feeling is important," Scarlett said. "It can be used. When you feel, it flips switches here." She put a finger to her temple. Her ring finger, its neighbors folded away, making the gesture odd but no less effective. "Not here." She moved the same finger to the back of her head, the vision center. "Like light."

"But," Lucy said, "when it… works, that's where I feel it." She tapped a finger (index, not ring) on the same area on her own head. "Back there. That's not where it is? Where it… comes from?"

"No. Not from there. Comes from here." Ring finger on the temple again. She tapped the same finger on Lucy's head, in the same region. "Here. That's part of what holds you back. Wrong focus. Focus here."

"That will help? How? How do I-?"

"Same way you focused in the back before. How you found me. You know how, just need to do it. When you do, it will get easier. Takes time, but gets easier."

"I don't—"

"Try now. Pull from me. Focus here"—tap-tap-tap—"and pull from me."

Lucy closed her eyes, tight. She fumbled at her frontal lobe with invisible fingers, like she was trying to find a light switch in a black and unfamiliar room. When nothing happened, she switched effort to recreating the image of the back road, a truck (smaller and slower) navigating over it with care. She saw it forming in pixels, like staring too close at a television screen or an early-generation video game. The road pitched and yawed in sloping curves until it wound its way into her ear. Scarlett was behind the wheel of this truck, her seat pulled far forward so she was crowding the steering wheel.

When Scarlett's truck, coated in a strange paint of marbled pink and white and gray (the colors of brain tissue, Lucy realized), made its way to the last stretch of road, dipping into Lucy's ear canal, she saw it. Something came to her. An image, like a blurry poster affixed to the backs of her eyelids. In time, it became clearer, taking on more defined edges, de-pixelating, until it refined enough for her to recognize.

A small object. Glass. Blue glass. Old, antique. A bottle. But rounded on top, not tapered. And short, three inches or less. Lucy worked, pushed, flexed a little more in her mind's eye to focus, and more detail came after some effort. There was lettering, wrapping with the curved glass, and embossed so it raised off the surface.

Baltimore, she read. Baltimore, MD. It was at the bottom of the bottle, curved around the base.

"Look," Scarlett said.

Lucy opened her eyes, and in the flickering light of the fire she saw Scarlett holding a small, translucent blue object between her index finger and thumb. The same bottle. Exactly as Lucy had seen it. She held it out and Lucy took it. There were embossed letters on it. Lucy read them. Top to bottom, it said:

Bromo Seltzer

Emerson

Drug Co.

Baltimore, MD

"Did you... send that? Send it to me?" Lucy asked.

"No. It was in my pocket. I held it, but that is all. You pulled it from me. I didn't show it, you saw it. You see details? Small points?"

"I did. I saw the lettering."

"Have you done that before?"

"No, not really. I've never gotten those kinds of details before; I've never controlled it like that before."

"Good. Progress, you moved forward. Focus coming from the right place, it helps. More of that, you'll get better. Stronger."

"Then I can send?"

"Yes, but before you drive in that lane, you need control over the *in*. The trucks. You see how to have control, right? It starts with knowing where it comes from, in you." Scarlett tapped her finger on her temple again. "Here. From here. Then you can practice and soon shape the road. Add signs and safety points and be ready for big scary trucks. Be ready to stop the wrecks."

Lucy nodded.

"Next, we try sending. You try going out, okay? But use the image of the road. Blue car, truck. If a truck is coming, if something comes in, don't let them collide. If they wreck, it's very dangerous. You understand?"

"I... I'll try."

"You must be sure, see the road. Picture the road. Drive the blue car and you will be fine." Scarlett walked past the fire, becoming a shadow that soon merged with the black beyond the perimeter of light. She called back: "I close my eyes, you send me something. Ready?"

"What do I send?" Lucy asked.

"Anything. Doesn't matter what. Just be clear. Firm. I'll tell you what I get."

There was silence for a few moments.

"Go," Scarlett said, insisting. "Now. Do not overthink. Just don't let them collide."

Again, Lucy fumbled at her own cortex with invisible fingers. She didn't know what to send, but tried not to be guided by that. She wanted to act from a place of certainty. She thought if she closed her eyes and pushed outward, an image would present itself. It did. It floated up from within her, a clear and detailed photo-quality image of the bracelet she had found in Anna's room. She drew down, into herself, crouching toward the ground now and projecting something that was part of her, but not of her body.

She saw the pieces of that bracelet as if she were touching it. The silver balls of the chain, linked with tiny studs, held closed by a round clasp like a shiny pill, open on one side. The typewriter keys, in Anna's initials. Their glossed plastic surfaces, domed and polished and clear. Brass housings, cupped around the sides like small collars. The white lettering inside them, set in contrast by black circles.

"Nothing," Scarlett said. "Are you trying yet?"

"Yes," Lucy said. "I'm concentrating on something. I'm trying to see it."

"Don't just see it. Send it. Get in the car. Drive it here. Bring it down the road to me. Careful, though."

Lucy kept picturing the bracelet, this time carrying the image further, expanding it. Beyond boundaries she felt but did not see. The humming in her head had moved to the front, where Scarlett had indicated. She saw more than the bracelet now. She saw herself, holding it, in the driver's seat of a car. She pulled in every available detail: the soft gray upholstery, the illuminated sections of the dash, one hand on the steering wheel, its surface warm from the sunlight settling on it. Then she looked in the side-view mirror, seeing the car's exterior: blue paint, of course, navy blue. Her foot set on the accelerator, gentle pressure. Eyes fixed ahead, ears trained for oncoming traffic.

She pulled back from the car's interior, like she was floating away from it, and saw the landscape split by her road. It was straight, with no intersections. She saw it plunging forward as the vehicle rolled that direction. Farther to her left, toward some artificial horizon, she saw Scarlett's face, or part of it. The makeup slathered over her skin parted, like a cut had opened across her forehead. Lucy pushed the end of the road into it, watching as the car moved seamlessly from the yellow-lined blacktop forward, disappearing as if swallowed by Scarlett's thick foundation, and all she saw were the fading taillights and...

"A," Scarlett said, calling to Lucy from out of sight. "I see letters. A... C."

Lucy's eyes jumped open. Her concentration slipped.

"No, gone. No good," Scarlett said. "Keep trying. Blue car. Blue car, drive it."

Lucy re-closed her eyes, bringing the image back to full clarity, with less effort already than the first attempt.

"A... E... C?" Scarlett asked.

"Yes!" Lucy said. "That's it. You see it?"

"I did, yes. You sent it. Good, that was good."

"That was... easier than I thought."

"Yes, like the man's heart. Good, but not a challenge. He will be harder."

"Robbie," Lucy said.

"Yes. Me? I let you in. That man today? He wanted help. This... Robbie will be different. He will fight back."

"Why? Why will he fight?"

"Doesn't matter. But he will. And it's much harder to send when they resist. Don't want to receive. But if you want to help, you must find a way. To push him and yourself. That is why it's dangerous. Why you must be careful. So careful. Or you won't be ready for something coming in, won't be able to move away in time."

"Did that happen to you? Did you have a 'wreck' like that?"

Scarlett's eyes darted toward the fire; a shadow of remembrance passed across her features. Lucy thought she may not answer the question, and second-guessed herself for asking it. She waited.

"Yes," Scarlett answered a small eternity later, with a quiver in her voice that Lucy deemed uncharacteristic. Her eyes came back to Lucy's, penetrating like needles, injecting a vaccine, as if trying to prepare Lucy for the fight with a mental virus. "It happens at the time you least expect. Be very, very careful. I feel how you want to help, to save him, and I see what drives you. You want to make her proud, the urge to prove yourself. All very noble. And you can succeed. Yes. Can come back, Lucy."

At the sound of her name in that voice, Lucy startled and goose-bumps raced down her arms.

"So much death in that place, though," Scarlett said. "When people die, at the precise moment, they cry and part of you will pay attention. Can't help that. Can't turn it off. But if you are into him, helping him, and someone else dying finds their way *into you* at the same time?" She shook her head. "Hear this well and don't lose it. To go in there, find him, carry him out? Is like walking onto a frozen lake to save someone who fell through the ice. And in that building, someone else may pull on you for help at the same time."

Lucy sat straight up, her posture rigid, muscles tensed as if the ground had become electrified.

"One mistake," Scarlett said, "and you will drown too."

From *Passing Through, Thoughts on Death and Dying* by Lucille Claremont, RN (p. 172).

"Dreams and Visions":

Because most of the dying process occurs beneath the surface, we should note the numerous meaningful experiences that occur outside lucid, waking moments. It is not possible for any observer to take part in these experiences, making it difficult to learn about or understand them. They are, however, critical to the person having them.

Research on this phenomenon is lacking, on both the causes and implications of end-of-life dreams and visions. Therefore, what follows is based on my experience as a hospice nurse. I believe in everything included, but must leave you to judge for yourself the validity of this information.

A previous chapter described two sides of the main variable that may influence the dying experience: whether the soul finds peace. The dreams and visions of a dying person are also shaped by this factor. It stands to reason as those same dreams/visions form a large piece of each person's individual death. What they see, hear, and feel outside waking reality forms their unique experience with death.

When a person can process their life events, dreams will be comforting. These can show that a person is facing death without fear, prepared to say their farewells, and sometimes they may even look forward to passing through. Their dreams may show not only their acceptance of death but also signs of hope, a focus on the desirable aspects of the next world.

The most common themes in hopeful death dreams can be grouped into loose categories. These include: reuniting with loved ones (most often children, parents, or siblings), preparing for a journey (organizing precious items, packing boxes, traveling to beloved places), or organized by their emotional core (most commonly love, acceptance, or forgiveness).

Some of the more touching examples shared with me are: a woman running with a child through a sunny green field (whose husband later told me that their only pregnancy had ended in a miscarriage), and a male patient riding in a car, reunited with his two deceased brothers.

In all cases, dreams with hopeful themes are a precursor to a good death.

Where dying persons cannot find peace, however, their dreams will take on a darker tone and can be associated with the sense of fear or perception of unfinished business. The themes for these would include violence, dread, terror, lack of forgiveness or acceptance, and most commonly, immediate physical danger.

Examples of discomforting death dreams would include: a man—wracked with guilt over his violent crime which was never discovered—who had visions of being stabbed repeatedly, and a woman who blamed herself for her sister's accidental death and had recurring dreams of drowning.

Whether they fall into the peaceful or tortured category, death dreams differ from those experienced during life in several critical ways.

First, they will increase in frequency and become indistinguishable from waking moments. This is because of changes in cognitive function that occur during advanced terminal stages, leading to irregular circadian rhythms and a blurring of the lines between lucidity and dream states. Death dreams often occur during mixed-state sleep when the patient cannot discern, even for some time afterward, whether they had been asleep or awake.

Second, death dreams are more impactful on the physical body because of their basis in emotions that have built for months or years. Even patients who have a tendency to forget dreams will remember their death dreams in great detail. In some extreme cases, for those unable to find a good death, dreams or visions become so profound they result in physical manifestations, movements, even marks on the skin or injury.

To pass through in this mental state, rather than having a peaceful death, is agony no human soul deserves to face.

CHAPTER THIRTY-TWO

They moved forward, Robbie pushing John along the cave floor as if he were a garden implement tilling the soil of his own grave, until they reached a wall. John didn't understand how Robbie saw anything, his flashlight held in his left hand, that arm clasped around John's neck so the light shone only behind them like a pipe streaming a cloud of exhaust in photonegative. Still, Robbie knew where he was steering.

John's protesting feet met the base of the wall, rounded into a non-angle from the floor. When he could push no further, Robbie twisted his hand to cast the light in front of them and John saw a small opening in the rock's surface. It was too dark, the light not holding still as he continued to thrash, and on closer look John noticed how tight that opening was. It was no more than a crack, a narrow crawlspace that started at the floor and rose up the cave wall in an inverted V, barely wide enough at its base for a human body to squeeze into. He knew something real about Robbie's intentions then.

John grunted in protest, a long and deep sound, formed more in his chest than his vocal chords. Robbie loosened the arm around his throat, enough for John to cough and grasp at the stagnant underground air.

"N-no," John said, sputtering the word as if his lungs were backfiring.

"Afraid so, buddy. We got to get you in there," Robbie said. "I'm sorry, I really am. But it's the only way. You have to feel what's happening out there. Embrace it and move forward."

John's mind wavered back to his terrible visions, all played back at the same time like the greatest hits of the past week. Dark thoughts whipped through him like a flock of bats, their wings leaving trails of sliver-like scalpel cuts. Robbie pulling the strings that brought his life crashing down. His brother, dying trapped and alone in a dark womb of rock. Mags, trapped too. Like him, in danger. But where? Somewhere dark.

The thought of her, trapped and alone and threatened as he was, brought John to action. His own safety was no longer pressing. He had to find Mags.

A surge came then, as if adrenalin had been injected straight into his chest. He placed both feet firmly on the wall, hoping to either catch Robbie off guard or force him to drop the arm around John's neck.

The arm stayed, locked tighter than its original position, cutting off his air. John's feet on the wall, one a few inches up, the other higher. He pushed with the full strength of both thighs as if he were jumping. He and Robbie went backward, landing hard and sprawling out, back-to-front, John on top.

The flashlight skittered away but remained on, coming to rest a few feet away, facing them and casting their shadows against the wall with the narrow crack where Robbie had tried to force him. Light sprinkled around them like chunks of yellow gore. Everything else was black.

"Stop," Robbie said with a bluntness that showed his steely resolve. "Stop fighting." His arm stayed locked around John's throat. John was choking, gasping with no sound. But his other arm was free. Robbie had shot a hand behind himself to break the fall, and his arm was now pinned underneath them.

John drove his now-free elbow into Robbie's right side, into the soft space between his bottom rib and pelvis. Robbie's breath came out in a whoosh. His arm loosened, John rolled to the side, and they both came to their feet like runners after the starting pistol.

John charged. Robbie stood his ground.

The impact hurt John more than it probably did Robbie. He'd been going for a low, football-style tackle, to wrap his arms around Robbie's waist and knock him to the ground. It didn't go as planned. John telegraphed his move and Robbie twisted his torso to the side, feet planted. John's collarbone collided with the protruding bone of Robbie's hip. The bone-on-bone contact was jarring.

Robbie lost his balance partway, his hands coming down in reflex to push John's shoulders away and absorb some of the impact. He called out something that contained no words, only a single elongated syllable. Something slammed into the back of John's head and his vision went white, a startling contrast to the full darkness he had seen since entering the cave. Then sight seeped back in, and he unwrapped his arms from Robbie's waist and started swinging them.

Robbie blocked the first punch, though John was not sure how he saw it. The second collided with Robbie's shoulder, and they cried out from the impact, in unison. Robbie swung back, hitting John on the chin, hard enough to send his teeth crashing together. One fell out, a bicuspid, and another, an incisor, broke clean through, halfway from the gumline. An orchestra of pain sang from John's mouth.

He swung again, this time his fist finding its way into Robbie's midsection, where the elbow had landed before. Robbie grunted but seemed unaffected. He dropped his own arm, catching John's in place. The fight was becoming hopelessly one-sided. Robbie rained a few quick blows, professional, calculated, on John's face and chest, released his arm and stepped backward, kicking the flashlight as he went, sending the light spinning in a mad, twirling strobe as if the only illumination in the world came from the top of a police cruiser. In one of its passing flashes John saw how close they had moved to another cliff. He saw edge and nothing past, knew there was a drop, but was unable to tell how far. For a brief second, the spinning light jumped farther out and came back. As the wall stopped, John saw a rivulet of water covering the floor along the cliff's edge, around twenty feet across. Then the wall was back.

Robbie hadn't seen it, John hoped. Blood was running from his nose into his mouth in a warm thin line. He combed it inward with his bottom lip like wiping a gruesome windshield. He walked forward, matching Robbie's retreat, coaxing him toward a fall he hoped would be enough to take the fight out of him (or more).

Robbie laughed, a bright, distinct, and offensive "ha." He looked at John with an expression that existed somewhere between pity and annoyance. "You're only making this harder, John." He moved forward.

In the dim light, John's rods and cones pulling in fragmented details like a drowning man sucking air through a straw, he saw Robbie move while his shadow stayed still. No, not his shadow. Another person? Surely it was a trick of the light, or lack thereof. There couldn't be anyone else in there, right? It would explain how John was pushed while Robbie was adamant he hadn't done it. How did they get in? If they followed John, he would know.

Which left two possibilities: there was another way in, or they were *already* in. Regardless of which, had Robbie known? Or arranged it?

No, John decided with a jab of instinct, it was a trick of his poor vision. It was the most likely explanation, which still left him at Robbie's mercy.

John struggled for breath after being throttled and then the fight, having trouble staying on his feet through the angry throb in his mouth. But he was still breathing, still standing. He held his hands up again, in a tired fighting pose. Robbie did the opposite, dropping his hands to his sides.

"What are you still holding onto, man?" Robbie said. "What's left? I took it all away, you have nothing left, and you're still fighting? Just quit, dammit. Let this happen."

"No," John said, wrestling with an impossible choice of survival. Goaded on by a drive he didn't understand, he decided that no matter what might happen, he would choose his own fate, his own end. "Not your way. No. I may die in here, but I won't be killed here."

"Woah, woah. Whoever said I was going to kill you?"

"Then what?"

"I'm just trying to show—"

"What is there to show me in that crawlspace? You're trying to cram me in there and leave me for dead."

"There's still so much you don't understand. This may sound like a joke, but"—he pulled a six-inch kitchen knife from some pocket or sheath hidden behind his back—"this is going to hurt me more... blah blah blah."

Robbie's face showed a mix of shame and glee as he covered the remaining distance between them with uncanny speed. In motion, he dropped fully into shadow and out again like he was skipping through darkness, or maybe John moved forward without realizing it. He caught Robbie's wrist, pushing the knife away to the side but leaving himself wide open to Robbie's foot. It came down on John's bent knee at a sharp angle, bowing the joint inward against its range of motion. There was a terrible cracking sound, like someone had wrapped discarded chicken bones in a thick cloth and rolled a car over them. Pain fired up the whole of John's body, alighting every nerve in his leg and jolting into his brain.

He fell and Robbie was on top of him immediately, swinging his free hand, hitting John in the face and chest. Again, again, again. John blocked with one hand, while the other clamped around his shattered knee, trying in vain to keep it from twisting further as the two writhed on the floor.

Robbie brought the knife up, high above his head, catching pieces of light from the small bulb a few feet away. Then it came down, sliding into John's side, piercing his skin with a faint *thuck* sound like sucking the pit from a peach, and skating between two of his ribs, buried to its hilt.

John felt it enter him in a detached, serene way. Instead of being painful, it was more like a switch deactivating his nerves, a circuit breaking. *Going into shock*, he thought, flashing back to his out-of-body moment hanging from the cliff. The broken leg was no longer his. The body stabbed belonged to someone else.

John relaxed.

Robbie pulled the knife out and stood. He looked over John like a conquest, a big game hunter surveying his kill. John's strained breath sluiced in and out, like air passing through a clarinet too slow to make music.

"I didn't wanna do that, you know," Robbie said, his voice discolored with rage or pain or something John couldn't place. "But you won't open your eyes. Why didn't you open your eyes, John? Why do I have to remind you of every single detail before you remember?"

John barely heard him, or was barely listening. He was sliding downhill, away from himself, on the slick, smooth rock.

Robbie stepped around and grasped John by the shirt collar. He was still talking, words muffling and blending, dragging John's limp form. John's shattered knee wiped over a bump in the floor and the pain came back. John came back. Robbie's words came back too.

"When I pushed you, you were supposed to fall, John."

I knew it, John tried to say, but his lips moved and nothing came out. Robbie wasn't dragging him toward the crawlspace, as John had first thought. He was moving toward the cliff.

"You were supposed to fall. That was going to be it, okay? No more endless, circular routine, no more hiding, no more forgetting. When you landed, that would be the end. We could both move on. Now I have to try something more extreme."

John's hand, as though possessed, made a fishlike flap sideways and slipped into his pocket, looking for the only thing in his possession that may be useful, the small key ring light. When his hand went into that back pocket, it found something else. Mags's hair ribbon.

"M-Mags," John said, choking it out, "where's... she." The stab wound in his side stopped him from adding the upward inflection of a question. His voice was flat and reedy.

"You tell me," Robbie said.

"You... said she... left."

"That's why we're down here, John. That's the whole reason. You know where she is. Don't you remember yet?"

John shook his head, pushing his eyes shut with the thumb and index finger of one hand.

"That's what I have to show you."

"W-what'd... you... do?"

"Not me. Us. And I can't just tell you. How many times have I said that? That won't be enough. You have to see it, John. You have to feel it. All. That's the only way back."

They reached the edge. Robbie stopped dragging and let go; John's chest fell to the floor. His head teetered over the drop and lolled sideways as he released the tension in his neck. He saw nothing in the void, but the effect was still dizzying.

"L-let... me go."

Robbie leaned in, as if readying to share a secret, and the light caught his face at an angle, distorting it like a pond reflection shattered by a thrown rock. Not distorted—maybe it was changing. John's eyes worked overtime to compensate for the lack of input, and they sent confused and frantic signals. He pulled the key light from his pocket and shoved the button down with his thumb. The light revealed a truth he wasn't prepared for.

It wasn't Robbie holding him down.

Chapter Thirty-Three

The face hovering above John's drawn into reality by the valiant strobe of his key light (before he dropped it in shock) was one he recognized but couldn't place. The face from a wanted poster, or the evening news. Police are looking for... wanted for questioning... person of interest... artist's rendering. Insert this face.

Gaunt, strong-jawed, unshaven. Dark eyes, like smoke concentrated inside a marble and clouding the iris out of being. A sneer coloring his entire expression. Perhaps handsome once, but buried now beneath a lifetime of hardship, rent by longstanding troubles and abuse, both given and received.

"Remember me?" the non-stranger asked, then laughed. "Your girl sure would."

His words brought a spark to John's memory, like kindling coming alight at the base of an enormous bonfire. It was smoldering enough to maintain its heat but not spreading yet. There was something there, he remembered. Something awful. Something deadly.

John fought back with a ferocity he hadn't dared unleash on his friend. No matter how badly Robbie had punished him, he hesitated to fight back, held a desire not to harm. That hesitance now gone, caught ablaze by that spark of memory. This man meant to kill him, there was no doubt.

Unsure of what had happened to Robbie or how he came to be pinned by this almost-familiar villain, John knew this was a death struggle. And he reacted the way anyone in the situation would wish to. Animalistic. Blindly vengeful.

There was a sound in the cave, one John hardly registered and never considered was coming from himself. Spurred on by the pain-vanquishing effects of shock on his body, he pulled himself to his feet and leapt forward with the fluidity of a jungle cat. He was rage incarnate, directed at the best possible target. This man had done something to him, taken from him, stolen part of him. Struggling to uncover it, John hammered his rocklike fists again and again. His broken leg was a numb shaft supporting him at an angle. The pain signals from his side served only to feed the red sheet covering his eyes, painting the dark of the cave in a maddening crimson glow.

There was no light. John lashed blindly through a blood fog, with only sensations of space and pressure and the motion of the swirling air around in trails behind his arms. Each landed blow only adding to his anger as fatigue crept in and the man he was beating grew limp, then still.

Swinging his arms in violent rhythm, John shot himself forward on his good knee, catching his target low, and then there was nothing left to strike. He swung again, only air, one last time, still no contact. He had vanished. No, he had fallen. In the flash of motion they had spun around, both of them, without John realizing it.

The cave was silent except for John's labored breathing.

He bent, fumbling around for the flashlight he had dropped. Or the one Robbie had dropped. "Robbie?" he called out. "Robbie, where are you?"

"Here," Robbie answered.

He was close. Too close, somehow. Where had he been a minute ago? John's foot moved forward and something skittered across the floor like an insect that was too big and too fast. The key light. He followed the sound, an act made easier in the dark so deep it honed his hearing, with more energy focused on the senses available. He found the light and pressed the button, his hand becoming a vise. He could not let the light abandon him. There was a sense of a tightrope; any lack of caution in either direction and he would plummet, trapped, alone, without hope of escape, on his way down and down.

What the light showed him this time caused that tightrope-sense to amplify. John saw hands, swollen from the fight, coming over the cliff's crest.

Robbie's hands. John dove, grabbed them, and pulled toward himself. He saw Robbie's face, one eye forced shut by the engorged tissue surrounding it, the other a blood-red circle. The nose was twisted, mangled, broken in a few places, skin scraped off one of his cheekbones in a big loose flap. Lips split and seeping blood onto his chin.

There had been no one else with them; it was Robbie that he attacked so savagely. The other person was a trick, an illusion. He had pummeled and beaten in the dark until he knocked Robbie back over the edge to hang on with the barest grasp. His hands trembled. John knew it wouldn't be long before their strength left and he fell. He held Robbie by both wrists, much like Robbie had done for him earlier.

One hand was slipping. John squeezed the wrist tighter, and Robbie's ruined face grimaced further.

"John," Robbie said, his words muffled by the obstruction of his own swollen lips. "Sorry. So sorry."

"No," John said. "Hang on, let's get you up first. Then we can both apologize. I can't believe I—"

"It's fine. What I wanted you to do. All along, this was it. It was all leading to this."

Robbie's wrist slipped further within John's grip, his fingers now wrapped not around the wrist itself, but around the palm. Robbie was still sliding, faster. John's grip was slick with blood. If one hand went, the other would follow. Robbie was falling, and John could not help.

"Sorry it had to be this way," Robbie said. "This hard. I wish it didn't, but nothing else was getting through. I had to bring you here and give you a target."

"Robbie, I still don't know what you're talking about."

"But you will, now. You'll see it all again. Feel it all. You'll remember. It worked, see?"

Slipping further and further, Robbie made no efforts to climb or even stop himself sliding away. Like he was headed somewhere better, or at least better suited for him.

"Just... hang on," John said. "I'll get you up. I can do it if you help me."

Robbie didn't reply to this comment, instead looking at John with an intensity made no less effective by his battered visage. All the swelling and torn skin and damage couldn't hide how stern he was, on the verge of an important message. One with real weight.

John knew what was about to happen even though he refused to accept it. A tear slid from his eye and rolled down the length of his cheek.

"John, just... just listen."

"No. No, don't. I'm sorry I did this to you."

"Listen."

"I'm listening."

"I knew you could do it," Robbie said, then pulled his wrists free.

Chapter Thirty-Four

Watching Robbie fall was like watching someone drop a mannequin down a department store elevator shaft. He didn't topple, he plummeted. Straight down, unmoving, un-flinching. As if he were already dead. Robbie fell in a way that resonated with John. It reverberated through him like the call of a bullhorn. *Why did he look so... lifeless?*

John called out after him, but Robbie had intended to fall. That was clear; he hadn't slipped. John hadn't let go or lost him while trying for a better grip. Robbie pulled away intentionally; a diving board wouldn't have made that more apparent.

He only saw a few dozen feet into the pit, the tiny moronic light doing its best as he shouted Robbie's name again and again, stopping only when the pain in his side grew too fierce. John heard him land, a dull thud, but the sound's quality made it impossible to judge the distance. When he landed, John stopped shouting and waited to hear something, anything else. Only silence.

John lay on his stomach, shoulders protruding over the drop. He darted the light back and forth looking for a passage to climb down. The walls on either side were not much farther apart than arm's length, and he realized there was no way down. It was only a steep drop-off buttressed by solid rock ten feet in either direction. Again John thought of an elevator shaft. He called down a few more times, denying its futility, his own desperation. Robbie was gone.

John was alone.

It coursed through him like an illness while his system sent frail antibodies in waves. Weakness came too. He stayed on the wet floor of the cave, the uneven rock pushing back in a few places, legs sticking out behind, arms propping his torso up. What were his options? He couldn't leave Robbie, right? Maybe he should, if Robbie lay broken at the bottom of that drop, bleeding to death. Whether he had survived or not, John could not get him out. He needed to find help either way.

What did he mean? "I knew you could do it."

He put a hand to his side where Robbie had stabbed him. The blood was warm, a little sticky, and copious.

John stood and clamped the key light to keep it on, then turned and tried to find his way back out. It was a slow, agonizing process, hopping to avoid putting weight on his damaged leg, leaning his hand against the wall to rest, then hopping more. The other hand kept pressure on his wounded side to slow the bleeding. His tongue traced the hole from the missing tooth and the too-sharp edge of the broken one. There were hot coals lying inside his lips.

He told himself to start by locating the sound of the waterfall again. If he found that, maybe he could find the large chamber they had climbed down to together. From there, he would backtrack, hobbling, crawling through the first tunnel, back into the cave's opening, and pull himself into the open air (if the rope hadn't fallen and his arms didn't give out first). Then, a simple matter of finding someone to report the situation to and shed responsibility. He would not be in charge of rescuing Robbie anymore. And what then? How could things be normal again? What was his path forward after this?

Even if Robbie was saved, pulled out and through some miracle recovered from both the fall and the beating, John had viciously attacked his only friend in some misguided act. Or was it misguided? He was still certain he had seen someone else in there, at least twice. And that other person's presence would help to explain other inconsistencies in the cave, wouldn't it?

John was hop-walking a few minutes with no trace of the waterfall or anything familiar. The only thing in the cave moving besides his legs (and moving more frantically, at that) was a gauntlet of questions and answers that came from dueling inner voices. The shock of being alone caused him to argue with himself for the company. He searched, knowing there was nothing else left to do.

The rock seemed to shimmer around him as he shone the light on it.

And the questions rolling through him now all shared a common thread. Robbie.

How could you do that to Robbie?

I didn't do it, he did.

But it wasn't him, was it?

It was, there couldn't be anyone else in there with us.

How do you know that?

Because he said it was unexplored.

And you believed him?

I had to believe him.

Isn't it possible someone either came in before us or came in a different way?

I can't rule it out, but that doesn't make it possible. Or probable.

Isn't possible exactly what that makes it?

I guess, but Robbie wouldn't have set me up like that.

Why not? Wasn't he always jealous of me?

No, you've got it the wrong way around.

Do you really think that?

Yes, he had it better than me. I was the jealous one.

Is that why he stole Mags from you?

He didn't do that, I set them up.

Do you really think that?

Yes. "Stop asking me that question." Without noticing, John had thought a question and then answered it aloud.

Aren't you getting a little defensive now?

"I arranged for them to meet."

When was that, exactly?

"A few years ago. I think."

Exactly, I said, when exactly?

"I don't remember, exactly."

Why not?

"Because it was so long ago."

Was it?

"So you'll keep making me answer the same questions more than once?"

Only if you give the wrong answer. Now, why can't you remember more?

"I don't know. I guess it wasn't that important."

If it wasn't that important, why did you steal that ribbon of hers?

"I didn't steal it. I wanted something to remember her by."

Aren't you tired of hiding from all this?

Now it was Robbie's voice arguing with him. John's guilt was manifesting to make Poe proud. *Tired of building all these elaborate backdrops to avoid the truth?*

Ice settled deep in John's veins and he coughed uncontrollably.

John had headed in the same direction, reaching nothing distinct. He moved the light to his left, hoping to glimpse something familiar and did, but not what he wanted. Not at all. There was a wall, a narrow crevice. It was difficult to discern in the questionable light provided, but he thought it could be the same one Robbie (or whoever) had been trying to drag him toward. Or was it? He was going in circles or getting farther into the depths of the cave. Either way, he could not ignore the spirals occurring both in front and inside of him.

If you can't remember when you set Robbie and Mags up, maybe you can remember how?

"Sure I do. That's clear, at least."

How?

"His sister helped, for one. She told me he needed some company that night."

What about my sister then, how well do you know her?

"Not that well, I've only met her once. I think."

You're sounding less certain with each answer, John. The voice had transformed now. He was holding an internal conversation with his missing (dead?) friend.

I'm not dead, John. So you can stop blaming yourself for that one too. It'll be good practice. Now, we can try something easier. What is this sister's name?

"Her name... her name... is..."

I don't have a sister, John. What about my parents, how did they die?

"They were in a car wreck."

That's the most manufactured death I've ever heard, John. Can't you come up with something less pedestrian?

"I didn't come up with anything. It happened."

How did we meet John?

"At work, we met at work."

Did we?

"Yes. We..." John hesitated.

Think before you answer, John.

"No, it was school. High school. Right?"

Now you're asking me? Feeling a little uncertain about these questions, John?

"I'm certain they don't matter."

They do, they really matter. Why do they make you uncomfortable?

"Because I don't know why you're asking them."

Is it because you don't have answers?

"I have answers, I just can't think in here."

So it's the place now, that's your new excuse for all this denial?

"I'm not denying anything."

Listen to yourself. Fine, why is it so cold in this cave, then?

"You told… Robbie told me that's normal."

It's not, and you knew that, didn't you?

"Well, I asked you and you said it was fine."

It's not fine, John. How many bogus pieces of information are you going to eat before you get full?

"I'm getting full of this shit, fake-Robbie-voice. How about you help me out of here?"

There is no 'out of here,' John. Point of No Return, remember?

"The tree."

Yes, the tree. What do you think that means?

"It means I'll die in here."

Okay, good. You're close, at least. Why does it mean that?

"You tell me."

I tried to. Are you ready to listen now?

"Tell me how I'm hearing you in my head, because I'm not asking myself all these questions, I don't buy that. How are you still here? How are we talking?"

At least you're asking the right questions now. All I had to do was bring you into this cave, attack you, and let you kill me. Why do you think you can't remember any of these details, John? Why is it all so foggy? Why can't you find your way out?

As that last question came in, John changed directions with his light again, finding the elevator-shaft-canyon that Robbie had fallen into. No mistaking that one. It confirmed that he had been going in circles.

John, Robbie's voice continued, *are you ready to see her again? Mags is waiting for you. You only need to remember.*

Definition of unknown origin:

Psychokinesis, from the Greek *psukhe (mind, spirit or soul)* + *kinēsis (movement or motion):* also known as PK or telekinesis, a term referring to the parapsychological ability to use mental energy to bring about effects in the physical realm. Most commonly attributed to non-living or non-human beings such as spirits or poltergeists, it is also believed that a very small percentage of humans that possess a hyper-developed frontal lobe have the potential to generate the mental energy needed for psychokinetic effect.

***

From: *Astral Projection and Tabloid Mentalities, a Pragmatic Interpretation of Paranormal Psychologies* by Dr. Arthur McGuire, PhD (p. 96)

The term psychokinesis (PK) is another used frequently by those who do not understand its origins or intended meaning. Often attributed to the infamous parapsychologist J. B. Rhine, the term was first recorded in use over forty years prior to Rhine's moment in the sun. It was originally applied to any influence over physical objects or systems, rather than merely describing the ability to move objects with the mind. PK was also designed as a categorical term to include various sub-forms such as bio-PK (see p. 144), psychic healing (see p. 168), or even pyrokinesis (see p. 283).

More recently, driven by the inability to produce results under controlled conditions, parapsychologists found a clever loophole to the empirical method by splitting the phenomenon into two groups. The first, macro-psychokinesis, is substantial enough to be visible without assistance. The second, micro-psychokinesis, is far more difficult to substantiate (or to disclaim).

One can gather dozens of historical psychokinesis claims revealed to be fraudulent, but as expected, this repeated exposure of its invalidity is outweighed by the blind acceptance of the masses. For them, the real evidence comes from glistening screens.

For example, I challenge you to poll a group of friends and see which of the following names they recognize more readily: Anna Rasmussen (a Danish medium exposed as a fraud in 1950) or Carrietta White (the protagonist from the 1976 horror film *Carrie*). Or perhaps sample their knowledge of Darth Vader versus James Hydrick (who after being exposed said, "My whole idea was to see how dumb America was").

Psychokinesis is an utter fallacy, but one that may never be seen as such. Which begs the question still, how dumb is America?

This author, for one, fears the answer.

***

From: "Effect of Consciousness on the Fall of Dice: A Meta-Analysis," by Dean Radin & Diane Ferrari, published in the *Journal of Scientific Exploration.*

This meta-analysis examined a straightforward hypothesis: Mental intention is correlated with the fall of specified die faces. Based primarily on the analysis of a homogeneous subset of balanced protocol studies, we conclude that the aggregate evidence suggests a genuine mental effect.

The mental effect evaluated in this study resembles similar consciousness-related effects observed in both microscopic (Radin & Nelson, 1989; Schmidt, 1987) and macroscopic (Dunne, Nelson, & Jahn, 1988) random physical systems.

CHAPTER THIRTY-FIVE

As she approached the hospital campus for the second time that day, Lucy was glad for the darkness that had settled. A moonless night was a willing accomplice to the secretive, solemn activities she had planned. Except she hadn't made a plan.

There was precious little time left to act, to save Robbie, so she had rushed bull-headed toward the scene in a manner different from her usual modus operandi. In doing so, she had failed to consider the amount of security lighting installed around the building. Breaking in (the sum of her plan) would take finesse.

She waited out of range of the discerning, xenon-burning lamps posted at regular intervals and hung high on metal poles all around the perimeter. Waited and plotted, mind reeling in desperate circles like a broken carnival ride that refused to slow.

There must be a way in. But how? Without being able to use the front door, I'm sure to set off an alarm, and the security guards are on duty twenty-four-seven.

The answer came as if it were a piece of ripe fruit falling into her lap from the canopy of trees overhead. She had been close with one of the security guards: Rick, the only person she maintained contact with after losing her nursing license. And she had seen him in her bus-mirror-vision. He was the key.

If I can... contact him, I can convince him to help me, she thought, with a more-than-modest bliss. *That is my way in. My mole.*

It was almost too obvious, so simple that it was suspect. She would call to him, try to send him a message, and if he was willing to help, she would have a way around all the obstacles. He could open an emergency exit, it was after midnight, there would be few staff on duty. Once she was in, she could wait out of sight as the attending nurse made his or her rounds, and slip undetected into Robbie's room. That would give her a few hours alone with him.

Could work. It really could, baby. She was talking to Anna in her head.

She set to it, not wanting any more time to pass by unused. Something in her ESP told her that his time was running short, as if a cloud-like gathering of his energy floated inside the building, growing dimmer and slower-moving with each ticking second.

Lucy put a hand to each temple and reached out to Rick. A wisp of dizziness came and passed. After a few seconds of pushing (her strength growing with each attempt), she mentally glimpsed Rick walking down one of the whitewashed and fluorescent-lit hallways of the building, turning a corner. He was whistling. She saw his face, bearded, showing deep lines of age more prominent than she remembered.

It was not a memory. She was seeing him as he currently was. His slacks were black with a permanent crease down the legs, the silver badge clipped to his gray polo shirt. The word SECURITY was affixed in large, white iron-on letters at his shoulder blades.

He was on duty tonight. She cocked one of her elbows down, pulling her fist toward herself in a motion of triumph.

Rick, she said without sound. *Rick, can you hear me?* She had spent several hours with Scarlett, practicing. The depth of its effect was surprising. She need only picture that blue sedan and drive on.

In her mind's eye, she saw him stop walking and heard his shoes squeak in protest on the cold tile floor. He looked behind, to each side, following his ears.

At least he heard it, she thought, then tried again. *RICK!* She pushed, trying to make it louder. He looked up, toward the ceiling.

You're getting closer, she sent.

"Someone there?" he asked. She heard it, despite being separated by a few dozen feet and two concrete walls.

It's Lucy, Rick. Lucy Claremont. Do you remember?

"Lucy?" he asked, again aloud.

You don't have to use your voice, Rick. I can still hear you if you just think it.

"What?"

Never mind, no time. I'm outside. Can you come out and talk?

He looked at his watch. "Oh man, I'm losing it. I got to switch back to days, this graveyard stuff is working me over."

Lucy didn't want to let him off the line. She had to keep working to reel him in, but carefully, if she didn't want him to snap off and bolt like a runaway bass with her mental hook still sticking out of his cheek.

I have to say something to prove it to him. But what? She ran through a remembered list of the conversations she had shared with him. As the list rolled by, like an internal stock ticker, she grabbed a few words and lobbed them at him.

Cigars, she sent. He liked to smoke cigars, she remembered. The next word she passed to him was *Pontiac.* He drove one and had complained to her about how unreliable it was becoming as the odometer wound up. *Ladder,* she followed with. He once told her about a fear of using ladders after a fall left him with limited motion in one foot.

Inside the building, Rick stood in place, shook his head from side to side, and delivered a few soft, open-palmed slaps to the sides of his face.

This sending one disjointed word at a time is not helping. I need to send something more coherent. Something that makes sense that will snap his attention.

Rick, she sent, *do you remember that time there was a fire alarm going off, and you helped me wheel a few of the patients out before we realized it was only a drill? Boy, did we get in trouble.*

Yeah, he thought, and she received it the same as if he had spoken. *That pissed Johanssen off, but you know what, Luce, I'd do it again in a heartbeat. I'd do it every time that damn alarm sounds.*

Same here.

He chuckled, then realization came. In the moment it was like conducting a normal dialogue, and hearing his own laugh aloud drew his awareness. None of those words had been heard or spoken.

"What the hell just happened?" he said, switching back to the verbal for comfort.

It's okay, Rick, it really is me. I'm outside.

How? How am I hearing you?

Well, you're not. It's more like you're receiving me.

Okay, get technical, but at least answer my question.

I can't. I don't know how it works myself. Rick, I need help and fast. I need to see a patient.

"Oh no," he switched seamlessly back to his voice, then caught himself. *We can't do that, Luce. If anyone found out I'd be fired for sure. And you... well, you'd go to jail. Remember the no-trespassing thing? They were kind of serious about that.*

I'm not worried about going to jail. It was partly true. What worried her was losing what little buoyancy she'd found in the last half day. *I'll make sure nothing happens to you.*

Can't you call and talk to someone? One of the other nurses or something? They'll help. They're much better at helping with that. What could I even do?

I need to get in. Today. Now. Please, there isn't enough time. They'll think I'm crazy when I try to explain it.

And I'm not thinking that?

Are you?

I guess I'm thinking more about myself being crazy.

Will you come outside and talk to me? Real quick, please?

I don't know, Luce. This is trippy stuff already.

Rick, I'm trying to save someone before it's too late.

Save them? You forgot what this place is for. Nobody in here can be saved. Unless, besides this mental-talk thing you can also do magical cancer surgeries or turn back the clock for people.

I don't mean save his life. Not like that. Come outside, okay? It'll be much easier to explain in person.

The strain of maintaining contact this long, in both directions, was wearing on her. Her time with Scarlett helped, but she was not strong enough to do these things for long. Fatigue came like the pressurization adjusting in an airplane cabin. Too much density built behind her ears, waiting for release. She exhaled sharply, and her image of him was lost.

She waited a few tense moments, then the emergency exit nearest her popped open.

CHAPTER THIRTY-SIX

Rick had put on a little weight, she noticed as he emerged into the halo of light cast by the security pole. And he hadn't started small. He was the type whose clothes never fit right, pulled taut in some places and baggy in others. That was still the case, only amplified.

"Over here," she whispered, catching his attention as he searched the shadows.

He walked over to her and surprised her with a hug, wrapping his big arms around her shoulders and squeezing tight for a few seconds.

When he released enough for her to breathe again, she laughed. It was good, long overdue. She cursed herself silently for having lost touch with him. Then he did it not-so-silently.

"Why the hell haven't I heard from you the last few years?" he asked in a tone of accusation overrun by what sounded like relief. Concern. She missed these things far more than she had realized. Her sense of companionship had atrophied like a large muscle behind that wall of apathy.

"Long story. I've been slipping away from more than just you."

"Well, where have you been?"

"Not far. I never made it far." She cast her eyes to the east. The direction of the cemetery.

"Did you ever make it in?"

She recalled telling him in one of their last conversations, which made it seem less distant than it was. It was surely last week, not years ago, she was crying in front of him, explaining how she needed to see Anna's grave but hadn't the strength to go after the funeral. Her self-constructed aversion to cemeteries, to all places of death, included the one they were meeting at. She needed to refocus; there would be time to catch up with Rick later. If she didn't drown in Scarlett's frozen lake.

"I did, but only this morning. Then I came back here for something important. I'm trying to help a patient, and he doesn't have much time left."

"How do you know that? Have you talked to someone else here?"

"No, but I'm sure of it. I can't explain how that works either, but it does."

"So you need to get in there."

"Yes."

"But you can't, because you're not allowed on the premises."

"Right."

"And you don't have time for proper channels."

"Mm-hm."

"So you need me to help you."

"Yes."

"Help you break in."

"Yeah, I guess so."

"To a hospice building," he said. Delivered flat, like a punch line.

"Right."

He considered this a few moments, even bringing a hand up to scratch the stubble on his chin demonstratively.

"You know, that may be even weirder than the voice in my head thing," Rick said.

They both laughed, loud, his voice booming over her smaller one.

"I guess it is. Bet it's the first time."

He shrugged his shoulders. It struck Lucy how easy it seemed to accept all these absurd claims once you had let the first one in. Once you had cleared the space for one, the others trailed in behind it like a line of ants.

"What's his name?" Rick asked.

"Robbie."

"Robbie what?"

"I don't remember."

"You don't remember his last name?"

"No, he was brought in right before I... left. And I wasn't exactly clear-headed at the time. All I really remember is that he was in terrible shape when we got him."

"That doesn't narrow it down much, Luce."

"He was *really* bad. Not like the others, who are sick with a terminal illness, or nearing the end of their time naturally. This man was young. He had been attacked... broken. Beaten nearly to death, thrown off somewhere high, maybe? Paralyzed, in a coma."

Rick's eyes moved in several directions, as if he was searching his memory.

She continued explaining. "If I can help him in time, it will fix me as much as him. That's the thing. I think it's as important for me as it is for him. I've..." She paused, looking at her feet, voice hitching. "... been struggling, you know? To find meaning, to be okay about... about me. Ever since..."

"Say no more." Rick excelled at reading the moods of others. That made his presence in the hospice wing more than one solely of watchfulness and security. Patients regarded Rick with much the same respect and admiration as the medical staff. He evoked the same responses in them. He cared, and it showed often. Lucy was sure that part of his easy acceptance of her monumental request (and the incredible story behind it) was because he could picture himself losing the purpose that his own work afforded. His job was part of his identity. And she was asking him to risk it.

"I just need access to his room. For a little while, that should be enough," she said, not sure if she believed that herself. It could take hours.

"We can do that," he answered. "We can do better. If you can hide out until Clarice makes her rounds past him, you should have at least an hour with him. Unless something goes wrong, and an alert goes or anything like that."

"That's all I need."

"Let's make it happen. I'll go back in, then you wait for my signal. I'll leave the door unlocked, and once it's clear, I'll flick the light in the room next to this exit. On and off three times, real quick."

Lucy nodded.

"When you see that, come to this door and slip in."

She nodded again, three quick bobs.

"After that, I'll keep an eye out and we can… talk, like we did before, I guess. And I'll let you know if anything goes wrong, so you can get out in time."

"Okay. That should work."

"I can't promise you won't be made. But we can at least try."

"That's all I ask."

"Here we go, then." He stepped into the white-yellow glow from the security lights and disappeared back inside.

He fixed the locking bar to stay propped open, meaning he had also disabled the emergency exit alarm. There was a small brick overhang, wider than the door itself, protruding five feet. This provided cover, but she would still be exposed by the lights for at least a few seconds, even if she was running.

She waited for the signal of the light flicker he had described. While waiting, she tried to chisel all of Scarlett's grounding images from marble, to make them permanent fixtures in her mental landscape, like statues.

The un-trackable rushing traffic on the highway. Country back road, blue sedan winding safely through. The aggressive approach of the truck and how the car had responded. Lucy sculpted them in bas-relief in some cognitive storage space. She was stockpiling mental weapons. Or shields. She was breathing evenly, poised like a gazelle awaiting the chase.

The light flicked. Twice. A third time.

Lucy shot out of the dark like there was a lion at her heels.

Chapter Thirty-Seven

She pumped her legs as fast as she could manage, which was not as fast as she wanted; it had been countless months since her last jog around the neighborhood. But it was fast enough. With the minimal staff on duty in these pre-dawn hours, there was no sign she had been spotted in her scramble across the xenon-lit clearing.

She shoulder-slammed into the brick wall, panting in rhythm with the throb of the massive light bulbs nearby.

She checked the door. It was still propped open, and when she pushed it gingerly, with one finger, it moved inward. She pushed further, enough to slide her slender form through, moving sideways. While clinging to a wall within the exit alcove, she saw only white paint and white tile and fluorescent light, but familiar smells came to her in waves.

Rubbing alcohol. Soiled linens. Vaseline and bad food.

She heard footsteps and made an instinctive move back toward the door, catching herself. Rick had cleared the way once; it wouldn't be clear again. She held fast, breath locked in burning lungs. Shoulders and fingers and butt and heels all pressed against the wall behind her. The footsteps continued, but no shadow approached, and soon they were moving away, getting quieter.

She exhaled, waited long enough to make sure whoever had passed was gone, then peeked her head around the corner at a dog-curious angle. When she saw no one, she swung her head, checking she was still alone. She waited a few ticks longer before slithering down the hall, her spine held against the wall before deciding it would be quicker (and easier) to walk, so long as her steps were soft. She leaned forward and pulled her shoes off.

Should have left these outside, she scolded herself. But it was too late now. She dipped into a room on her left, placing her shoes on the floor just inside the doorway and making a mental note to come back for them before she left.

Lucy didn't know which room she needed. She tried to remember where Robbie was when she left and failed. There were still too few details about him.

The room was dark, a few low-grade nightlights that allowed staff to see, LED lights on some equipment. But it was enough that she found the patient's chart. She checked the name. Tiffany. Wrong room.

How am I going to find him? The answer came before the question finished forming.

Rick, she reached out, hands to her temples again. *Rick, I'm in, but I don't know what room.*

Good. I'm not too far away. Let me check.

She sensed him thinking, their connection more solid with use, like someone was tracing the curves of her skull with a finger.

Okay, the guy in room 6 sounds closest to what you told me outside.

I'll try there, thanks.

But Lucy, he's not—

Rick's last message cut off. She had a glimpse of someone approaching him, probably the nurse on duty, and then it was gone too. He must have been distracted and broke the contact.

She needed to keep moving, couldn't afford to wait for him to come back. So she checked the number she was in. Room 14. Which meant the room Rick mentioned was on the opposite side of the building.

Lucy crept back into the hall as if her body were filled with greased ball bearings. She was silence incarnate, the merest whisper floating through the halls. She knew she would find him then. Something grand was on her side, far bigger than herself or her patient. He needed her, and she needed him, perhaps even more so. She was ready, she was cognizant, she had a plan. It was going to work.

CHAPTER THIRTY-EIGHT

She rounded a corner, the numbers on the patients' doors moving down in a slow but steady pattern. Room 12, on her side of the hall, 11 on the opposite. Her path was still clear, but for how long? Sufficient, which was how she felt.

More prep time would have boosted her confidence. The final picture of circumstances was far from ideal. But sufficient. Thinking that gave her strength, aided her stealth, guided her steps.

She breezed past rooms 10, then 8. She saw the number *7* on a door as she approached with feet wrapped in smoke. She paused at the wall next to that door, pressing herself backward again as if trying to merge with it. To be absorbed. A voice came from her left but it was small, distant. The on-duty nurse making rounds. And she hadn't yet reached Robbie's room. It was too soon to go in. Lucy took in her surroundings with a firm glance.

There was nowhere to hide. The voice came again, louder. She was either in the hall or a closer room. Lucy had time to search options, but not much.

Ducking into another patient's room would not help. If the nurse was rounding this direction, her hiding place would be temporary. She could either move from room to room or find somewhere within the room to disappear. Either was risky.

The medical supply closet was a better option, but it was a few turns farther ahead, down another hall. She could make her way there, then wait until the nurse had passed and completed her checks. Navigating that far was dangerous, but time was on her side. Each patient check should take at least a minute, perhaps two. There were still two or three patients left before they would cross paths. That gave her somewhere between two and six minutes. Ever cautious, Lucy preferred to allow herself less than two minutes to hide.

The voice moved toward her, following the trajectory of the hall Lucy had left.

She moved toward the supply closet, which seemed miles away. Because of the lack of activity in the building, she reached it without incident.

The problem started when she tried to open the door.

Chapter Thirty-Nine

T he closet was locked. She stepped back, surprise almost winning over urgency. She pressed the handle down, again, careful to minimize the noise it caused. It moved slightly and gave no sign of changing its position. She tried turning it up—no help either.

The supply closet had never been locked when she worked here. She hadn't thought to ask Rick, and he hadn't mentioned it either. It would seem that neither of them anticipated her having to duck inside to wait for the all-clear.

She tried to call out to Rick, but couldn't reach him. It was as if he had vanished, their tentative line of communication broken. Lucy thought of the B-movies she had watched with Anna (her request, always), the ones where the phone line always got cut right before anyone got hurt. But she was not facing dismemberment by a knife-wielding maniac; she stood on the brink of another arrest, one final setback that would send her spiraling back down into the depths that invited only suicide as a way out. She was her own stalking killer.

Rick, she sent, loud. Rick, *are you still out there?*

No response.

She jiggled the door handle a few times, neglecting the noise. Should the nurse on duty hear that, it would replace one problem with another, far worse. She needed to get herself in, fast.

She remembered some TV show where someone slid a credit card between a door and its jamb, at the same height where the bolt of the lock would be. If she found something thin and rigid enough, maybe she could coax the lock open. It seemed possible, except she was in an empty hallway with no time to search.

The sound of footsteps edged toward her like an approaching forest fire. Panic swarmed around her thoughts, but before she let it rush in, Scarlett's voice came to her.

You could learn to do things you've only seen in fantasies.

But what does that mean? Lucy thought. *Does that mean I can... move things?*

No answer.

She grasped the door handle, using both hands, and tried to picture the inner workings of its mechanism. Springs and metal wheels and small brass teeth that slid into place when you inserted the key. Next to that, the bolt. Long and smooth, six sides but not equal sizes, making it more cylindrical. It protruded from a hole in the door's side, sized perfectly to move in and out as needed. There was a small metal clip at its base, holding it fast until the key came to release it.

That was where she focused. The image in her mind became more solid, increasing in clarity, same as the image of Robbie's hospital bed in the field had. She was pushing herself much harder than previously. She wished for darkness in the hallway. If she had seen anything at all, it might have prevented her from mustering enough strength. If only it were dark.

A single drop of blood slipped from her left ear. A shadow drew out on the tile floor a few feet to her left, its owner only steps away from rounding the corner.

She traced every curve of that metal clip with her mind and tried to sculpt a scene of herself holding it, bending it. The door held fast, both her arms pushing the handle downward. If the door opened she would fall.

The shadow in the corner moved sideways; its owner may have detoured into a patient's room. Lucy dared not allow herself more time—if the door didn't open now, she would run.

She tried another angle, reverting to the slip-a-cred-it-card-into-the-jamb idea. She formed the image of a small metal plate and defined its edges in her mind. Rounded, not sharp. No, one was sharp, the one that would lead. Like a wedge, it would slip with ease between the edge of the bolt and its home. The precise size and thickness of a credit card, but far more sturdy. A mix between a surgical instrument and a pocket tool.

She held it, gripped it, turned it over and examined all sides, using a hand not attached to her body. Placed the pad of her index finger over the minimal gap between the door and its frame. The other hand was still pushing down on the handle, should anything move she wanted to capture it.

Pressed. Focused. Saw the plate slide in. Pressed her finger. Focused her thoughts. Drove her little blue car.

The footsteps returned, the shadow reaching the opposite wall and sliding up it as the person approached.

There was a click. The handle moved down. Lucy pulled the door open a few inches and dropped into the safety of the closet, hitting the floor in an unorganized lump like a runner gone one mile too far.

From *Passing Through, Thoughts on Death and Dying* by Lucille Claremont, RN (p. 159).

"Peaceful Deaths vs. Troubled Souls":

There are infinite variables that together form the overall perception of dying for each person. It is easier to comprehend the dying process by focusing on one variable in particular, as it is the most influential. By down-scaling possible deaths this way, though over-simplified, we can group deaths into two distinct categories. This variable is the presence (or absence) of troubling circumstances, and its effect becomes much more pronounced the nearer to the end of life.

As so many of the steps in dying occur at a subconscious level, the conscience needs clarity for a peaceful detachment. If the conscience is stained, it becomes necessary for the subconscious mind to remedy this. At the moment of death, a troubled soul, possessed of unresolved past issues or with distressing events contributing to their death, will encounter a far different experience than someone at peace with the major events of their life.

Often a troubled soul is eased through prayer or the request for forgiveness from a higher power. Having past sins absolved by whatever powers one expects to encounter in the afterlife can be of profound comfort. However, some psychologists have claimed that religion or spirituality can, at times, be an obstacle to mental health.

There is little research or documentation on this phenomenon, so to those dealing with the expected loss of a loved one, I can only offer the sum of my experience on this topic.

Through years of witnessing both types of deaths, and continuous effort to facilitate a peaceful transition, to ease the passing through, I have learned four recurring (if not constant) truths.

First, the subconscious mind has more awareness of death's approach than the conscious mind. Second, the subconscious has an insatiable desire to clean itself to prepare for death. Third, if it cannot do so to satisfaction, whether because of a lack of time, proper information, or other resources, the subconscious can enter a desperate state. And finally, in this desperate state, the subconscious can go to extreme lengths to cope with the troubled nature of the conscience.

These extreme lengths, like death itself, can take infinite forms (I would fail to contain even a fraction of them here), such as tricking the conscious mind with false sensory input, rearranging memories, or even artificial constructs.

A fractured, unprepared subconscious can wreak havoc on a dying individual in ways that most of us will never experience or understand. This is the single biggest obstacle to a good death.

CHAPTER FORTY

"Remember what?" John asked the voice in his head that couldn't be Robbie's but somehow was. Silence. The desire to leave the cave, to flee, grew into a need. It was something tangible inside him, a large, debilitating splinter. Survival was all that mattered. He needed out, needed light, needed sky. Needed free.

Pain from his mouth and leg was coming in stereo flashes. The blood from his side was slowing, drying. He released pressure from the hand there, waking the sliced nerves in an angry flash.

But there was nowhere to go. He had spent too long blundering in circles in the blackness, wondering how much battery his light had left. A wasted effort.

He stood, canted on his damaged knee, motionless beside the elevator-shaft-canyon for an indeterminable time. Then came a voice.

A woman's voice. Mags's voice.

It drifted toward him from behind, her words too soft to keep their shape as they traveled, but their caliber uniquely hers. He turned, stabbing the light in several frantic directions around him like a dagger against the dark, calling back to her.

"Mags!" John said around an orb of red anguish. "Mags, that you?" But he was sure; her voice registered in him as a grand memory.

How is she in here? Robbie didn't even tell her where we were. Unless that was a lie too. But did she follow us? Or did Robbie bring her down here first?

He gauged which direction her words had come from, measuring the sound waves like an untrained bat. Far enough to be indistinct but remaining trackable, if she spoke again.

"J-John... please... hurry... hurts."

"Where are you?" John called out, already finding a sliver of confidence in the direction her voice was coming from.

He moved around in a frenzy, keeping most of his weight on his good leg, the light shooting from wall to floor to wall to ceiling in desperation. In this whirling state, unsure if he was moving forward or sideways or how far, what little bearings John had left scattered like fallen leaves in a strong wind.

He spun in a full circle, or tried to, training the light at a level heading on the smooth, unbroken wall. Only uninterrupted rock in all directions. He dismissed it, certain that was impossible. If he had wandered into a different part of the cave, a smaller chamber, there would still be a path back out.

Another circle, more slow and deliberate, but the same result. No, not the same. The walls were still a flawless cylinder of rock, but they were also closer.

It's shrinking, John thought, letting out a strained laugh. *What the hell is this place?*

Mags's voice came once again, repeating the same desperate idiom. "J-John… please… hurry… hurts."

Now that the voice's direction was clear, John's frenzy became tinged with a sense of being led. He pointed the light where the sound originated and saw a break in the rock. A small one, only a crack. It may have been the same one Robbie had tried to use.

Wasn't there before, he thought. *It could have been, though. I didn't aim the light low enough, or I looked too fast. It's so hard to see anything.*

"Mags?" John said again, warm blood on his tongue.

"Hurry," her voice said. "I can't move."

He dropped to the floor and crawled in.

CHAPTER FORTY-ONE

Once he coaxed his shoulders through, it was easier to pull himself all the way in. His hips presented resistance, but by then he learned that any part of him too wide to fit in straight-on, fit at an angle with effort. He tilted his shoulders, then righted them as if the opening's edge was a limbo stick. On the other side there was room enough to keep them straightened. He was glad for the foresight to enter with his right arm stretched in front; it would be impossible to bring that up from his side had he slithered in headfirst like a snake. Using an arm to crawl was critical, even more so with only one leg to push himself.

All this bending and stretching and distorting his frame to get inside pulled his knife wound further open. Wetness ran down his side. He held the light in his extended right hand, ribbon in the left. He pressed that one to the wound but failed to get much leverage when his elbow butted against the rock above him. Blood soaked into the ribbon and dripped from its end.

He had less than six inches of extra space in any direction. Half the surface area of his body was wedged against the walls.

He shone the light in front of himself for a few seconds, then dropped it and used that hand to pull himself farther in. It would have been easier if he could squirm on his belly but the crevice was too narrow. His feet slipped into the opening like they were entering a vertical pit of quicksand.

John stopped pulling once his feet were in and decided the light was no longer useful. What little he saw weighed on his resolve like an anchor. There was no visible opening ahead. It looked as if he were pulling himself into a funnel. But her voice had come from here, and he pressed on.

He released the light, and the darkness swarmed around him.

With only one hand and one foot to pull-push himself, he inched forward. The farther he pulled himself in, the tighter it became. More and more confining until he could barely move.

Mags is hurt. I have to help her. She needs me. He goaded himself to keep moving against the strain in his muscles. Lactic acid spilled into him like boiling water dumped from a vat.

He stopped to rest, already wondering if he had the energy left to keep going, knowing that his muscles would continue to betray him.

He heard Mags's voice again.

"J-John… please… hurry… hurts."

John snapped back into motion, limited though it was. She was close and in pain. Or dying. He would rather die himself, and yet he was helpless. Stuck. Made to listen as she cried out for him.

He wanted to call back to her, but spared the effort, directing it to his fingers as they flexed to pull his entire weight farther into the crevice. Thought evaporated, leaving only the will to get to her.

A few more inches. Another. Each movement was more exhaustive and strained. Again. Again. He pulled. Pushed. Strained. Pushed more. Pulled again. Bones ground against the rock walls forcing their way tighter around him. Again. Tighter. Struggled. Wrenched his body in unnatural contortions. Another push. And another. Another. And another. And then...

He could go no farther. The tunnel was too tight. His shoulders forced toward each other in a V shape in front of his chest, butted up against rock, and he could not contract himself any further.

His heart was trip-hammering, his breathing too fast to supply oxygen.

He pushed himself backward, meaning to retreat and look for another way, a different tunnel to reach her, a back door, anything.

His good leg became caught behind him, his foot wedged into the rock like an ax head buried in dense wood. He pushed harder, trying to knock it free, but it only forced in deeper behind him. He had no leverage to push or pull it. All of his muscles were exhausted and useless. His entire body trembled against his will. The foot would not move and he could not free it.

His broken knee was pinned beneath his good leg, left hand clutching his blood-soaked side, his right arm stretched straight out in front of him. His shoulders were pulled toward each other but still pressed firmly against the walls beside him. He couldn't shift any of his limbs. Couldn't go forward, or go backward.

A jarring weight filled his stomach, then his heartbeat and breathing shot out of control. His body held fast at all points like he was inside the pressing fist of a giant. And the only person who knew his location had attacked John and fallen to his own death.

Surrounded by untold millions of tons of rock in every direction, alone, crippled, unable to help Mags. Immobile. Useless. Trapped. He cried out, frantic and primal. Muscles cramped in painful harmony with each other and he was powerless to relieve them. Again, he screamed, the sound echoing back at him mockingly.

He fought to maintain some piece of calm as his tortured mind fed him an image of Mags lying broken and bloodied. Next to her was the tree. The tree from outside the cave. Robbie's "Point of No Return." He saw it in his mind as clear as he had seen it outside yesterday, stabbing viciously toward the moonlight.

He grasped Mags's hair ribbon, dripping with his own blood, as consciousness trickled away from him in a rush of tiny pieces, like sand escaping through a hole. As he drifted from the confines of the cave, its walls, pressing in on him from all sides, were replaced by the pressures of memories. Lost memories that were now resurfacing. Robbie had been right. There were buoyant remnants from an ancient sunken ship, freed from their watery resting place by the slow and steady erosive combination of time and solvent.

Mags's voice filled in the gaps as his head dropped to the floor. He recognized her voice, her words, because he had heard them before.

Definition of unknown origin:

Psychic healing: also referred to as energy healing, a phenomenon characterized by the ability of a psychically sensitive individual to channel energy into another person, resulting in some level of healing effect in the recipient of that energy. There are various methods of psychic healing, the most widely known being contact healing, non-contact healing, distant healing, and therapeutic touch.

***

From: *Astral Projection and Tabloid Mentalities, a Pragmatic Interpretation of Paranormal Psychologies* by Dr. Arthur McGuire, PhD (p. 168).

Psychic healing is, without a doubt, the most dangerous avenue of parapsychology. What makes it so is the susceptibility of those who believe their illnesses and injuries can be cured, or even affected, by the transfer of psychic healing energy. This belief delays any true medical intervention. Of course, there is no conclusive evidence of its effects under controlled conditions, but as with all aspects of pseudo-science, this is not enough to satiate the faith-based desires of the uninformed masses. Therefore, propagators of this ridiculous and harmful practice seem only to increase in numbers.

There are thousands of devices worldwide claiming to heal by "energy," either at use or being commercialized. Most of these are illegal and marketed under false pretenses. All of them are dangerous.

So dangerous is the concept of psychic healing that several countries have enacted laws with the express purpose of curbing its use. Most prominent is the Fraudulent Mediums Act of 1951, enacted in England and Wales. This law prohibited a person from claiming spiritual or psychic abilities for profit. Knowing that all prosecutions under this act (before its repeal) resulted in convictions reveals the unfortunate truth that such a law in other countries would also prove effective.

At best, psychic healing results in prolonging minor or uncomfortable conditions and placating the ignorance of an ailing individual, while the healer or medium deceptively profits from their victims. At worst, the delay of medical treatment can cause serious complications or death.

However, one can't help wondering if losing someone prone to such ridiculous notions as energy healing has any negative impact on our species at all.

***

From INDTG.org, website of the International Nurses Diagnosis and Terminology Group:

Therapeutic Touch: A recognized healing method performed by practitioners sensitive to the energy field that surrounds the receiver's body, detecting and manipulating that energy field, often resulting in profound therapeutic effects.

CHAPTER FORTY-TWO

Lucy's vision swooned as if she were underwater with her eyes open. She registered she was still in the supply closet, on the floor.

She heard footsteps approaching. Her breath stopped—*What if she needs something from in here?*—before she reasoned the sound was passing her, going in the opposite direction. Either the on-duty nurse was skipping Robbie's room, or Lucy had been so close to passing out she hadn't noticed the nurse go in there.

To be sure, Lucy made herself wait for silence, then counted to one hundred, just shy of eternity, before she opened the door.

After checking both directions with more forced patience, she slid into the hallway, careful to close the door behind her. It clacked shut with the perceived volume of a grenade explosion.

The earlier sensation, of gliding through the building making no sound, was gone. After the near miss, every move she made seemed to create noise. Her socked feet clumped on the floor like they were filled with lead. It was a few steps to the room she sought, and each rang out like a gong. Her perceptions were dialed to new heights, fed by something freshly awakened in her.

The door to Robbie's room now glowed with a strange, foreign energy. It was a cry for help that only she could receive. She closed her eyes and the frame of the door stayed, shining all the brighter against the back of her eyelids. She turned the handle, another grenade to her ears.

To her eyes, this room was dark. To her mind, it gleamed with a soft but perceptible energy. It was like every surface was made of TV screen glass and all projected toward her. She held in place, a shiver running down her spine as vibrations from a shattered mind in the throes of death moved into her. Once she could, she spoke, not sure he heard but unable to approach his side without first breaking the silence.

"Hey there, Robbie," she said, her voice a calculated whisper. "You've been waiting for me today, haven't you?"

His machines answered for him, with their patient and steady bleeps and hums, IVs pumping nutrition-rich fluids. She went to him, touching the clean white sheet that covered his withered form.

His face looked nothing like she remembered. Once, he had borne a resemblance to her younger brother. Handsome in a way, defiant of his non-exotic German-Catholic genealogy. Hair dark and shining like an oil slick running from his scalp, complexion somewhere between pale and fresh-tanned.

Now, he looked as if he were mummifying even as she watched, retreating into himself as everything internal sputtered in and out of function, pulling together and rotting like a piece of old fruit or the time-lapse footage of an animal decomposing. Limbs curled up in atrophy, face sallow and drained of its shape, cheeks sunken, hair thinning and lifeless.

His time was shorter than she had hoped, but it might still be enough. An aura framed his body, a brighter blue glow against the softer yellow one filling the room.

Lucy looked through his window and saw it was raining. A flash of lightning came, followed by a distant clap of thunder.

A storm coming out there to match the one coming in here, Lucy thought with a twig of detached humor.

She dropped seamlessly into a routine she hadn't performed in years, and reached toward the foot of the bed and took the clipboard with his chart in her hands.

Scribbled on the pages was an assembly of information that did not surprise her. All items she had expected and had seen before. Vitals—blood pressure, temperature, oxygen saturation, pulse, respiration, fluid intake and output—all slightly below normal but holding steady, until recently when they became sporadic and unpredictable. His height and weight had dropped little by little, shown by graphs that moved downward in gentle slopes. The dull regularity of checks by his many caregivers showed through the repetition of tick marks in various square boxes scattered over the pages. Each mark looked precisely the same in a telltale constancy.

But, on the topmost pages, this constancy had broken down. His vitals spiked or dipped as his life force ebbed and flowed.

He started passing through a few weeks ago, she told herself. *It could be a matter of hours now.*

About to return the chart and climb her Everest, Lucy gave the top page another perfunctory glance. She noticed something that, unlike the details of his body's condition, surprised her. On first look, she had skipped the basic information at the top of the sheet. Admission date, insurance details, and other facts that are non-critical for nursing staff. Buried in there, waiting for her notice, was his name. His actual name, not the one she had given him.

This triggered a memory flash as if it were the lone obstacle to her full recall of him. That name unplugged a dam of information in her.

From the day she first treated him, Lucy had formed a stronger, quicker attachment to him than most other patients when she noticed his resemblance to her younger brother. For several weeks, it made him a safe harbor in the terrible storm that was her life immediately after losing Anna.

Lucy's brother's name was Robbie and this patient's middle name was Robert. She had referred to him as "Robbie." Her lost little brother. "Robbie" fit him better than his birth name in Lucy's opinion, and so she had used it around him repeatedly in the short time they'd had together. She had convinced herself that he was responding to it, showing slight variations in brain waves when she used it aloud.

It seemed so natural, and she was with him a few times before being fired, so that name stayed as the rest of her thoughts and feelings melted to the self-loathing depths that trapped her. Her immediate kinship with him flooded back, a sisterly concern, formed all the stronger by the similarities in their experiences.

That common ground of being stuck.

The page on the clipboard in her hands revealed the long-forgotten truth. His full name was Johnathan Robert Camden.

Chapter Forty-Three

L ucy took his hand in both of hers. It was cold, too hard, lifeless, like a skinned piece of chicken pulled from a refrigerator. She shuddered, unable to stop herself, and pressed her focus into a point. She closed her eyes and pictured herself stepping into that blue car once again and closing the door. Turned the key, checking the road ahead and dropping the transmission.

Robbie? she thought at him, much like when she had reached out to Rick. *Or John? Are you in there?*

Through the windshield of the imagined vehicle of her mind's eye, she saw a sharp curve ahead, turned the wheel at an angle to match it and stopped short. Saw the horizon blocked by an enormous wall of what looked like rock, as if she had driven into a tunnel that dead-ended. Or a cave.

John? she called out to him again. *John? Are you in there? Can you hear me?*

There was no response. But for the readings on the machines, and her vast medical experience, Lucy would have thought him dead. He looked dead, he felt dead, he was out of touch even to her strengthening mental probes.

Lucy moved a hand to his head, one to her own. Index fingers on each temple, as if she were trying to complete some bizarre circuit to allow energy to pass between them, uninterrupted. Because something was interrupting her transmission. That was certain. She called out a few more times, sensing each one bounce back at her as if he were secured inside a soundproof chamber while she clamored to him from the outside, unnoticed.

She opened her eyes, severing the line between herself and his defenses in a tactile way, like letting go of a rope that disappeared into a well before pulling the bucket out. She scanned the room, retracing what happened when she had managed to exercise her control over the homeless man's heart attack.

What did I do? she thought. *It was like I was seeing the medical procedure. But he's not having a heart attack so how can I use that?*

A phrase from his chart cropped up: *full paralysis*. He had suffered severe spinal damage and could move nothing below the neck.

If I can help him move, there's a better chance he'll be able to pull out of this coma. And if I can get him back to consciousness, even partway, I could try to learn what happened before he came here, or learn what's happening inside him right now. Help him cope with it.

She thought back to her time in nursing rotations, lifetimes ago and worlds away. She had spent a few weeks learning from the staff at a spinal surgery center a few hours north, in Ohio. During that time, she had observed two spinal operations. A minimal amount of information, but it would have to do. She wondered when the on-duty RN would peek in on him. It may not be long.

As she struggled to emulate what she had done that afternoon, under the highway, Lucy focused on recreating any images she dug up from those spinal operations. They came slowly, and not well-formed. She saw the operating theater, had been sitting in the stands with a clear view of the square section cut open amid a sea of blue surgical dressings. The surgeon crouched intently over the operating table, asking for someone to wipe the sweat from his forehead.

He was left-handed and a stainless steel tray, populated with stainless steel instruments, had been set atop a stainless steel cart to his left.

That was the landscape of the operating scene: white tile, blue cloth, clean light, stainless steel. She drove her focus in on the square opening, where the patient's skin had been separated and exposed, his vertebrae and the tender cords of nerve bundles like the wires inside a car dashboard brought to light. She zoomed in to a more micro-view of them and imagined a cluster that had been severed clean, these pathways to motion rendered impassable.

She slid a hand beneath his back and left the other on her temple, working to send energy straight to the base of his spine, where the damage was. In her mind's eye, the severed nerves bent, twirled, entwined with each other, all moving on their own like a colony of agitated worms. Then they reformed, like string fused back together by heat, melting into each other and forming a solid mass. Connections remade, pathways restoring. Soon it was a near-flawless harness of wires able to send nerve signals to all corners of his being. And she was—

Interrupted, by a strong shout from Rick, not verbal but mental.
Lucy!

It jarred her, and she went straight to the scene of the oncoming truck narrowly avoiding the stopped car. She saw Scarlett's look of disapproval in memory and heard her words: *If that was a death cry, you'd be a goner.*

But it wasn't, he was trying to get her attention, not crying out for her help.

Lucy! Rick sent again. *She's coming. Get out!*

Who? Who's coming?

Clarice, the night nurse. There's some alert coming from that room to the nurse's station, and she's headed there to check it out. Go. Now!

She looked down at Robbie (*John,* she reminded herself) with careful consideration. Nothing had changed, he looked no different.

How long do I have?

Not long. Thirty seconds, but you'll run into her in the hall if you don't go right now.

In defiance, Lucy used two of those seconds to look once more at John. She nearly squealed when she saw that one of his hands was moving. He was pushing the fingers to half-extension, knuckles popping, then rolling the fingers into a fist. It was a slow, shaky motion, driven by deteriorated muscles but it was visible all the same. And then he did it again.

Lucy was transfixed, watching this miracle she had induced, and didn't hear the door open behind her.

"Hey!" Clarice said, her voice lined with alarm. "You. What do you think you're doing in here?"

PART THREE

Death In Life

From *Passing Through, Thoughts on Death and Dying* by Lucille Claremont, RN (p. 191).

"Facing Past Trauma":

Psychological research has determined that all emotions stem from six core feelings: happiness, sadness, anger, fear, disgust, and surprise. Everything a person feels can be traced back to one or more of these, in varying forms of intensity. It is also well understood that all emotions occur for a reason. They are a natural attempt to inform us, guide our thinking, or influence our behavior.

When intense emotions are denied or suppressed, and therefore not allowed to run their course, they do not disappear. They will persist under the surface and reemerge in unplanned, sometimes strange ways. When doing so they can cause damage to our relationships, and in extreme cases, can be harmful to the psyche. This is usually in proportion to the intensity of the emotion and the length of time it has been ignored.

The most extreme cases of emotional harm to the psyche are evidenced when severe trauma, eliciting more than one of the negative core feelings (sadness, anger, fear, disgust), has been suppressed for a period of several years or longer. Post-Traumatic Stress Disorder (PTSD) is one example of the psychological impact of suppressing trauma rather than confronting its effects. Combat veterans and first responders are frequent examples of patients who have spent years suppressing the traumatic events they have witnessed or been involved in.

For those that have experienced traumatic, life-changing events, it is of the utmost importance to face those events head-on and come to terms with their outcomes to die a good death. If they have avoided or suppressed their emotional reaction to trauma, especially for prolonged periods of time, it can transform the dying experience, including their end-of-life dreams and visions (see p. 172–176), into a terrifying and tragic one.

Physicians may recommend the use of medication to ease the psychological pain associated with reemerging trauma. However, the true nature of this reemergence effect is such that it can only be relieved through a direct confrontation. The soul must be healed, perhaps by acknowledging a guilty conscience or forgiveness for events of the past. Therefore, to provide medication to someone who is reliving past trauma near the time of their death is often another means of subversion or denial of the emotions festering beneath the surface.

To face past trauma, with a determination to experience all the emotions it conjures, is the only therapeutic path for someone in this state. It is their only means of reaching a good death.

CHAPTER FORTY-FOUR

On the greatest day of his life so far, John Camden got a new job writing parking tickets and met Margaret Ivers. That day stood out in his mind like a bold black state line on a road map. There were consequently two sides of that line: Before and After. Old and New. Born and Reborn. To use the word "different" to describe the map's landscape on one side of that line versus the other was quite an understatement. "Drastic change of direction" was closer, but it would be more appropriate perhaps, to say that meeting her had cultivated a change in him on a molecular level. After that day, every cell in his body changed. To look at this road map of his life, with that day as the dividing line, there were two separate states of being: old John and new John.

But somehow the events of that day had become twisted, and everything that came after was forgotten. Now, it was all being dragged back in place, like bodies pulled from an inferno. Robbie had spoken truthfully once, at least.

They had gone deep.

Chapter Forty-Five

*I*t *started with the eyes. Remember that now?* Robbie's detached voice, so like his own, came to John as he lay trapped, balanced between sleep and wakefulness and perched near the brink of a lonely death. *But doesn't it always? A person's whole self, their being, it's in their eyes. "Window to the soul" isn't even the half of it, right, buddy? Her eyes were a window to the universe within. One you should have shared.*

As Robbie spoke to John, with his own eyes shut to the world around him, John saw what Robbie described to him. He was reliving moments in his own life like a spiritual spectator. He had suppressed these moments and their surfacing now came with a focused emotional pain, which surged like sunburn on the inside of all his skin.

Started with the first look into her eyes, all right, Robbie continued. *But it ended with that sound. That awful, three-dimensional sound. I can tell you don't remember that yet. But you will. We're going to watch it all. And I'm sorry, but it's the only way through. It's for the best, okay?*

John couldn't respond. While he knew of this monologue on some distant, fractalized level of himself, he was a passenger in its proceeding. He could naught but listen as his nightmares reemerged.

Pervasive numbness spread over his body as if his extremities were being taken by frostbite. He tried to move, prodding and examining all of himself, sending desperate signals to force movement. There was little space, making this task more difficult, and as Robbie continued to speak at him about the past, he found he could only move one hand. In his confinement, he kept moving that hand, as much and as far as possible, forcing his fingers straight, then curling them far enough to leave nail indentations in his palms, straightening again, with a deliberate strain that caused a few knuckles to pop.

Don't turn away, John. We've come too far for that. It was your, our, first day there—such good news, remember? The job. You'd been looking for a job for so long it was a relief. You had already missed a few car payments, about to lose your apartment. Then you met her and that was the day it all turned around. No wonder that's where you got stuck.

Robbie's voice faded, each word lilting farther out of reach, until John was alone with this mental telephoto version of his past. Stretching and splaying the fingers of his right hand as each memory promenaded itself past him, slipping free from where he had buried it.

CHAPTER FORTY-SIX

They had met his first day on the job. His shift almost over, evening falling uneven but swift across the landscape like a bedsheet pulled high in the air and left to parachute down. He was driving back to turn in the truck and was radioed to take a student to the impound lot, to release her vehicle.

Looking out his window as he waited, John saw a memorable scene. The kind that stayed with you based solely on a charming resonance. There was a couple walking on the sidewalk with a small girl, not far from him. The man was a few years older than John. They were each holding one of the girl's hands. She was jumping, and with each jump they pulled up, holding her in the air for a few seconds.

John smiled at this, turned to look through the passenger window, and saw her approaching, the student he was called to pick up. He sat bolt upright in the seat as if caught doing something he shouldn't, then told himself to relax and leaned toward the passenger side for a better look.

He guessed she was a few inches shorter than him but still taller than average. *Perfect height,* he thought. Even with the dark and the distance between them, he saw a high grace in her walk, her steps nimble but sure as she moved into the radius of light that spilled over from the lamps along the street. Her hair was blonde, shoulder-length, and turned slightly outward at the bottom into half-curls that bounced with each step. She was dressed in dark blue jeans, a pastel yellow sweater with two white horizontal stripes, and white tennis shoes. As she neared his truck, her face came into the light enough for him to see. She had a warm, genuine smile.

He stretched over and pulled the handle on the passenger side door to swing it open before she got to it. He didn't push it open hard enough, and it swung out a few inches, caught, and closed again. She had opened the door herself before he got another chance.

"H-hi," he said, frustrated that one of the smallest words got itself stuck in his throat that way. "Are you Margaret Ivers?"

"Yeah," she replied. "Mags is fine, though. And your name is John?"

"That's right."

With one arm on the truck's door frame, she used the other to point back toward the office. "OK, Annette in there said you can take me to get my car back?"

"She's right. She radioed me and said that it was all right to release it, so I can give you a ride over to the impound lot. Hop on in, Ms. Ivers."

She sat and closed the door. "Thanks. But call me Mags before you make me feel old."

"So, are you a student here?"

"Yeah, down to my last two semesters. I think. I'm on one of those five-year plans, I guess. Couldn't decide what to study."

"I have the same problem myself. What did you land on?"

"Liberal arts. Sounded lucrative."

He laughed. "I can relate to that too. I ended up picking psychology and now I have no idea what I'm going to do with it."

"I'm sure you'll figure something out."

"Let's go rescue your car."

"How long have you been doing this?"

Distracted as he pulled into traffic, John did not understand her question and answered with an inarticulate "Hmm?"

"Working here, I mean?" She seemed embarrassed at having to repeat the question and made a furtive hand gesture toward her face, then used it to twirl the end of her hair behind an ear. It struck him as quite a playful movement.

Wait, he thought. *Is she flirting with me?*

"Started today, actually."

"I can't believe my car got towed. I mean, I know it's not your fault, but it sucks. The person I'm mad at is my roommate. I kept letting her borrow it. She's late for everything, so she'll park wherever, but I don't have a pass and suddenly I had, like, seven parking tickets I didn't even know about."

"That's too bad. I hope she pays you back."

"Yeah, really. She's one of my best friends, though, so I'll let it slide. I'll get back at her. Plus, I've got you to help me."

Their eyes met and his stomach churned.

She said, "And it only cost me a hundred and sixty-four dollars to meet you."

A grin came across his face and he willed it away, only to have it settle in further. He signaled a left turn.

A few moments later, they were pulling into the entrance of the impound lot and John fretted about not seeing her again, enough to push himself into taking a shot. She opened her door, thanked him, and stepped out. When she turned to close the door, he spoke.

"Hey. Would you like to... go... out? Sometime?"

She smiled. "Sure. I'd really like that."

"How about tomorrow?"

She hesitated while his heart pounded.

"You'll have to pick me up," she said with a playful laugh. "Believe it or not, I promised my roommate she could borrow my car."

"You did?" he asked, with a laugh of his own.

"No. Not that one. Never again, that one. My other roommate."

"Well, okay. How about I pick you up around seven?"

"That's great."

The attendant at the impound lot made a gruff, insistent noise from her booth a few feet away.

"All right, I'll see you then." John put his arm over the passenger seat and backed the truck out, like a criminal fleeing the scene before anyone realized what was missing.

"John!" she called.

"Sorry. Did you forget something in here?"

She laughed. "No. Shouldn't you get my number or something?"

Chapter Forty-Seven

Having her phone number had been helpful. They had gone to dinner and followed it with a simple, moonlit walk around campus. Though neither elaborate, nor creative, the evening was framed by an unspoken agreement of comfort and enjoyment. One date turned to two, then a third, and John found himself wanting to spend as much time with Mags as possible.

Somewhere within those first few weeks, she asked about his family. It was the first time he spoke of them to her. To anyone. They had been sitting together in John's apartment. Her small hands cradled in his, their breaths coming in unison.

John guarded the topic. He tended not to share much about his past, his origins. Whether from humility or regret, perhaps both, it was not an easy subject for him. But for her, he tried without hesitation.

"Well," he said, "I don't talk to them much anymore. Lately, I mean."

"How come?" she asked.

"I guess we've grown apart over the years."

"Oh. That happens to a lot of people, I suppose."

"It did. It just sort of happened."

"Grew distant?"

"Yeah, I guess that's what we are now. Distant."

She said nothing, but offered a frown. It hadn't taken her long to learn how to coax things out of him. An ability few had gained, and none so well.

"It started when my dad left, I think."

"Oh. Where?"

"Not sure. Just gone one day. I was young, but I don't think it surprised me. That seems like the strangest part when I say it out loud."

She frowned again and gave him a light kiss on the cheek. He continued, voice trembling slightly. "Yeah, one night, he just... vanished. I remember my brother waking me up to tell me that my mom was crying."

"Brother?"

"Yep, just the one. And one sister."

"Hmm. Older or younger?"

"Older, both of them. Karen was the oldest, then Scott. He was four years ahead of me."

"Was?"

"Scott died. About six years ago. He was working in a coal mine and there was a cave-in."

She gasped, then moved a hand to stroke his upper arm. "Oh, that's terrible, John. What a terrible way to die."

Until then, he had lent little thought to his brother's death, aside from how it affected himself.

"It *was* terrible," John said. "There were two others trapped in there with him, but the debris separated them. My brother spent two days trapped in a closet-sized chamber by himself, and by the time the rescue crew made it to him through all that rock, it was too late."

"How awful. I wouldn't wish that on anyone."

Jesus, he thought, *is there a worse way?* He was fixated. Slight claustrophobia arrived, tightening his lungs, ice in his veins, sensing a fractional version of what his brother had experienced.

Mags spoke again, pulling him mercifully from the path of this dangerous thought spiral. "What about your sister? What's her name?"

"Karen."

"Where is she?"

"Not sure. I haven't talked to her since Mom died."

Mags moved her hand to his cheek, wrapping her thumb under his chin and guiding his face toward hers. He gave a clumsy half-smile.

"Keep going. Tell me about your mom and sister?"

"Well, Mom did her best after Dad left. Karen helped. Things worked out as well as possible."

Mags nodded as he spoke.

"For about eight years, but we all knew Mom couldn't keep it up forever. She was pushing herself too hard, even with my sister's help. She worked constantly. Had to. Kept it up until she died of a heart attack when I was eighteen. That was the catalyst, I suppose. Things... crumbled after that."

When he stopped talking, Mags waited a few moments, then squeezed both of his hands with both of hers. Her eyes grew bigger in anticipation, pressing him with silence. So he continued the story, further than ever before.

"Mom was the glue. After she died, everyone went their own way. It's good to talk about this."

And it was. Relieving, liberating even, to work past how he had never mourned for the near-complete loss of his family. To release it, he had only needed to find someone to share it with.

He talked for nearly thirty minutes without stopping, and Mags interjected twice more when she sensed his pace waning. She listened, absorbing every word with silent support.

She made it so easy for him to let go. Tears came toward the end—few, but more than any recent memory. And when he finished, she placed her lips first on one cheek, then the other, taking the final tears with them.

He kissed her back, firm. One hand found the side of her face, the other on her shoulder, as if fearing she would run. Instead, she curled her fingers into the hair at the back of his head and pulled him closer, driving the kiss deeper. His blood rushed up and down through his body, like it was traveling in an errant elevator. Her hands grasped at his shirt tail and pulled it off, and he was regretful having to pull away from her long enough to shed it.

His hands went for her shirt, much more clumsy a motion than hers. Soon they were together on the floor, clothes strewn in all directions like a protective circle from the world. They made love with a soft impulsiveness. Her eyes fixed on his, and there was nothing else in existence. There was no time and no end to it.

Until there was, and they stayed intertwined atop the carpet. Still but breathing, quiet but sharing all. In that moment he never wanted to be without her. The need to live as part of her, and she part of him, had gelled into a solidity that could not be dissolved. Not by all the time and pressure and solvency and terror of the world.

CHAPTER FORTY-EIGHT

The brief time they spent together wisped by with the transiency fate reserves for the purest things.

Being with Mags made John a better version of himself. He saw their future clearly, sprawled out before them like staring through a panoramic window on the observation deck of his own personal skyscraper. That future stretched on, out of sight in every direction. It was glowing with a million points of light, and he wanted to present each one to her over a lifetime together.

Before two months had passed, he planned their first trip together. He would leave work on a Wednesday evening and pick her up. His bag would be packed and already placed in the trunk with his grandmother's wedding ring in a white hinged box, hidden underneath the clothes.

He would take her to Chicago because she loved crowds and busy days. Neither of them had been there before, but it was only a six-hour drive and it suited them, her especially. He had little money for lodging, but found an acceptable hotel online near the 'L' train line, and all that was left was arrival. Inspired by his vision of their future, he would take her to the observation deck of Willis Tower, drop to one knee, and ask her to marry him. He would find the words to articulate how he felt about her, the depth of it. How she had shaped him into something more. He would explain his view on their future together and his "million points of light." That sounded catchy.

She would respond with an emphatic "Yes!" and they would return home the next day to a new life together and set about the very rewarding work of telling every person they knew. Then the wedding planning, a house, fulfilling careers, children, them united into old age and beyond. Together and wanting nothing more than time.

This dreamlike future he planned was ready to topple into place like a line of dominoes, starting with a weekend getaway.

But in reality, that first domino fell wrong.

Definition of unknown origin:

Psychography: also referred to as automatic writing, a psychic phenomenon wherein a sensitive individual or medium can dictate language or expression from a removed source with no conscious effort of their own. This is accomplished through a type of channeling, wherein the medium receives energy that allows the source to control the medium for a short time.

***

From: *Astral Projection and Tabloid Mentalities, a Pragmatic Interpretation of Paranormal Psychologies* by Dr. Arthur McGuire, PhD (p. 195).

Automatic writing, or psychography, is often viewed as equal parts parapsychology and spiritualism. This practice involves movement that is not self-directed and results in receiving words or symbols that compile to form messages "from beyond." I must note it is closely related to using a Ouija board (currently available from the children's toy maker Hasbro) and trust that is information enough to expose this phenomenon as no more supernatural than a child's board game.

When supposedly transcribing language from another source, without consciously lifting a finger on their own, mediums may claim their muse was a higher power, a spirit, or an extraterrestrial. Unless they are more devoid of imagination or intelligence, in which case the writing may be attributed to another, living human. This alone proves the act to be a farce because it is not possible to conduct a controlled experiment when one person claims to be writing words received from another. To invalidate the data, they need only be jointly aware of the words to be used, before the experiment begins.

It has also been used by zealots as a tool to feign credibility for their absurd claims of divine intervention. In fact, several widely recognized religions or faith-based organizations have their origins in psychography. As a result, their founders have achieved a rare form of notoriety, reserved only for our most unstable, sociopathic personalities such as cult leaders or reality TV stars.

To those of us more enlightened, all claims of psychography can be explained by one of three clear possibilities. First, that the claimant has an overactive subconscious, resulting from prolonged suppression of the id, leading to the manic manifestation of base desires. Second, that the claimant suffers from an advanced form of schizophrenia. And third, simple fraud.

Should you, being a true scholar of psychology, ever find yourself confronted with supposed evidence of automatic writing, know that you need only respond by asking the individual which of the following labels they would prefer: animal, crackpot, or liar.

***

From: "The Strange and Mysterious History of the Ouija Board," Smithsonianmag.com

The makers of the first talking board asked the board what they should call it; the name "Ouija" came through, and when they asked what that meant, the board replied, "Good luck." An advertisement in a New York newspaper declared it "interesting and mysterious" and testified "as proven at Patent Office before it was allowed. Price, $1.50."

Though truth in advertising is hard to come by, especially in products from the 19th century, the Ouija board *was* "interesting and mysterious"; it actually *had* been "proven" to work at the Patent Office before its patent was allowed to proceed; and today, even psychologists believe that it may offer a link between the known and the unknown.

CHAPTER FORTY-NINE

"Security!" Clarice called, before Lucy could react. She was focused on John lying in his bed, despite Rick's warning. Not prepared and now in a jam.

In the seconds it took Clarice to see if someone was on their way down the hall, Lucy reasoned through her options. If anyone was on duty besides Rick (there was one guard per overnight in her recollection, which was about as reliable as the unlocked supply cabinet had proven to be), they would hold her for the police. Unless she ran.

As Clarice added an urgent "Down here!" to her earlier shout for security, Lucy decided she had better not stick around to see if it was Rick who would respond. Not wanting to jostle the bed (between her and the window) gave her only one option.

She charged.

This surprised Clarice, which helped because Clarice had fifty pounds on Lucy. Lucy knocked the nurse backward, and she rolled to the side, leaving enough room for Lucy to slip past. In the hall, she glanced left, toward her hiding place, and saw a tall, slim man (not

Rick) in a security uniform looking back. When their eyes met, he jogged and called out, "Stop! Stop!"

She took around the corner, in the opposite direction, glad he was coming from that side of the building. It meant the back entrance was still unguarded. She ran, almost colliding with a wheelchair in the hall, folded and left to the side. A near miss, she skirted around it like an athlete running agility drills.

And learned she'd been wrong. The hall back toward the emergency exit wasn't open. But this time it was Rick. When she saw him, she didn't slow. He looked angry.

"What the hell was that?" he asked. He sounded angry too.

"Huh?" she asked, between heaving breaths. "That's what I came for. What do you mean?"

"I told you she was coming. You should have split by now."

"I got sidetracked, sorry."

"Well, what the hell now? They'll be here any second. What am I supposed to do? This wasn't what I agreed to."

"Rick, I have to go. Please."

"I let you go and they fire me. That wasn't what we talked about. I said I'd make sure the hall was clear. And I did that. I'm sorry, Lucy, but I can't afford to lose my job. I can't just let you go."

"You're... you're not serious? I have to go, they're on the way. They'll arrest me, I have to go."

She looked back, saw both the nurse and the other guard pulling around the corner, closing fast.

Rick put his hand on her shoulder. "I'm sorry, you know? I want to help, but I can't make your problems my problems. What will I do if I get fired?"

"Damn you. After what I've lost, you give me that nonsense."

Rick said nothing, but held her by the shoulder.

She imagined she heard sirens approaching. She had come so close, had even proven to herself that Robbie (*John, his name's John*) was still in there, waiting for someone to help. *Even now, heaven knows what he's going through. He needs me. May have only hours left. So, it's bigger than just me now.*

"Down here," Rick said, as the other two closed in. His free hand went to wrap Lucy's wrist, as if he were preparing to subdue her. "Did you call the cops?"

"Yeah, they're on their way," the other guard answered, his face firm and staunch as he neared. He was older than Rick, had full, gray hair. But his height (perhaps a foot over Lucy) made him intimidating. "Be here in a few minutes, I expect."

They were a few steps away, she'd soon be cornered. But she'd come too far. Risked too much to let go now. Lucy gave Rick a mischievous look, her eyes narrowing as a stealthy smile passed by.

"Thanks for opening the door," she said, then drove her knee into his crotch.

His breath came out with a sound that was part whoosh and part howling tenor. His hands released and she was running again, the door in sight.

CHAPTER FIFTY

Lucy made it a few hundred feet into the woods past the building, branches whipping at her bare arms and roots colliding with her socked feet, rain falling cold on her face and arms, until she collapsed from the strain of pushing herself further and faster than her alcoholism-depleted body would allow. There were sirens; they cut off once they sounded close, wary of disturbing everyone's rest. Thunder rumbled in the distance. The storm she had seen through the window was waiting nearby, not ready to begin its attack. The rain was slow and steady, patient.

She kept walking, her steps careful without shoes, having trouble seeing well enough to avoid all the obstacles the woods were throwing at her, but knowing she needed to be farther away. She wasn't clear yet. A leafy branch brushed at her face, and she pushed it aside. The ground was getting muddy; she heard it splash beneath her footfalls.

It's not like they'll be sending the bloodhounds after me, she thought, conjuring an image of a cinematic chain gang escape scene. *But they'll look for a while in the exact direction I headed when I ran out of the building*. She scolded herself for not making a more clever getaway, though considering it was her first time trespassing, at least she had a head start.

No one was near her yet, so she searched for a place to stop. To hide and catch her breath. She found a pair of trees close enough to secure her body between their trunks while obscuring most of herself. It gave a view of the path behind her, a suitable place to see what kind of tail she had.

A few seconds after settling in between the trees, Lucy heard leaves rustling nearby. The rain wasn't hitting her, beneath the canopy as she was, but the water was seeping into her clothes.

The low light moon hiding between two clouds much like her, would only reveal the outline of a person, moving in her direction. Lone. Lucy held her breath, pinching her lips together and squeezing the rough bark of her hiding place. She strained her eyes to get a better view of her pursuer. Her heart thrummed unevenly in her ears.

They looked away, shining a flashlight in circles. It wasn't Rick. Their dark form could be a navy police uniform, but that wasn't certain. The light swept toward her; she crouched a little further to hide her face, legs burning and shaking. She thought of sitting, but that would make it harder to get away before they... what? They would not shoot her, surely.

Yeah, but they may have one of those Taser things. She decided to stay put, let her legs protest the position a little longer. She gritted her teeth and clenched her jaw.

They moved toward her, and in a flit of escaping moonlight she saw it was a female police officer. She looked young, and a little nervous. Lucy hoped that would lead her to abandon the search more readily.

The officer stepped toward her, two feet from Lucy's tree while she crouched squirrel-like on the other side. The light passed by her in an arc, revealing nothing but shed brown leaves and dirt becoming mud as the rain continued.

Had she been sitting down, the light would have found her feet and forced her to run on shaky, uncooperative legs. Lucy took a slow, deep, quiet breath and zipped all her muscles together to brace herself.

The light stayed beyond her safe boundary and Lucy counted to herself (*1... 2... 3... 4...*), trying to maintain her state of inanimation.

"Grismer!" a male voice said, farther away in the woods.

"Over here!" the officer near Lucy called back.

"This way, I think I found a trail."

"Right there." And she was moving away.

Forcing herself to hold still and keep counting, to make sure it was clear, Lucy waited. When she finished counting, having heard no further noise, she rose and walked, perpendicular to her original path, trying to reach the tree line and head back to the road.

Then what? she asked herself, stepping over a large root that protruded from the dirt like a compound fracture. *I don't know yet, I guess. Not the how, at least. I know* what, *but I have to figure out* how.

She had to get back in there, to finish pulling him out of his coma.

How the hell am I supposed to get anywhere without Rick's help? It was hard enough last time. To get in there for half an hour and get started. I didn't even reach him, just started... building the road. I don't have anyone on the inside to help, I'm on my own. Plus they'll be looking for me for a while, and I can't afford to wait for them all to leave. He may not have that long. If he's gone before I can get back in, the whole thing was for nothing. I might as well have...

She didn't finish the sentence in her monologue, but she thought about the bottle of pills, waiting for her in Anna's room. *It would be so easy. Go to sleep and wake up in a better place. Anna might even be there. Maybe that's all that separated them, a bit of courage to do what was necessary. Not all this planning and running and hardship. And for what? To be betrayed by someone she had trusted and thrown back to the wolves?*

A rumble of thunder reminded her of the coming storm and interrupted her thoughts. More cold rain water invaded her clothes, seeping in from the bark of her hiding trees.

But, she corrected herself, *if I took that way out and Anna was waiting, could I face her? What would I be to her then? A failure, a crazy, stupid coward. No,* she corrected herself. *Look at what you just did. That was something. He was moving, you healed him. Anna would have been proud of that.* It was a certainty that splashed over her like warm light. She was on the right path still, had been since walking out of the sheriff's office that morning.

She waited longer, with no watch, knowing time was short. Which made the waiting not only tedious, but anxious. She had heard rustling at one point, then voices, but nothing since. Wrestling between the risks of moving out too soon or staying still too long, she stood and surveyed.

Saw nothing. Heard nothing. Counted to ten, an eternity. Then moved back toward the road. She approached the building, pausing in a far corner of the parking lot to get a sense of any remaining activity.

The police cars were still there, dome lights circling like futuristic scanners. But it was quiet. She saw someone in a dark uniform walk out of the front door. A policewoman. A second officer followed, this one male. Lucy ducked behind a nearby bush, grateful again for the cover of night, shielded from the moon by the gathering storm clouds. She heard car doors closing, then saw the cruisers pull out of the parking lot and drive off, in the direction she had come from. They were still looking for her, but headed the wrong way. She had doubled back on them.

Which gave her a chance. The biggest problem left, though, was that the building would be on alert. Until they heard she was caught, the guards (Rick included) would be a little less sleepy.

No, that wasn't the biggest problem. There was one far worse.

Without Rick's help she was blind, and even then she had barely enough time to form a tiny connection with John/Robbie. To determine what was happening to him and make a real difference, she would need more time. Or would need some scouting report on what was taking place inside his broken consciousness. Worse, she would likely need both.

Lucy waited more, crouched behind a bush in the parking lot, organizing her thoughts and watching raindrops fall into puddles. First, the problems.

One, it will be harder to sneak around without being seen. Two, I can't count on Rick. Third, I can't get back in. Fourth, even if I could, there's no way I'll have enough time to help him. Fifth, he'll probably be dead in a few hours, so I have to hurry.

Okay, that's everything I'm up against. Now what do I have to work with? I could "talk" to Rick again. But that would only make things worse. She didn't believe that he would come after her and try to catch her, but he would stand in her way now. *He probably expects I'm coming back, but he might not think I'll do it tonight. Strike one. I could try that side door again. But they must have locked it by now, and no one to open it this time. Plus, there's no way for me to know when it's clear inside. I might run right into someone again. Strike two. I could try to go in through his window, now that I know where his room is. But that still wouldn't give me enough time. Not to mention I'd have to either break the glass or the window frame, which is sure to be loud enough that none of the rest would matter. Strike three.*

A thought came to her, built of this tragic list of obstacles, finding a common thread in them that could be removed. And once that thread pulled out, everything in her way might unravel. A slim chance, but there it was.

The problem is the building. If he wasn't in there, I'd have a chance.

Since breaking in to help him had failed, her next best option was to break him out.

CHAPTER FIFTY-ONE

Lucy slung any near-rational thought at her ridiculous idea, trying to give it enough substance to act on. She was building a house of cards from a list of questionable justifications.

But she wasn't giving up. If she did that, or if she failed, she cared not to imagine how torturous John's last few hours of life would be. At the same time, she worried about her own newfound, precarious strength. Lucy knew that crumbling beneath this challenge now, just short of reaching her goal, would send her crashing back to the bottom like a chunk of flaming wreckage. And the odds against her climbing out again were microscopic. Nonexistent. If she fell now, she would not rise, would not find the will to return. Could never recapture Anna's admiration.

Lucy acknowledged these notions, then pressed on.

If I get him outside, in the woods, I may have time enough to do something. Before anyone finds us. What about his machines? I can't take him off those. Well, I'm bringing him into the woods to die, so that's not a problem. Except that he needs oxygen. That is a problem.

I can't have him suffocating before I can help. I could breathe for him manually, but not without paying attention to it. And I need my focus on the other... thing. Or I could get hurt, like Scarlett warned. What if I can get him breathing on his own? I got him to move his hand. I could even bring a portable CPAP for backup, there should be one in his room for emergencies. Like this.

Well, not exactly like this. Has there ever been an emergency like this?

What about the storm? That could be a problem. But will it? Whatever is about to happen will be in a different space than the one where it's raining right now. I'm not even sure what that means, but I can feel it. He's imploding; it's all internal.

All this reasoning left one glaring billboard-sized question. *How the hell do I get him out here?*

Okay, I can tackle that one too. No idea is too far-fetched, especially today. There must be something useful in it. What's the most likely thing to stop me? The other people, sure. So I need a way around them. Or through them. No, no violence. I won't sink to that. What, then?

What if I can get them out? No, that would raise more alarms, bring more attention. But it's too risky to wheel him, bed and all.

There's something right there. I don't need the bed. He can't weigh much more than a hundred pounds, all atrophied and dried up like he is. But I still can't pick him up and carry him to the door.

The bed isn't the only thing with wheels, though.

Was there a wheelchair in his room? No, not in his room. It was right outside it. Okay, that's a start. Sneak the wheelchair into his room, disconnect everything and get him in that. Then slip out before anyone knows what happened.

Two problems left. When I disconnect all those machines, they'll raise hell. That other nurse will come running. Lucy barely noted that she was thinking of herself as a nurse again.

I'll never get in the room to load the wheelchair, anyway. Let's start there, that's bigger. What can help me? I think it's just the three of them, Rick, Clarice, and the other guard. And I'm not going swinging in there like Batman to eliminate them one by one. No, better to go the smash-and-grab route and hope I can get it done before we're caught. So, how do I get them away long enough, without them calling the police again? And putting no one in harm's way?

What if I can... trick them into thinking they called the police? It might work. If I can first pull that bit off, I guess.

That only leaves the machines. I can't just yank them loose, that'll set them off. The IV, catheter and feeding tube won't matter, no alarms on them. The ventilator, heart rate monitor, and EEG won't be so cooperative. I'll have to deactivate those. That will take a few minutes. Which means I'll have to distract them long enough to get through the front door, to his room, turn off the machines, get him in the chair and out the back. Maybe five minutes, assuming all those steps go smoothly.

If I can buy time before anyone comes after us, I can give it my best shot. Try to pull him back and make sure he's not alone at the end. That he understands what is happening to him and why. Help him make peace with death and whatever he might be experiencing.

It doesn't matter what happens after that. All or nothing. Just need to get through to him. And I can try that before I go back inside, scout around in his head and get the lay of the land. That would help.

Her legs were burning from all the time spent crouching, but her brain was as clear and focused as a pilot's.

CHAPTER FIFTY-TWO

There was no more activity in the parking lot, the search had moved away. She wondered what Rick had told them. If he shared any details, they would not believe him. Most likely he had feigned ignorance, and she looked like a disgruntled former employee, or a junkie after pills. Both shared a border with the truth.

She stood, the rainwater invading her clothes more with the movement. It was deep into the night now; a chill breeze passed through the open air outside the building and made her more alert, cooling the moisture in her jeans and T-shirt and socks.

Lucy strode along the building's side, following the exterior wall like a cat burglar, as it wound toward the back of campus. She counted the windows until she reached the bricks outside John/Robbie's room, then pressed her ear to the wall as if she were listening to a secret conversation. She added her palms, reaching out with her mind's eye to try to... what? Gauge the energy in there. To get a sense of his placement, if anything had shifted since her scuffle with the nurse.

She tried to recall the image she had last seen while worming her way into his head. Rock. An endless wall, in all directions. Unmarred, impenetrable. She focused on that. She pictured herself touching it, transposing the brick beneath her palms, as if the countless tiny holes in their surface were filling in and becoming smooth.

Robbie? she sent to him, then corrected herself. *John? Can you… hear me in there?* This hadn't worked before, but she was at a loss for how else to contact him.

Nothing. She pressed herself further against the walls, both physical and mental. She pushed her probe further out, imagining a straight-ened wire coat hanger searching the surface for entry. A soft spot. Anything. Then she sensed his voice. Someone's voice, at least. But it had to be him, who else? She had already sensed he was calling out, searching for help from someone. She couldn't make out what he was saying. It was faint, like an actual voice heard through an actual wall. Faint, but it was there. She trained her ear to it, tracing it back, to find the source, follow the line he was feeding out.

Suddenly, her hands pulled away from the wall, as if on their own. She reached into her pockets and produced the pen and paper Scarlett had given her. Her eyes were still closed. She was not in herself, not in control. As if she were channeling, the voice she strained to hear was coming in through her hands. They wrote. Scribbled, more accurately. The pen in her right hand, though she was left-handed, danced around the page in a measured fury, the page held captive against the brick by her normally dominant left hand.

A word here, a few there, in flittery, spastic movements. The pen tip punctured the page, leaving small tears when the hands (no longer her hands) became too fast. Soon it was over, and she was left breathless and unsure of what she had done to catalyze this transfer, this reception of his voice through her hands.

Taking deep breaths to calm herself, she opened her eyes and looked at the page. It was mostly errant lines, nonsense. But there were several lone, intelligible words amongst the scribbles, and those were elucidating. "Help" appeared twice, as did "MAGS," the only one in capital letters. The others were "cave," "can't," and "trapped." Most telling, though, was a fragmented sentence dead center of the page, machine-precise. It drew her eye and held it.

"Robbie tricked me, now gone."

He didn't seem able to hear her, and she hadn't been able to understand him when she "listened" through the wall. There was something blocking them from connecting, a formidable barrier, probably of his own making, intentional or not. But as Lucy scavenged the words he had somehow written through her hands, she unearthed something of shape. An important fossil, a critical clue.

He was doing the same thing she had done herself, until this morning when her self-constructed wall of apathy crumbled.

It's not to keep me out. He's keeping himself in.

From *Passing Through, Thoughts on Death and Dying* by Lucille Claremont, RN (p. 217).

"Final Hours":

It has long been a consensus that the start of a person's final days or hours in this world before dying is marked by a noticeable increase in energy. This is evident across different cultures, bridging gaps between varied theologies. Like many aspects of the dying process, it requires a strong faith because it cannot be quantified or measured.

As previously noted, confusion and lack of orientation to person, place, and time are usually present throughout the days leading to death, as the dying person works to separate their spiritual self from their physical self while internalizing most of the process. However, within the last hours, it is common for this to change. The confusion and disorientation lift, sometimes suddenly, and there is often a strong sense of a return to normalcy. Many of the physiological changes described previously may revert within moments. Demeanor, expression, eating habits may return. Vital signs such as blood pressure, respiration, even skin color may be restored to their established base levels. Social desires and communication style will also return, and the dying person's loved ones will find comfort in this. This stage of the dying process represents a brief respite from the coming finality. It is an opportunity to share one more story, one more wish or thought. Most times, this may be a last chance to share a lucid moment with a loved one about to leave this world.

This final, momentary relapse in the progress is commonly attributed to the arrival of spiritual energy. It is this energy needed to allow the dying person to complete their conversion from a physical being to a purely spiritual one, as they pass through into the next world.

With tortured souls, however, the final hours are believed to be trying and frightening experiences, which means this arrival of energy will be directed negatively, apt to cause severe psychological torment and damage, at a time critical to their attempts for resolution and finding peace.

CHAPTER FIFTY-THREE

You're doing good, John, Robbie said, his voice pulling John from the train of memories and back into the oppressive darkness of the cave.

John tried to move again and found it still impossible. His limbs were edging to something past numbness, closer to detachment, blood pooling in his core, as if even his brain had given up and redirected its focus to the parts that mattered more. He thought how even a trapped coyote is free to chew its own foot off, and yet he was confined so tight in his prison of rock he'd be unable to bury his face in his shoulder to cover a sneeze. And still Robbie goaded him, prodding him toward some self-serving spectacle of pain and loss.

What happened next, John? Robbie asked from nowhere but as loud as if he were speaking lip to ear. *We can't stop there.*

John closed his eyes, finding that the darkness was stronger with them open. He pressed the lids closed tight, trying to push Robbie's voice away. He wasn't there, couldn't be. Even if that fall hadn't killed him, he couldn't make it back up. His voice was a figment. Yet it was in control.

Keep looking, John, keep looking. The important part is on deck.

John did, against his own will. He saw a sunset, flowing pink and purple and blue lines of cloud the color of early spring flowers in the distance. He was driving on a six-lane highway, Mags next to him, their hands clasped together between the seats. The radio was off but she was humming a tune he didn't recognize.

The image blinked away, replaced by... nothing. He opened his eyes again, or thought he did. In the absolute darkness of this crawlspace, he couldn't be certain.

I can't, he told Robbie, not sure if Robbie heard. But there was nothing else to do. He had no other ability, at all, but to respond to the phantom voice of his surely dead friend that may or may not have tried to kill him. *I don't know what you want from me, please. Please stop.*

Can't stop, buddy. You know that, now keep trying.

No, no more. I... please. Leave me alone. Let me out.

I'm trying to let you out. That's the whole point.

I don't know what that means. Please. Please stop this.

Only you can stop it, John. You have to see it. Remember what happened next.

I don't—

Stop doing that. No more denial. No more running. It ends here. It ends now. You want to see her again, right? This is the only way, John.

That part, at least, was true. He wanted to see Mags again.

John's eyes closed on their own, or maybe they hadn't been open. When he tried to open them, he failed, or maybe he had them open and couldn't tell. All his senses were betraying him. Nothing seemed real. He was in a dream on the verge of waking, the nightmare moment when you begin to fall and jerk awake, safe in your own bedroom, but turned perpetual. His mind reeled for answers, pinned like a butterfly in a shadowbox.

Robbie's voice returned. *It was our fault. That's what you need to remember. Our fault she died.*

Died?

There was no response. John gave in and let his resolve to be free slip slightly. And Robbie's horror show started again. As he watched, John found that he indeed remembered it all.

Chapter Fifty-Four

It was around ten miles from Mags's apartment to the interstate and they made it that far without incident. But a little over thirty minutes later, driving on the interstate, they approached a disabled car on the right shoulder. The sun was setting, evening shedding its skin into night and there was little traffic headed in either direction, so they both saw the blinking hazard lights of the beige two-door as it came into view half a mile ahead of them.

"Look. Do you think they need help?" Mags asked.

"I don't know if it's a good idea to stop," John replied. By nature, he was hesitant to help someone roadside, the product of a mother who fought hardscrabble raising children alone, watching too much Dateline, and too gulled by the perceived sensational danger of the world around them. *There are always those stories you hear,* she would say.

Mags persisted. "There's not many cars around, they'll be stuck a while if we don't stop. It looks like a flat tire. If nothing else, I can let them use my cell phone to call someone for a ride."

He didn't want to stop, but it was hard to disagree with her desire to help. It was the part of her personality that appealed to him most. That open, curious, socially willing state he himself was incapable of. He found it admirable, as though it gave him an example to live up to. Without her eagerness to help other people, she would not have let her careless roommate borrow her car and park it illegally until it was impounded. In a way, this side of her had brought them together.

John shook his head in a feigned sign of protest, if an obvious one, clicked on the turn signal, and guided the car carefully onto the shoulder, the tires crunching over pebbles and debris. He shifted into reverse, to back up the distance they had driven past the other car, and stopped twenty feet ahead of it. He opened the driver's side door, stepped out, and leaned his head back in.

"You stay in here, OK?" he said. "I'll check on them and be right back."

"Don't be so worried," she replied. "I'm sure everything is fine, but I'll feel better knowing we tried to help. If I was stranded, I hope someone would do the same for me." She added a flash of a smile. That was when John noticed the red ribbon tied in her hair, holding it up in a casual but playful sprawl. The image stuck like a dart in his chest.

"Point taken." He smiled back and closed the door.

Approaching the disabled car, he noticed a lone woman, no one else around. His apprehension lessened as he walked closer, and the woman got out and waved to him.

"Hello?" she called out.

"Everything all right?" he asked.

A large van passed by, speeding. John did not look. His eyes were fixated on the scene before him. The van was in the farthest lane, unimposing, but drowning the woman's response to his question.

"Is everything all right?" he asked again.

She nodded this time. As he approached, the dim post-sun haze made it difficult to mark any of her facial features. But she seemed non-threatening enough. A slight woman with long, dirty-blonde hair and a slouched posture.

"Not hurt or anything," she said. "Just need some help, ya know. Can you help me? I'd really appreciate it, I'm not sure what to do here."

She spoke quickly, nervously, pointing with her left hand. John followed it and saw a flat tire. He chuckled, the irony not lost. He'd been waiting weeks to get Mags and skip town, only to be interrupted so soon by something he would have done at work.

"How'd that happen?" John asked. He stepped into the grass and kneeled to check the tire.

"Well, man, I think I, uh, hit a pothole a little ways back. It didn't go flat at first, though, ya know. Just a loud noise and then seemed like everything was fine, so I kept driving, ya know." She paused and glanced past her car, away from the highway, toward the dense woodline.

She continued talking with no pauses, one sentence strung after another.

"On my way to pick up my kid, ya know. She lives up in Indianapolis, but I'm already late and I'm really trying to hurry, ya know."

"Mm-hm."

"Yeah, I haven't seen her in like, six months almost, ya know. So I'm pretty excited. Then this, and I don't know how to change it, ya know."

"I can change it for you. Do you have a spare? And a tire iron and jack?"

"Yeah, they're back there. I appreciate this, man. You're really saving my ass out here, ya know."

She opened the driver's door and pulled the lever for the trunk. As she smiled and the light from the car interior splashed out, John noticed several teeth missing behind severely chapped lips. Her face was pale, eyes sunken, and cheeks sagging. She wore a thick canvas jacket despite the lingering summer heat.

Her appearance gave John pause, and he considered leaving right then. She was likely a drug addict, and experience told him that could make her desperate and unpredictable. But he decided to stay and help, to stop making negative assumptions based on appearance. Trying to live up to Mags's example.

He pushed the trunk open further, the rusted metal workings whining in protest.

"Yeah, I get it," he said. "We're on our way out of town too."

She looked toward John's car and waved. Mags waved back with a warm smile. "That your girl in there? She's real pretty. Hope she doesn't mind you being out here with me, ya know."

Another, longer glance shot toward the bushes. A nearly imperceptible nod. John thought this strange but dismissed it like his previous biased thoughts.

John leaned into the trunk of her car, searching for tools, pulling aside clumps of dirty cloth and plastic bags. It was getting darker and he couldn't see well inside the trunk. He stubbed a finger against something metal, the tire iron. He heard a sound like shuffling footsteps around the passenger side of the car and looked up. The woman was closing the door; it clapped shut as he watched.

John returned to digging in the trunk.

"Found 'em," John said, popping up with the tire iron in his left hand and the jack in his right. He walked around to the flat and a car whizzed past in the closest lane, jarring him. He paused, startled, and looked back at Mags, sitting in the passenger seat of his car. She had opened her door, the dome light coating her hair and shoulders, highlighting them against the night. She turned back, smiled, and in that moment, he missed her intensely. It was an effort not to drop these strange objects and run to her.

He took a deep breath. Mags winked at him, red hair ribbon dancing in the light flow of air produced by the car's dashboard vents. He broke his gaze with effort, turned toward the car, and kneeled to loosen the wheel's lug nuts. He set the tire iron down to his left side, toward the driver's door, and positioned the jack. It was a struggle; the jack was also rusted and stubborn and the surrounding light was fading by the second. No other cars in sight. Once it was in place, he reached for the tire iron again, where he had set it down seconds ago.

It wasn't there.

He heard more shuffling footsteps before the tire iron struck the back of his head. His vision flashed out with the speed of a popped light bulb, replaced with pure white light and furious orange pain. He thrust forward, and his face thudded against the fender of the car, above the flat tire. He fell sideways and heard Mags scream. The white soon broke and jumbled sensory input tumbled through what remained of his field of vision, like he was looking through two pinholes at blurry pictures. Then he was struck in the chin, hard enough to send his teeth crashing together. One fell out, a bicuspid, and another, an incisor, broke clean through, halfway from the gumline. An orchestra of pain sang from John's mouth. His cheek hit the pavement and the shock of impact seemed to restart his eyes—his vision returned in groups of pixels that didn't quite form a picture, like an unfinished jigsaw puzzle.

He saw the car. His car. The headlights were still on, but Mags wasn't in the passenger seat anymore. Where was she? The door was open; he heard the engine running but saw no one around. It was painful to turn his head. His limbs were slow to respond. He pushed his chest up, away from the pavement. It was cold to the touch when it should've been warm.

He heard voices, close but on the other side of the car. There were... at least three. The flat tire woman. A man, there was a man's voice. He heard Mags's voice next.

"Help... John... help me."

Little more than a whisper, but laden with emotion. A weighty mix of fear and pleading. It was faint, but stood out to John. They were attacking her too.

He pieced things together, thoughts returning to a state of semi-cohesion. He forced himself to his feet, struggling for balance and catching himself with a hand on the woman's car.

A man was searching through John's backseat. The woman saw John standing.

"Carl!" she called out. "Look!"

The man pulled his head from the backseat, locking eyes with John. He was wearing a dark sweatshirt, hood up. His mouth and most of his face were covered with a white and black bandana. He was easily four or five inches taller than John, but much thinner. He shoved the woman aside and barked, "I'll handle it, you shut up." He walked toward John, the tire iron still clutched in his right hand.

John still couldn't find Mags. Heard her voice again.

"John... help."

Clarity came back like a quick-rising tide, on the heels of adrenaline, and his feet moved without command, propelling him forward. Carl moved toward him at the same time, raising the tire iron above his head. John struck first, with a dark guttural sound flooding from his mouth as his fist flew at the man's throat. He missed the mark, barely. The tire iron clanged on the pavement as his hands clasped around the man's neck, his breathing impaired but not disabled. John lashed out, hitting again, striking the man in the chest.

Carl wheezed, air whistling in through a crumpled passage. He stumbled backward and fell. John dove on top of him, striking again and again and again. Blood spattered over his fist as it connected with the man's nose. The bandana loosened but stayed on. John had a glimpse of a shattered tooth lying in the grass next to them, then struck again, unaware he was growling and ignoring the pain in his hands.

Carl had stopped moving but was groaning. John stood and scanned the grassy area around him for Mags.

The woman was hovering over her, grasping a handful of Mags's hair. John started toward her. He saw blood on her face and the blur in his vision flowed red. He was still growling as he strode toward the woman, left arm reared back in attack form.

John's gaze fixed on Mags's face, echoing her expression of terror. She shouted, straining, "Behind you!"

John turned in time to see Carl pulling a six-inch kitchen knife from behind his back. He caught the other man's wrist as it swung, pushing the knife away to the side but leaving himself wide open to Carl's foot. It came down on John's bent knee at a sharp angle, forcing the joint to bow inward against its range of motion. There was a terrible cracking sound, like someone had wrapped discarded chicken bones in a thick cloth and rolled a car over them. Pain fired up the whole of John's body, alighting every nerve in his leg and jolting into his brain.

He fell and Carl was on top of him immediately, swinging his free hand, hitting John in the face and chest. Again, again, again. John tried using one hand to block his, while the other clamped around his shattered knee, trying in vain to keep it from twisting further as the two writhed in the grass.

Carl brought the knife up, high above his head, catching small pieces of light from the lone headlight a few feet away. It came down, sliding into John's side, piercing his skin with a faint *thuck* sound like sucking the pit from a peach as it skated between two of his ribs, buried to its hilt.

John felt it enter him in a detached, serene way. Instead of being painful, it was more like a switch deactivating his nerves, a circuit breaking. *Going into shock*, he thought. The broken leg was no longer his. The body stabbed belonged to someone else.

John relaxed.

Carl pulled the knife out and stood. He looked over John like a conquest, a big game hunter surveying his kill. John's strained breath sluiced in and out, like air passing through a clarinet too slow to make music.

Mags cried out and John turned toward her. He tried to stand but crumpled into the grass as his ruined knee gave. Then he crawled ten feet between them.

His eyes met Mags's, tears running down both cheeks, pain and terror swelling her hazel eyes. She did not blink, neither did he. The hair ribbon had been pulled free and lay discarded nearby, trampled, its color matching the stream of blood from a cut on her forehead.

Pain jolted him again as the man grabbed his bad leg and dragged him back. John flipped himself over and the knee screamed in protest, splintered bones grinding against one another. He took a swing up with his right and missed. Something hit him in the cheek, hard. Tire iron again.

"Doesn't feel so fucking good, does it? Asshole." Carl stepped over John, toward the woman and Mags.

John was struck again, in his back, harder than the others. His limbs went numb, and his vision reddened further. He lay on his side and saw the other three ten feet away. They were sideways from his point of view, like they were standing halfway up a wall covered in blood.

"Not supposed to be this hard, ya know," the woman said. "Carl, we was supposed to be quicker than this."

"We're not done yet," he replied. "This hasn't been worth our while. Too much trouble to walk away with what we found in their dumb shit car. Now they're gonna have to pay."

"We need to go! Someone's gonna come, ya know. Carl?!"

"You shut the fuck up, you dumb cunt. I'm running this shit, now shut your mouth and back off." He stepped over, grabbed Mags's hair out of the woman's hand and shoved her back. She stumbled away. "And quit sayin' my fuckin' name. Dumb-ass cunt."

He looked at John, lying helpless and seething on the grass, arms and legs sprawled asymmetrically like a noir chalk outline.

Rage came out of John's body like microwaves.

Carl leaned closer to eye level, turning his head sideways to match. "You still in there, guy?" His face was gaunt, strong-jawed, unshaven. Dark eyes, like smoke concentrated inside a marble and clouding the iris out of being. A sneer colored his entire expression. Perhaps he was handsome once, buried now beneath a lifetime of hardship, rent by longstanding troubles and abuse. And John's fists.

John only growled, unable to move.

Carl spat thick blood into the grass. "You messed me up a little too bad. Can't let that go, just can't."

John commanded his arms to move, and they refused. He was disabled, stuck within his own feeble body as everything that mattered to him teetered on a cliff just out of reach. He wanted to rip Carl's throat out with his teeth, like a quadriplegic zombie, blood raining on his face and clothes, warm and infectious. A thousand more angry thoughts swarmed like hornets and his vision ran crimson like a blood storm.

Carl laughed and took a step away from John, toward Mags. He grabbed her hair again. The woman he was with whimpered and took one cautious step backward, toward their car, as if longing for escape herself.

Carl raised his left foot, clad in a large brown work boot with the laces untied, and kicked Mags across the jaw. She sprawled limp on the ground. It was so swift and brutal Mags didn't make a noise.

John did. John made a terrible noise.

His hornet swarm of thoughts found his mouth and spewed forth as a shriek, startling the woman. She jumped and ran toward their car. But shriek was all he could do, no other part of his body functioned. Paralyzed, spine damaged, frayed nerve endings disconnected from their terminus, signals not relayed. Could not even turn his head away.

Still no other cars in sight.

"J-John... please... hurry... hurts." Mags's voice as she tried to crawl toward the bushes, obviously disoriented. The tire iron swung again, landing next to her shoulder blade. She collapsed and John heard her sobbing, and he was sobbing too.

"I-I'm coming, just hold on," John said, words muffled by the swelling in his mouth.

Mags stopped crawling, lying still and broken in the grass.

"You ain't doing shit and you know it," Carl said, his eyes fixed on Mags. "You can't even move."

"Ring!" John said, remembering it was in the car. "Ring, there's a ring in the car. Diamond ring, take that and go."

"Yo, we found that already," the woman said, leaning on their car, next to the flat tire, smoking a cigarette. "Looks fake as shit, ya know."

"Shut up," Carl said. "You done enough talking already."

"Come finish me off, if that's what you want," John said, red spittle flying out. "Get it over and let her go, you piece of shit."

"Nah, not gonna do that, guy. That's not good enough anymore." Carl brought a hand to his nose, pinched it and winced, then spat a thick clump of bloody mess straight into John's face. John tasted it, leaking into his mouth as Carl cried out feebly. "I really liked my nose, and I'm pretty fucking sure you broke it. Hurts like shit too. I can't walk away from that, you see. Has to be hell to pay. Has to be."

Carl looked at John. Then over to Mags. Back to John. "You ready to pay?"

John scowled back, eyes gleaming, numb from the neck down. Devoid of senses as his body had become, there was still ice spreading through his heart as he watched and screamed.

Carl grabbed Mags by both shoulders, picking her up violently. She was limp and moaning, though her timbre changed slightly as her small frame jostled. He tossed her against the side of the car, held her up with a hand under her armpit, and looked toward John, who lay still and stuck.

He pulled a silver, semiautomatic handgun from the back of his waistband in a strangely graceful motion and held it down, his arm rod-straight against the side of his leg. "You ready to pay yet, asshole?"

John screamed again, voice cracking and giving way. His mind commanded his body again and again. Wanted something, anything to move. Yet the message would not travel; it was like shouting down an empty well, a soft and indifferent echo the only reply.

Why didn't I leave? When I knew I should? This is my fault.

John could only watch, unable to turn his head, daring not to close his eyes because that would be tantamount to leaving her alone. One final, hot tear slipped sideways across the bridge of his nose and ran into the opposite eye. The world was crimson and throbbing in tune with his wayward, monstrous heartbeats.

Then it was happening. The gun raised to Mags's stomach. Stopped. Carl leered at John, raised his eyebrows and opened his mouth partway as if he would ask a question. He moved the gun up farther, to her chest. Another leer, another questioning expression. He shook his head. "No," he said. "Too quick."

Carl dropped the gun halfway and shot Mags in the knee. The sound was solid as if it had shape in three dimensions as it traveled to John. It was true thunder, the sound of the end. Of his ultimate, perpetual failure.

Mags became animated again with the shot, flailing and screeching with an emulsified mixture of terror and pain. Carl watched with a smile, breathed deep, pushed the gun against her chest, and fired again.

John tried to scream but all that came was a dry, mummified coughing sound. Time blurred worse than his vision and he closed his eyes, but the sound of the shots was echoing, overpowering, filling his consciousness. It erased all else like a tide smoothing the sand over, pulling down all structure.

No cars passed. No help came.

John watched and tried to scream and failed to move and heard the repeating sound of his own abject failure, as Carl dragged Mags toward the woodline off the side of an empty road, two hours short of their whole life together. An inestimable time later, he came back, gun still in hand.

As he neared, John looked from the barrel of the gun aimed at his forehead, to the blood-red hair ribbon lying in the grass in front of him.

Then a third shot came, and all was black.

PART FOUR

Life In Death

Definition of unknown origin:

Remote viewing (as distinguished from clairvoyance): a psychic ability wherein an individual, through focused concentration, can receive impressions about a target in an unseen or distant location. The target remotely viewed may be an event, object, or another person, and the impressions received can range from physical characteristics to emotions, sensations, or even ideas. Additionally, the barrier separating the receiver and the target can take various forms, including darkness, physical separation, or different states of consciousness.

***

From: *Astral Projection and Tabloid Mentalities, a Pragmatic Interpretation of Paranormal Psychologies* by Dr. Arthur McGuire, PhD (p. 302).

Besides being one of the lesser-known forms of parapsychology, remote viewing is also often confused with the more generic term of clairvoyance (see p. 9–11), and in fact, was given its name by parapsychological researchers Russell Targ and Harold Puthoff in the 1970s to differentiate the two phenomena.

As the term implies, clairvoyance deals more with the "clear sight" of events, implying that someone with this ability could observe more depth and detail in any instance than those of us relegated to using only our five senses. Remote viewing describes a psychic ability to perceive specific facts about an object or person who is removed from the viewer's physical line of sight. A necessary distinction, indeed.

By concentrating their psychic energy with enough force, an individual capable of remote viewing can theoretically describe whatever level of detail they perceive regarding the "target" they are viewing, without being aware of that target's location, shape, size, distance, etc.

Discussion of remote viewing reached a new level of prevalence several years ago, a result of the US Federal Government releasing documents related to a series of experiments conducted to research potential military applications of psychic phenomena. Code-named the Stargate Project (fitting), the experiments were abandoned following a total investment of some $20 million and the resounding conclusion that there were no conceivable military applications.

Somehow, though, belief in remote viewing persists, yet another demonstration of the abject lunacy of parapsychological studies. It is nothing short of absurd to perpetuate the existence of this phenomenon, considering our own military gained nothing from their enormous investments, both financial and otherwise. In that context, it is difficult to understand how anyone could maintain an opposing point of view with any level of confidence.

Quite simply, if remote viewing existed, would we not be implementing it in our military intelligence efforts around the globe?

***

From: "An Assessment of the Evidence for Psychic Functioning" by Professor Jessica Utts, as reviewed by the American Institutes of Research (AIR), at the request of the US Congress and CIA following Project Stargate.

According to *Webster's Dictionary*, in law, *prima facie* evidence is "evidence having such a degree of probability that it must prevail unless the contrary be proved." There are a few examples of applied, non-laboratory remote viewings provided to the review team that would seem to meet that criterion for evidence. These are examples in which the sponsor or another government client asked for a single remote viewing of a site, known to the requestor in real time or in the future, and the viewer provided details far beyond what could be taken as a reasonable guess. Two such examples are given by May (1995) in which it appears that the results were so striking that they far exceed the phenomenon as observed in the laboratory. Using a post-hoc analysis, Dr. May concluded that in one of the cases the remote viewer was able to describe a microwave generator with 80 percent accuracy, and that of what he said almost 70 percent of it was reliable.

CHAPTER FIFTY-FIVE

I need to figure out where they are, Lucy thought. *Locate someone inside the building. Without going in. Then I can sneak in the front, time it for my best chance to get him in a wheelchair and through the back door before anyone notices. Plus, if I'm going to trick one of them into thinking the police are on their way, it would help if I figure out who is most suggestible. Then if they don't come after me themselves when the emergency exit alarm goes off, I can get him far enough away, fast enough.*

If I pull all that off, I might have enough time to help him. But that's a lot of "ifs."

She was standing outside John/Robbie's room, still in wet socks and jeans. The rain stayed steady and patient, but the thunder was crawling closer. The electrical activity in the air was noticeable. It was boosting her, as if she could pirate its bandwidth to increase her own signal. Or she was getting better that quickly.

She pressed herself against the wall, forehead on brick, as if peering through glass. Closed her eyes tight. Her hands to both temples, she pictured the hallway she had run through, outside his room. The wheelchair had been knocked sideways but still there, upright.

The image was clear. Well-formed and vivid. Light reflected off clean white floor tiles. The wooden bars set hip-high along the walls to prevent damage when beds were wheeled around. She saw fine details, like the grain of the wooden doors. Two open, one closed in this corner of the hallway. The faint red glow of an exit sign at the opposite end with part of the T burned out. Not the one she would use for her escape, though. It was closest to him, but led to the wrong side of the building, and she wouldn't get far fleeing that direction. It was too likely someone would see her, and a woman in rain-soaked street clothes running through the parking lot at three a.m. with no shoes, pushing an unconscious man in a wheelchair would bring questions.

No, best to avoid the nearest exit and quietly move toward the one she had already fled through.

Despite the clarity and detail, Lucy was unsure whether this image was from memory or if she was seeing inside the hall, when Clarice came around the corner. She looked frazzled, and a little angry, but back to routine, likely content knowing the police were after the lunatic who broke into a patient's room then attacked her when confronted. As she passed John's room, Lucy tried to "talk" to her, the way she had first gotten Rick's attention, to see what happened.

Clarice continued down the hall, undeterred, unaffected. Lucy considered that contacting Rick was easier because they were familiar. He would be the easiest target for her now. She scouted the hallways with her mind's eye, trying to locate him.

It was more difficult, at first. It had been easy to pick up things right past the outer wall, but to push herself toward the farther reaches of the hallways was more taxing. She crouched down, the effort making her legs unreliable. As she "moved" around the corner, into the adjacent hallway, what she saw was clouded, as if thick fog had rolled into the building. With more effort, she dispelled that fog and approached a clearer view. Not clear for visible texture and surface condition anymore, but enough to orient herself and continue navigating.

Her breathing became more even, deeper. The fog in the hallway thinned.

Even with a clearer view, she struggled to determine where the people were, to note their movement. She couldn't hear anything, could only bend her mind's eye around the interior of the building until some movement drew her attention.

After a few minutes, she located the other security guard and tried to probe him, to measure his defenses, his mental susceptibility. Again, she assumed it had worked with Rick because of their shared past, expecting the same result as she had earned from Clarice. But Lucy surprised herself.

She found him seated behind the nurse's station, reclined in an office chair, his feet up on the desk, and watching recap videos from a baseball game on his iPhone. She poked at his mind, without sending words—more of a "flick" at his brain. He responded immediately, swatting about his ear like a fly was near.

Outside, Lucy laughed and then her breathing returned to its trancelike rhythm.

She decided to take it further. She needed to plant a suggestion and see if it would cause some behavior. And, hopefully, stay implanted if she relaxed her attention.

She noticed her mouth was open, long enough to grow dry. She pushed that sensation out toward him, to make him thirsty so he would go for a drink.

The guard coughed, smacked his tongue against the roof of his mouth a few times (she saw this, rather than heard it), then stood and walked into the break room, a few doors past the nurse's station. When he got there, he turned on the counter faucet, cupped his hands and drank from them, like an overgrown child stealing water from a garden hose.

She kept pushing the sensation of thirst toward him, curious to see if a few sips would undo her suggestion. When she did, he turned his head and put his mouth directly under the running water. From her safe distance, Lucy saw it spilling across his cheek, some drops escaping and moving down his neck, soaking into his shirt collar.

She left him, wanting to determine where Rick was hiding. She roamed down hallway after hallway, picking up speed as she went, but light-headed and moving to kneel, leg muscles strained from her crouching position.

Her search came up empty (except for Clarice, a predictable distance farther into her rounds). Lucy made a quick list of places Rick might be, assuming he was still inside.

Her first guess was correct: he was in the men's room, near the lobby. A potential problem, if she waited much longer. He was in a stall (seeing shoes and bunched-up pants beneath the door was plenty close), which could leave her time to get past the lobby unseen, before he finished.

If she went right now.

That, however, meant she couldn't further test the duration of her "thirsty" suggestion; she would have to trust it. She dare not wait for another chance to present itself. No certainty in that.

Now or never, she told herself. She ran to the building's front, passing through the automatic doors and out of the rain.

CHAPTER FIFTY-SIX

The silence in the building was unsettling. Lucy had spent little time here during these long red-eye hours. She was accustomed to some minimal level of activity in the halls, people milling in the lobby, the occasional flyby of staff as they hurried about. Now, it was dim and silent. No background music, no movement of any type. The effect was eerie, even more so when coupled with the unstable status of her overactive consciousness.

But at least she had made it in, unnoticed. During her approach she was certain the front doors would be locked, despite hospital protocol. *Hell, locking the doors would be smart under the current circumstances. There's already been one break-in tonight, and the culprit is still loose.* She smiled at that, finding a surge of energy when considering her rebellious actions from that detached angle.

She checked her mental tabs on the three other occupants, no changes. That meant she could rush past the men's room and make it to John's hallway before Rick came back out. She moved swiftly, gliding down the tile in her socked feet, her slight frame held narrow and close to one wall. She crept around a corner and saw the wheelchair waiting at the far end.

The other three were still unaware of her reentry. Clarice was moving to another patient's room, Rick was still in the stall but standing, the second guard had returned to the nurse's station and switched from baseball recaps to hockey. Lucy was astounded at her own luck. At this rate, she had a clean shot at his room. She could wait in there for several minutes until she was certain of her exit route.

Not luck, Scarlett's voice said. It could have been a projection of her own confidence. *It's not luck, you're ready. It's time. He waits for you.*

Lucy nodded, striding down the hall to his room. There were hunters on her tail, but this hallway was her territory. She knew it well and pressed that advantage. She was smoke.

When she entered the room, the window drew her attention as lightning struck and thunder rattled the glass with a force that seemed barely short of shattering it. Rain drummed against the façade of the building as the storm winds swept through, oppressing the night and bringing a sense of shelter to the building that made her second-guess her decision to move John outside. But it was needed. She had no chance of finishing her task before she was discovered in his room. The storm could be helpful in covering her escape.

Then a second spat of lightning revealed a new problem.

The bed was empty.

Chapter Fifty-Seven

Fighting to maintain rational thought, Lucy first assured herself that she had the correct room, then reminded herself she had already been in there once tonight. Or maybe that was yesterday by now. And she knew, with his being comatose for years, they wouldn't move him out of bed, for any reason. It was counter-Hippocratic for God's sake.

Would they move his bed? To protect him from me?

Nothing else around the bed had changed. His machines were in place, still running. How could that be?

Lucy scanned the room, leaving the light off for fear it would attract someone's attention. The lightning came again, keeping her pupils from adjusting to the darkness.

What am I looking for? Clues, I guess. The mystery of the disappearing coma patient. If I was unconscious for four years and suddenly regained movement, where would I go first? It was a joke, though. Absurd. She had seen his hand move, but it was impossible he could go anywhere. Wasn't it?

One more flash of lightning revealed the clue she had thought wouldn't be there. Her joke wasn't so far-fetched. He couldn't go anywhere, no, and had not tried to, most likely. But he had, all the same.

She saw one corner of bedsheet still tucked under the mattress. The sheet was pulled off, hanging from the opposite side. She squatted down to follow its path.

John was lying on the floor. Crumpled, limbs disorganized, face-down. Still connected to his machines, miraculously, but motionless except for shallow, assisted breathing.

I must have fixed him more than I realized, she told herself, moving around the opposite side of the bed to collect him.

He was mumbling, moaning. When she approached, a surge of energy filled the front of her brain—strong signal received. His cries for help still rang out to her, the universe, anyone listening or capable of tuning in.

She skidded around him to the cabinets against the wall. She was seeking a small, portable emergency CPAP machine and found it in the third drawer she opened. It was half a loaf of bread's size, smaller and denser than those she had used before. She turned it on to check the battery; it was full and made a too-loud beeping noise. Lucy caught herself short of "shushing" the little machine. She set it on the bed and returned to John's side.

She stooped, removing the IV lines that delivered his medication and nutrition, then reached inside his open gown and disconnected his catheter line. Her hand brushed against his skin, and she let go a guilt-ridden shudder. His skin was cold and had taken on the texture of soggy paper.

Oh God, there's no time to waste, she thought. *He may have only minutes left.*

She used both hands to pull out his endotracheal tube, disconnecting him from the machine that had been breathing for him since he stabilized. Lucy knew an alarm would sound instantly, which she disabled before the second beep. She "checked" again on Clarice's position, and the other guard's. Still safe, but hard to tell how long until one of them would start moving in her direction.

She coaxed him onto his back, pulling his knees up to give herself somewhere to hoist him from. His bottom jaw fell slack. He looked not just dead, but skeletal, and her heart jumped. The lightning came again, thunder joining to scrape her nerves at the wrong moment. She stood, turning to run, to leave this place, give up.

There's nothing for you that way, Scarlett's voice scolded.

Lucy's mind cleared. She bent down to pick him up, careful not to strain her back. He was alarmingly thin, but still weighed enough to cause damage if she were foolish about moving him.

Now, with all of his life support disconnected, she slid her hands under his neck and knees, bending at her own, and lifted. It was a strain, and she thought she might drop him when he slipped. But she fought through, picturing Anna in her mind. She was dedicating all her reserves to this second, final chance. She had removed his life support and was taking its place; she was his death support. She would not fail him now.

As she cradled him in her arms like a distorted and malformed child, she sensed signs of life, his meager heartbeats against her own chest. His arms dangled away from her, but one of his hands had moved again, clawing at the air. He mumbled and was breathing on his own. This shocked her so much that she nearly dropped him again.

More lightning came, thunder louder and closer, rattling the window and prompting her to keep moving. She stepped back into the hall, each footfall a struggle to keep silent as she moved with his extra weight on her tired legs. She made it to the wheelchair, pushed it against the wall with her shin, and deftly pulled it open with one of her feet.

She stood beside the wheelchair and set him in it, like she was unpacking someone else's collectibles. Without warning, too late for anything but a push through, the gravity of her actions dropped on her. But she took no pause. Her break for the emergency exit became a blur, her socked feet moving nimbly as if no longer attached to her hips, hands choking the wheelchair grips. She burst through the emergency exit, and it clamored its tattletale report.

Lucy pushed the wheelchair through the damp, rainy night at a jog, a flash of lightning revealing the path she had fled to earlier. The wheels tried to protest in the rain-soaked earth, but her resolve denied this and she shoved onward, disappearing into the trees and leaving the jarring sound of the alarm behind her.

CHAPTER FIFTY-EIGHT

Once sure she was hidden, Lucy stopped, abandoning John in the wheelchair and turning her attention back to the weak-willed security guard. She projected herself, her mind's eye, back into the hallway and caught him striding (not running) to meet Rick at the back door.

Lucy watched, unable to hear but sensing both men were shouting. Clarice had not joined them yet, and Lucy fretted she was phoning the police already. She did a quick sweep and found Clarice in John's room. Taking stock, inventorying whatever was missing or stolen. Surely, she noticed the patient himself missing first, Lucy thought. Then, as Clarice's head darted about the room, something caught Lucy's eye, sending a cold chill into her chest.

On the bed, next to the one tucked-in sheet corner, was the CPAP machine. She had left it behind, cutting her time to a fraction. He would be brain-dead in a few minutes if he stopped breathing. She turned back to the chair, put her ear to his bone-bare chest, and listened. Still breathing on his own, a small miracle that she dare not depend on. A grace sure to be short-lived.

First thing's first though, she reminded herself, turning her attention back to the alarm. *I've got to stop them from sending anyone after me.*

She concentrated on the other guard, sending a mental probe of a ringing phone. Again, she shot at him like an arrow, hoping to skewer his attention and drive him to movement. He shouted something she couldn't hear, and Rick nodded, clear to her mind's eye. He turned and strode back down the hall, headed toward the nurse's station.

"Hang on, John," Lucy said. "Just keep breathing for me. It's almost time."

He mumbled something unintelligible.

She watched from her wet perch in the woods outside, lightning punctuating her thoughts, hoping she could misdirect the guard and earn herself enough seclusion to do what was needed. All the while, her window was closing.

Lucy saw the guard approach the nurse's station, making his way down the hall in a posturing non-hurry. Were anyone watching (besides her), it would take a considerably larger effort to convey urgency. To him, tonight was no different from the previous. No matter how many times some crazy bitch broke into the building, his paycheck would have the same numbers on it next week.

His gait conveyed all this to Lucy, and she smiled in return, knowing she had chosen the perfect vessel for misdirection. Arriving at the counter, in a haphazard effort to phone the police, he reached for what, in his mind, was unquestionably a phone, and pressed the correct sequence for 911 on numbers that were unquestionably represented by buttons on its receiver. He waited until a voice on the other end confirmed his call. He explained and paused while the voice (a man's, calm and reassuring) on the other end informed him help was en route.

He set the stapler he'd been holding to his ear back on the counter and returned to the commotion at the violated exit, without hurrying.

He said something to Rick. Lucy assumed it an ETA for the police, that she had bought herself some time, hoping it would prove enough. She could not fall short this close to the finish line.

Beneath the canopy of trees, thick and occluding as the deepest rainforest, she turned to her patient and asked, "Ready?"

She bent forward toward his wheelchair, and went in after him.

From *Passing Through, Thoughts on Death and Dying* by Lucille Claremont, RN (p. 256).

"Understanding Death":

Many have tried to understand or explain how mental preparation for death may manifest itself, with infinite opinions and speculations. Perhaps the most accurate way to explain it is to say it *cannot* be clearly defined. It is believed that most of the preparation takes place on a subconscious or near-subconscious level.

Because of this, among a myriad of other possibilities, how a person mentally prepares to transcend their mortal remains is unpredictable in any clinical or scientific way. It is as unique as their fingerprint, and malleable as their life's experiences.

Therefore, we return to the age-old conclusion that it is impossible to know what a person undergoes mentally as they pass from this world, into death and what lies beyond it.

There is only one true method of learning what death is like.

Chapter Fifty-Nine

See why we had to do this now? Robbie's voice came to John from nowhere, bringing him back to nowhere. *It's the whole reason I came. You needed me. You needed this. To remember it and face it. And be held accountable.*

John drifted around the rim of consciousness like collected pond scum. He didn't respond and Robbie didn't relent.

You should have run. You should have gotten the hell out, but you didn't. You made that choice. He was right, you see? There was hell to pay, and you've escaped it for too long.

In despair, John had abandoned all attempts at movement, coupled with an inability to control even his breathing. His heart beat with a wild ferocity as if it were trying to escape on its own and damn the consequences to the rest of his body. Numbness had long since changed to a full physical detachment and was now transcending into a strange balance of phantom limb awareness and petrification, like he was a large doll given a human brain. A creature of thought only, no longer designed for motility.

As a creature capable only of thought, he found that sole purpose drawn toward a black hole topic. Alone, trapped and hopeless in the cave, John thought only of Mags. Her face, her words, her warmth. He saw her, fully, as a construct of his fondest memories and then as the bloodied result of his greatest failure. Live Mags, dead Mags. Prime Mags, mutilated Mags. There was much difference between them and yet little distance. One poor decision had been the only dividing factor.

His need to see her again grew until it overtook his desire to move. And he remembered he carried a piece of her. A small, perhaps ineffectual piece, but the last one he possessed, which made it precious. Her hair ribbon was still in his pocket.

If this is it, he told himself. *If I'm dying like this, I at least want to hold that tiny part of her again. To clasp onto her as I go.* But he couldn't retrieve it. Moving his hand that far, pivoting and shifting and shoving and negotiating his arm into the right position, was impossible. There was a sudden sensation of rolling, falling sideways, then impact, yet he hadn't moved.

That doesn't matter. If I can't get it back out, and touch it again, I'll die trying.

He funneled all his attention back to his right hand, still the only part he could move.

His breathing was unreliable, lungs filled with heavy wet cloth, or cinched in half, or collapsing. He stretched them to pull in more air and found that impossible, too, as if the depth of his diaphragm had changed.

His heart was betraying him, falling in and out of rhythm, for one moment stopping altogether. This was the end. He knew he was dying and surrendered to it, a mercy. A jolt arrived, ringing through him loud as a gong, and his heart jumped back into motion, uneven and straining.

Robbie had won; he had what he wanted. There was no one else to help him. None who knew his location. The cavalry did not exist.

John wallowed, hoping for the last moments of life to trickle out like infected blood to be washed away and cleansed by greater forces.

Definition of unknown origin:

Astral Projection: a paranormal phenomenon that deals with the distinction between the physical body and the astral, or spiritual, body and refers specifically to the act of willing the astral form to leave the physical body (also referred to as an out-of-body experience) and enter another plane of existence. While it is believed that certain psychically empowered individuals can project their astral form repeatedly, a common speculation is that all persons have some ability to achieve astral projection. However, without a significant level of psychic ability, most astral forms will only become separated from their physical counterpart at or near the time of death.

***

"The whole problem with the world is that fools and fanatics are always so certain of themselves, and wiser people so full of doubts."

—Bertrand Russell

***

"The door to the infinite lies just outside your belief system."
　—Bumper sticker

Chapter Sixty

Lucy watched, breathless, as the man she had "rescued" from the safety of a specialized medical facility was dying in front of her. His breathing grew troubled, and she had forgotten the CPAP machine. His skin grew colder and deep blue. His heart was failing, and she had no EKG or defibrillator to monitor or restart it. He was so near the end now, any disruption in vital signs could become a permanent cessation. If his heart stopped and never started again, she was equipped to do little in response.

In her hurried planning, she hadn't properly considered these details, and he was now paying the price. She held a finger to his wrist, monitoring his pulse, and felt his heart stop. Her own skipped in response; she allowed a fraction of fear through her. She closed her eyes tight, calling forth an image of his weakening heart. The striations of the cardiac muscle, the waving pink valves that let blood course from its chambers to his arteries and then back in from his veins. With an invisible hand, she squeezed his heart, seizing on this vision to pull him back from the edge, for a few more minutes. He deserved to understand what was happening as he left this world.

The pulse returned in his wrist, uneven and straining.

She sharpened her mental point yet again and formed the image of her blue car, an open stretch of six-lane highway, devoid of traffic, imagined herself in the driver's seat.

And found the unending rock wall again. He was still blocking, keeping himself cut off inside some self-designed prison. She reached into her new bag of mental tricks, trying to implement the other feats she had already accomplished. One thing that was clear: she could bring about effects on his body to some extent, but it did nothing to penetrate his consciousness. She realized she would need to be more adaptive if she were to reach him inside the cocoon of rock.

Lucy thought of the words he had "written" through her. The page was still in her pocket; she unfolded it and read.

The prominent sentence fragment caught her attention again. "Robbie tricked me, now gone."

What does that mean? she thought. *If I'm going to get to him, I'll need to find out why he's keeping himself trapped in there. Why he's blocking me.* But turning his transcribed words over in her own frame of mind, examining every angle, she found no reliable interpretation. It was not enough information.

Must be something else I can use.

"Help" and "trapped" provided no direction. Nor did "can't." The only real clues she could explore were "cave" and "MAGS."

What is "MAGS?" A name? Is that why it's in all caps? I remember there being talk about someone else with him. Hadn't the investigation dismissed that when no other body was found? Yes, that seemed right. More hunch than fact. But investigators chased hunches usually, right? And that meant it was a viable lead. So she followed.

It looks like he's projecting this wall; I've already considered that. And it seems to be made of rock, which implies that his self-imposed prison cell may appear to him as a tunnel. I (we) wrote "cave." Does he think he's trapped in a cave?

She was taken back to the newspaper headline the officer outside her cell had been reading. About a man trapped in a cave, and how terrible it sounded. How frightening it was even to think about, let alone to inflict it upon oneself.

Shifting focus back to her mind's eye, Lucy tried to leverage the two words from her transcript that seemed most useful. She envisioned herself touching the rock wall again and called to him.

John? she sent. *Or Robbie? I don't know if you can hear me, but I'm here to help.* There was no sign this was having effect, but she proceeded, too aware of the closing door. Too much time had been lost already. *I'm here to help, okay? My name is Lucy. I'm a nurse. Are you in a cave? Is that where you are?*

In her mind's eye, she envisioned herself placing both her hands on the strange rock wall, palms flat. It was cold, slick. And solid. Impenetrable. Stretching in all directions. She looked up and saw it growing. Soon it was all she saw unless she turned backward. She pushed on it, still calling to him, waiting to see if there were any signs of it yielding.

I'm here to help, okay? John? I know you're trapped, and I can help you. But you have to let me in. Open up and let me help. I can get you out. But I can't do anything if you don't let me.

She dropped her hands, backed away from the surface of rock, and waited. Strained her concentration, slipped further and further from her physical self into this landscape of little substance. This came as a strong sensation, like the realization of height when peering over a balcony. This prompted her to turn and look behind her.

The blue car was gone, that image abandoned, by her, she supposed. Instead there was only a bleak and endless desert, a sea of what looked like dark sand. Some imperceptible distance away she saw herself, her physical body, crouching next to the wheelchair. John was in it, leaning crumpled and pathetic and dying. The image was stark enough to reinforce that sensation of height, of gravity. She felt pulled down, perhaps being pulled back into her body. But she must not return. She needed to press forward. To find a way in. The part of her mind that enabled these feats was allowing this physical separation, but the rest of her was giving its strongest protest yet.

She looked down at herself (not her physical self) seeing an ephemeral glow. It was emanating from inside her as if she were incandescent.

This isn't reality, she reminded herself. *I'm not reaching out to him on the... plane that our bodies are in. I'm here, but he's here too. He's not in there. And if that's true then we, THIS, is all some different kind of... energy. Mental energy. I've been learning how to control that, haven't I? I can do this. I have to keep pushing harder. I need to get his attention.*

She turned back to the wall and called to him again.

John? John Camden? Let me help you. The rock was as unyielding as ever.

Lucy played her final card.

Mags. Does that mean something to you? Who is Mags? she sent to him, still unsure if it was a name or something else. She waited, fighting the urge to call out to him again.

She put her left hand on the wall. It sunk into the pale rock, disappearing to the wrist as if a section had become quicksand.

Chapter Sixty-One

Lucy pulled her hand from the wall, noting the effort needed. At first, her fingers held fast in the quicksand-like substance that had changed place with solid rock. Then her hand came free, leaving a hole she thought would snap closed. Instead, it stayed, and she saw through the barrier. Not much, and not far. But she had visibility to the other side of John's self-imposed prison.

She looked in, like peeking at some astral locker room, with torrid and juicy details awaiting. Her vision found only a shapeless black cloud on the other side, like thick smoke from a house fire. It was no use; there was nothing to see.

Another mental shout would fail, so Lucy tented the fingers of her left hand together, forming a point, and slipped them through the opening. As she did, she focused all of her thought on sending him warmth, on showing him her intent through the energy she had seen coming from her own form in this strange place. She cast her light into the hole and the effect was much like walking out of a movie theater into bright midday sunlight. She was blinded, but continued her attempt to illuminate whatever may be on the other side of the wall and waited for her vision to adjust.

Green, she saw. Grass. The wheel of a car. She heard a woman's voice.

"Well, man, I think I uh, hit a pothole a little ways back."

As she watched, outside her physical form, peering through an opening the size of her hand, forced into what appeared to be a wall of manifested denial or guilt, Lucy learned more about John Camden's last waking moments than anyone that had helped treat him or clean up or investigate it. She learned what happened to him, what had sent him to the hospital clinging to the last strings of life. She learned "MAGS" was a name, learned to whom it belonged, and why John was keeping himself prisoner inside his own mind. She learned what he had been putting himself through as he neared the end of his life. She also learned the role Robbie played in this end-of-life tableau of self-punishment.

And she learned what would lead John to a good death.

CHAPTER SIXTY-TWO

When she finished watching, and had taken a few needed moments to compose herself following this specimen of the atrocities that humans can commit against each other, she pulsed the light coming from inside herself, fueled by the confidence of having found her way through. The knowledge that she was getting closer.

The opening in the wall grew wider, crumbling around its edges, as if he were readying himself to accept her. She was being allowed in.

John? she called, stepping through the hole as it became large enough. *Robbie?*

She found herself inside an apparent cave, matching the information she had extracted so far. When she looked back to where she had entered, she saw only light, an impenetrable whiteness. There was an unearthly separation between light outside and void inside, as if the two were shielded from each other. Ahead of her was crippling darkness and more rock on all sides, but the energy she was generating was piercing through and guiding her to him.

John Camden? she called again. *Can you hear me?*

She walked forward, through a tunnel barely high enough to stand, emerged from its mouth, and saw him, wedged inside a crawlspace, as if her seething light rendered transparent the rock pinning him in place.

From *Passing Through, Thoughts on Death and Dying* by Lucille Claremont, RN (p. 239).

"The Role of Hospice":

For patients with serious, life-threatening illnesses, it is common practice for the focus of their care to shift from curative to hospice. The difference being that, for hospice care, the primary intent is relieving symptoms, rather than curing the illness or ailment. Therefore, hospice or palliative care is administered to improve the quality of life for patients when no cure is realistic and the curative treatment itself can cause undue hardship or trauma.

This is as important for relief of psychological effects as it is for physical, as most terminal conditions cause severe psychological distress to patients and their families. This distress is brought about by the primary emotional and spiritual concerns of hospice patients, which include: severe pain, loss of independence, the perception of being a burden, concerns about the afterlife, and most prominently, fear.

It is critical to address each of these concerns if present, to ensure patients can find true comfort, and experience a peaceful end. With the varied nature of these concerns, hospice care takes many forms, some quite unconventional.

Chapter Sixty-Three

John heard something in the cave. A voice, but one he didn't recognize, traversing through the cavernous nothing encapsulating him. Not Robbie's this time, nor was it Mags's. Another female voice. It floated angelically toward him from behind the endless cold rock. The voice called to him.

John Camden? it said. *Can you hear me?*

"He-hello?" he answered, with mousy hesitation. "Someone there?" The words slid toward the wall inches from his mouth and bounced back at him as if mocking.

John? the voice said again, and he realized it was not coming through his ears. He turned his head instinctively but its direction was unclear. He saw the white tree again, in his mind, and had a churning in his stomach.

"What the hell is happening?" he screamed.

Everything is all right. The voice was indeed skipping past his ears and directly into his head. *I'm here to help you.*

"Who are you?!" he cried out, a tear slipping by to accompany each word. "Where are you?"

I'm here with you, John, I'm here to help.

"How? How are you here? How am I hearing you?"

With your mind, John. And you can talk the same way.

"What?"

Take a deep breath and try to calm down.

That request yielded the opposite result.

"Help! I'm trapped. I'm going to die!"

Take a deep breath and try to calm down, John. You're not where you think you are, and if I'm going to help you get free, you need to calm down.

He screamed until the sound lost shape and morphed into unintelligible cries. Then he sobbed.

There, that's a start. Now, how about that deep breath?

John complied, and found that it calmed him. Inhale deep, pause, exhale.

Good. One more, please?

Again, he obeyed, thinking the voice had a distinct air of caring, empathy, like it belonged to a teacher.

Nurse, actually, it said. *I'm a nurse, John. Your nurse.*

Holy shit, he thought. *She heard that?*

Yes. Are you ready for me to help you now?

Who are you?

Good, you sound more level. I think you're almost ready, that's good. My name is Lucy. I'm one of the people who've been taking care of you.

What? The calm settling over him lifted some, was transient, as though it were imposed by someone else but he could override through exertion.

John, I need you to stay calm. Please.

Semi-imposed serenity washed back over.

There, the voice continued. *Can you stay that way for me? This will be much easier if you can.*

John surrendered further as his battered cognition accepted that he was neither in danger nor in control anymore. *Did you do that? Did you calm me down? Did you... make me feel that?*

Yes, I did. At least, I think I did. I tried to, definitely.

How is that possible? How can you do that? How can I hear you and talk to you this way?

I'm not sure of that, John. But I know one thing. We're, neither of us, inside our bodies right now. We're... well... we are somewhere else.

He shook his head from side to side, added a silent mental *no*.

What do you remember last? Before this place? This cave?

CHAPTER SIXTY-FOUR

What do you mean? I remember... I... This isn't real. It can't be.

John, Lucy replied, *listen carefully. I need you to understand what is happening. If I'm going to help you, you need to know what you've been doing to yourself.*

To myself? You think I did this to myself? I'm finally losing it, I guess. I've flipped my shit and now I'm having conversations with dead people and voices from nowhere. Is that what this is?

John, we don't have time to argue. I know there is a lot you don't believe or understand or want to explain, but you don't have much choice. So you might as well listen, right? Let me explain what you're doing to yourself and then we can talk about why you're doing it. What do you remember about today before this cave? How did you come to be here?

It was Robbie. His idea. His decision, really. I was having these... attacks, and he thought I needed to face it head-on. Confront the fear behind them. That's what he said, at least. Then he tried to kill me.

Good, that's a good start.

I'm so confused! Why am I having these... Are they memories? Of Mags and I together? Her dying, and me...? She married Robbie. Where is she? I just want to see her again. Even if that means...

We'll put all the pieces together, John, you have to trust me.

Why? How? I'll die if I don't get help soon, and I'm supposed to trust a voice in my head?

I understand it's asking a lot. And that this is... difficult.

Difficult? he said, scoffing.

Would it help if I told you about myself some? About what I've been through?

You've been through what I've been through. You're a voice in my head. What's that Dickens line? "More of gravy than grave," or something?

I'm not, John. I'm not part of you, and I know how that sounds. But I'm here to help. No gravy. And no grave either.

How are you going to help me? I'm trapped. Unless you've got twenty other people with you, or some giant construction equipment, I'm fucked.

My name is Lucy. Lucy Claremont. I'm a nurse. I've seen a lot of death, and I've experienced some personally.

What does this—?

I had a daughter. She was killed. I couldn't stop it, John. I failed her.

John was silent so Lucy pressed on.

I know a little about what you're going through. She was taken, kidnapped, by her father. While I was at work. They disappeared for a few days, and I tried to help the police look for her. But they didn't find her in time.

What... what happened?

He took her away, in the middle of a class field trip. I dropped her off, watched her get on the bus, and never saw her again. I got a call at work that afternoon from the police saying she was gone. For days, John, three days, I waited and agonized and prayed and hoped for something. A sign, anything. On the fourth day, I was called to identify their bodies.

After the funeral, the police told me more about what happened, and I sought out more details even though they hurt. I guess it was just too much, so over time I shut down. I didn't talk to anyone about it, not really. Then I started blocking it out. I called it my Wall of Apathy, I stayed behind this emotional barrier, drank all the time, trying not to block it all out. But I realize now, all that denial and hiding, that was making it worse, not better. And once I accepted that, all the details I had blocked out came... came back. I know it all now. I've felt it from her view. Earlier, I... I lived it with her, in a way. I know that sounds crazy, but here we are, I guess.

What do you mean?

I... I guess I have this, ability, you'd call it. I picked up her bracelet and it just... it just happened. It came over me, like I was there. Like I was her.

How is that even... how is that possible?

I don't know, John. I'd love to explain it but I can't and we don't really have time anyway. But this... ability of mine is how I'm talking to you.

What happened to her? Can you tell me?

He had driven her to a roadside motel, about two hundred miles from Frankfort, where the field trip was going. They stayed there together for a few days, and then when he—Chris, her father—thought the police were close to finding him, he took her swimming in the motel pool. It was late, nighttime. Chilly. They didn't have bathing suits. Now I can picture her little teeth chattering, her blue lips. Her desire to make her daddy happy. She was such a sweet girl, John.

How old?

Eleven. My Anna was eleven.

Keep... Will you keep going?

Yes, I want to talk to someone about it. So badly.

Well, I'm not going anywhere.

He, Chris, had a gun. Carried her into the pool in his arms until the water was almost up to his waist. He looked up at the moon and tried to explain things to her. Why he hadn't been around, how I had kept them apart. That he had gone to jail for a short time for embezzling money from work, and how it was a mistake but not something he should lose his whole life over. How much he loved her and missed her. She felt his sadness and even though she was shivering, she didn't want to interrupt him because she knew he was telling her something important. She listened, even to the parts she didn't understand. He told her nothing would come between them again, ever, and that made her happy.

After he spoke to Anna, she looked up at the full moon too. There were no clouds. While she was looking, he pulled the gun from his waistband and shot her. In the back of the head. Lucy was sobbing, the incandescent light of her form was fading, dimming.

Then he shot himself.

I'm sorry. So sorry, John said.

Thank you. It's been a long time. Such a long time, and I didn't know all those details myself until just yesterday, when I went into her room for the first time in years. I picked up that bracelet and I felt what she felt. I lived her death, and facing that is what started me back on this path to you.

She paused, and there was a weighty silence between them.

I had so much guilt over it, John. I knew he was dangerous, he'd threatened to take her before. But he never had the mettle to go through with it. Or I didn't think he did. So I blamed myself. I let that ruin me, John, so much that I couldn't even go visit her grave. And I drank. All the time. She would have been ashamed of me, I think. I can see this all so clearly now, and saying it to you makes it that much more clear. I could have started healing years ago. Started moving on years ago. But I chose not to. I see that I've been in such denial. I've denied Anna and myself. Denied my purpose. I denied my responsibility.

What responsibility?

To help people. People like you. And the strangest thing is that I'm more prepared to help you because of her death. Because of what I've been through. I don't think I could have reached you without that, without what happened to her, to me. Without the time to pull through it. It's like I needed all of that to get to you. And now that I'm sharing this it's probably helping me as much as anything.

Get to me? What does that mean?

Are you ready to trust me yet, John?

I... I guess so. I don't have much choice.

That's good enough, because we're out of time. Now, listen carefully.

Chapter Sixty-Five

John's voice had a meekness that wrenched Lucy's heart. He was desperate, tired. But he was trusting her. She had a small hope now.

Please, please. I don't know what's real anymore, he said. *Just help me. I want to get out of here. I want to see her again.*

You will, John. You will. I'm going to help you. But you need to understand what's happening.

I don't... he replied, unable to finish. He shuffled minutely within his confines, then tried again. *You're just a... can't be... don't know...*

You don't understand. That's what I'm here for. We're going to get you out.

How can I get out? I can't even move.

That's part of what you need to understand. You're not trapped. At least, not the way you think. John?

Hmm?

You're not in a cave, she said. That seemed to give him some momentum as she had hoped.

What?

What happened after you were attacked? Can you remember that?

I... I... no. That wasn't real. It must have been a... a dream.

I'm afraid it was real, though. And that's the missing piece. You almost died. You didn't, but you came close. Very close. When the ambulance arrived, they kept you breathing and took you to a hospital. You were unconscious, beaten, clinging to life. They put you on machines, life support machines, to breathe for you, feed you, keep you alive until you wake up.

Wake? You're telling me I'm not... awake?

No, John. You're not awake right now.

What? What does that...? Surprise pulled at his facial muscles like there were strings attached to them, twitching and searching to show the depth of his shock.

You've been in a coma for four years. You still are. Right now.

She waited for him to absorb it.

What the hell does that mean? I'm not... I'm trapped in a goddamn cave and I'm going to die and you're not helping me.

No. No, you're not in a cave. Not really.

What do you mean? Of course I am.

Can you see me, John?

NO! I can't see shit. How the hell do you even know my name?

His trust was slipping, as his defenses raised anew.

I'm your nurse, I've been taking care of you. I still need you to trust me, okay?

Taking... care of me? Why?

I'm trying to explain that. First, can you see me?

He moved his head again as much as the confines would allow.

No. No... I can't see anything.

Try to, John. Try harder, but not with your eyes.

What? That doesn't make any—

You're not hearing me with your ears, right? You know that. So you can see me without your eyes.

He closed them.

That's right, focus on my voice. Deep breaths. Listen to my voice and you'll see me.

I... I see. Light, I see light.

That's good. Keep looking.

The light grew brighter and the surrounding rock... relaxed as if it were breathing, softening, dissolving, turning to foam. The light pierced his eyelids. He opened them again and found that he was floating. The cave was... gone. Nearly gone. He looked around in time to see several large rock shapes dissipating and floating upward as if they had turned effervescent. He gasped.

Then he saw her and realized she was the source of the light. She had no clothing, but her shape was not defined like he would expect. There were no clear borders to it, except for her face. The rest of her blurred into the light as it escaped, leaving only faint impressions of her skin at the edges. She looked ghostly, flowing and nebulous.

She was floating, too, like him, around five feet to his left. With the rock walls dissolved there were no points of reference for distance.

Distance doesn't work the same in here, John. At least, it doesn't seem to.

You don't know?

It's kind of new for me.

He saw that no part of her face moved while she was speaking, though the light she was casting grew brighter. It was pouring out of her, several beams shining through to his own form, which he noticed was alarmingly dark in comparison.

Am I dead? he asked.

No, she replied, *not yet. You're close, though, and that's why I want to help you. I know you want to see Mags again, and I can help you get to her. But I also want you to get there the right way.*

I'm not dead, but I'm dying?

Yes. And then this will all be over. But we need to make sure you're at peace first. That you're okay with the things that happened to you. There's not much time left. We have a lot to do, John, so I need you to focus. All right?

He nodded in agreement. As her form swayed up and down in his view, the light left glistening trails in both directions.

Good, she said. *I have to explain first. This won't be easy to hear. I have questions and I need honest answers. Can you do that?*

He nodded again, the light trails dancing. Her form sparkled, and the light pulsed through her like brilliant white fire.

***

Lucy told John everything.

She explained to him what she had learned about his self-torture. How he became stuck inside his own fractured consciousness, reliving the days before he had met Margaret Ivers to deny the pain of his memories, the permanent echoes of watching her die from the confines of his own shattered body, and the similarities to Lucy's own loss and grief and denial. How he could not contain those memories indefinitely, and when they resurfaced, how he had constructed Robbie to reset the skipping record of his thought patterns. How Robbie started as a projection of the life he had wanted, then had become a vessel for his crippling guilt, then took on the role of his tormentor, punishing John even as he forced him to face the memories so long repressed.

How, to remove John from the endless cycle of repeating his pre-Mags memories, Robbie had systematically taken everything that gave John stability. Had unmoored his delusions one line at a time, while John became more susceptible and dependent, allowing Robbie to progress his manipulation to the point of no return. To lead John down a path of terror and guilt and pain until there was no way out but through.

His form darkened as she spoke in contrast with her own, the last of his life force fading while hers fed it as if they were connected by spiritual jumper cables. He was passing through before her eyes; she wouldn't keep him tethered much longer. Though she had gained his trust, she still had one undeniable obstacle to delivering the good death he needed. They both needed.

Lucy realized how to get there, to mount this final obstacle and keep him from falling short of the end he deserved.

She would beat Robbie at his own game.

CHAPTER SIXTY-SIX

John was wallowing in deep self-hatred, encompassing enough to distract him from the fantastic things happening to him. But her voice kept coming, pulling him back when he wanted only to slip away, left alone with the fate he deserved.

Robbie was wrong. About a lot, she said.

You just said Robbie wasn't real.

He was real enough. And he was right about some things. He was right to break that cycle, and he was right to push you into facing the past.

He's a fucking gem, isn't he?

But do you know the worst thing he was wrong about?

He should've finished me off himself.

No, no. Listen, okay? He was wrong about blaming you.

I blame me.

That's what I mean. That's wrong. You can't do that.

Just let me go. Can't you stop my heart, or something? Switch me off for good? If anything you've told me is true, you can do that.

I can, I guess. But I don't think you want that. Not really. I know it's not what you need. If I did that, I'd be betraying us both.

It is what I need. What I deserve.

You need to forgive yourself, that's what you need. To stop holding yourself prisoner and admit that her death wasn't your fault.

Shut up and kill me, please.

No. You don't want that end. Not on the level where things are true.

I do. It's all I want now. I don't want to wake up, and if this is the alternative, I don't want this either. I want to die, for it to be over. I want to see her again. I need that.

If you chose that, how would it feel facing her? To tell her you took the easy way out? Did the cowardly thing?

That's not...

Lucy gave him a moment to digest her words.

Right? she said. *I can tell you don't believe me. Not all the way. Call it a part of this whole crazy thing. I can see your doubt. It's like a gray worm inside your head.* She pointed, casting a small beam of light at him. *But even though you doubt, you understand there's a better way. I was the same. I blamed myself for Anna's death right after you were admitted, and I just faced that blame down this... yesterday morning.*

He turned, facing away from her.

That's freedom, John. I've been there. I know what I'm telling you isn't easy, but it's the only way. The best thing. It's what you want. But, unlike me, you don't have to do it alone.

She reached a hand to him and held it there.

Take my hand, and I'll help you get there. You can see Mags again, and you can be proud of what she sees. That's the way I'm choosing for myself now, and I think it's what's best for you too.

No. Put me back in the cave and let me die. It's what I deserve.

What else could you have done? Tell me that.

I could... should have left. I knew it, and I ignored my instinct and she paid the price. She did, damn it. So I need to pay mine.

Why did you stay, then?

What?

You knew you should leave and chose not to. Why?

It was... it was for her. I didn't stay for me, I thought I was doing something right for her. Being who she wanted me to be.

Then be that now, John. Be who she wants you to be now.

I'm not a coward.

It wasn't your fault. You were trying to help someone that needed help. You chose to be a better person for the sake of someone else. And you're blaming yourself for what happened?

That's not the way—

It is. Yes, it is the way. You can see that too. But you aren't letting go of the blame. Let it go, John.

She held her hand closer to him, her light flowing while his ebbed. She saw a drop of brightness run down his dark cheek like an impossible tear. *Come full circle. It's time.*

For a few beats, he didn't move, and her hand stayed. She watched as his face contorted and the gray sliver in his head worked around, like a snake excited by a disturbance in its nest. It grew thinner as if stretching out longer. Thinner still. Then it was gone.

John looked at her, deep into her bright eyes.

It's time, she repeated, smiling.

He reached his hand out.

Lucy pushed the sum of her focus toward him, waiting for their hands to touch. When they did, she would hold tight and pull him out, like she had talked a suicide jumper back from the ledge.

Her fingers were inches from his when another patient's death cry came at her like a runaway truck.

A woman inside the building was dying at that precise moment. She shrieked from surprise, grasping for firm ground as her life force left her. Lucy had enough time to realize that her physical body was defenseless.

Then the cry struck her and she shattered through the ice.

CHAPTER SIXTY-SEVEN

Mommy? A voice floated to Lucy from the void. *You're okay, Mommy. You're okay.*

Lucy registered this voice, but found no context around it. Crippling disorientation weighed on her like a wet coat, and a slick pain ebbed from side to side in her head. She had no eyes, no hands. Could not feel her... self, her *being*. She was a mind with no vessel, her consciousness escaping like air released through a crack in a pressurized chamber.

Unseen, her body crumpled to the drying ground next to the wheelchair. Her neck twitched violently, jerking her head toward one shoulder again and again. Her mouth was open. John's withered body was deathly still next to her.

Remember what you told me? Anna's sweet, lilting, detached voice continued.

Lucy felt a drifting, a sense of leaving her body farther and farther behind. Like she had become detached from outside a space station and was wafting toward a cold and lonely infinity.

You said, "Sometimes, if we open up too far, hurtful things can come in."

Blackness swirled around Lucy like ink in water. It swarmed and pulsed as she drifted, blocking out everything.

Except Anna's voice.

It was there like a tether. Lucy reached for it. Pulling.

And when that happens, the right thing to do, Anna spoke.

Lucy listened and pulled. The swirling black was now pierced by a winding stream of silver light, like a river painted on black canvas.

—is to not close up.

Lucy tried to speak back, to finish what Anna was saying. Because she *did* remember those words. *Her* words. Her daughter. Her self.

If we close up, Anna and Lucy's voices in tandem now, *what happens is we block the good out too. Then we shrink.*

Lucy pulled on this tether, her anchor, her Anna, leaving behind that sense of drifting. A firmness came to her, like her form were a ripening fruit. She was the bloom and Anna's voice the vine. Feeding life, awareness, sanity back into her.

Be strong. Stay open. And get up. Get up, Mommy.

Get up.

Lucy got up.

CHAPTER SIXTY-EIGHT

Drawing strength from her daughter's voice echoing her own past words, Lucy forced herself back into place. That strange place where she had been a few moments ago, a being of light, without edges, crooning to John to let himself go.

She saw his eyes reform like blown dandelions in reverse. His face followed, translucent and frail and darkening. She was not too late. Very close, but still time left to bring him back.

His glass-like face questioning, and his voice came through, asking if she was all right.

Okay, she answered in a weak tone. *I'm okay... now.*

What happened?

A... collision, she answered, falling back on Scarlett's analogy of the road leading both into and out of herself.

I was reaching, and you just... you disappeared. Blinked out like a light, almost. I was alone again. Scared. How did you get back?

I heard her, John. I heard Anna. I think part of me was... was shoved to the... other side, and she sent me back.

She was there? Like she was waiting for you?

Yes. I think so. And I think that means—

—Mags is too, he finished.

Lucy nodded, trails of bright white light flowing around her like blond hair underwater.

Ready? she asked, holding her hand out, palm up.

He reached his hand toward hers.

When they touched, his hand in hers (which was somehow larger), Lucy was overcome by that sense of weightiness again. The high-dive feeling of an impending plummet and the mind's preparation for what followed.

This time, she chose not to resist it. She held onto John's hand in a true death grip.

A rush of sound came, like an inverted waterfall.

They both held their breath and closed their eyes in unison.

From *Passing Through, Thoughts on Death and Dying* by Lucille Claremont, RN (p. 225).

"Final Minutes":

As with earlier stages of dying, the final stage can be best observed through changes in major bodily functions. This is logical, as the physical body is the epicenter of the process, the part that is dying. When life leaves the body, it is most often displayed through the final breaths.

Accordingly, the ultimate breaths become more pronounced and separated, with abnormally large gaps between them. So much so that the inexperienced viewer is prone to thinking the process has stopped prematurely. The second- or third-last exhalation is often mistaken for the final breath.

When breathing has ceased, the non-physical part of the dying person has completed its passage from this world. It has become separated from the body, unencumbered by a vessel that is no longer needed.

Chapter Sixty-Nine

Lucy came to first, opening her eyes to see morning near. The sun had not yet crested but the dark was waning. A few errant bird chirps replaced the nightly cricket song. The security lights had turned off. Her earthly senses continued realigning. Her bearings returned, and she looked upward, through the canopy of trees covering them. The rain had stopped, the storm clouds were breaking up. She wished she had checked the time when they'd come outside, to know how long they'd been in that... other place.

Next to her, John gasped, his withered body trembling in the chair. They were holding hands here too. She looked down, her left clasped over his right, and saw his pulling free and swinging in a tight semi-circle, his range of motion severely limited. He took her hand in his now, and even with its shrunken, atrophied, malnourished quality, his was larger than hers on this side of reality.

One of his eyes came open, partway, giving a sleepy quality to his gaze. The right, closest to her. He moved it around in a slow, confused way. He was searching.

"I'm here," she said. "I'm right here."

The corner of his mouth curled, near-unnoticeable.

"I…" he pushed through mummified throat tissue. His voice was a croak twisted by premature age and disuse. Lucy heard it more in her mind than in her ears. "… hear birds."

"Yes," she said, sounding overwhelmed and croaky herself. "Yeah, John. There are birds."

"Thank you," he whispered. His breathing was getting shallower with each exhale. She felt the weakness of his pulse through the back of her fingers as he held them tight.

"No," she said, and he twitched his eye up to her face. She wondered if he saw anything but haze. He was likely just following the sound, but maybe he saw her enough. She wanted him to. To see a caring face. "Not just yet, you don't."

His eyebrows became a V, forehead crumpled in a questioning but shaky look.

"You have to say it. I need you to say it out loud, so I know you mean it."

The questioning look stayed, his open eye moving up and down. Searching again.

"Tell me it wasn't your fault, John. Tell me that before you go."

He stopped breathing. For a moment, she cringed, then her years of training and practice guided her.

His breath came back, and he opened his mouth, slight enough to mouth words. He stopped breathing again.

"Louder, John. I need to hear it."

He did, showing great effort. The words were stilted, staccato, but growing in volume as they passed.

"It was... not... my fault," he said.

"What wasn't?"

"Mags's... death..." He breathed out. Then used his final inhalation to give voice to his last three words, so he was pulling them into himself rather than releasing them to the world. There was a strength to them that made Lucy's chest swell.

"... not... my fault," he told himself. His last breath came out, and he grew still.

Lucy sat with him, holding his hand, and crying as the sun came up.

Epilogue

Not many flowers was her first thought upon arriving. *Not many people either* followed close. She walked down the center aisle, passing a cluster of people she assumed were related to him in some distant way. There were some faint resemblances in their faces, causing Lucy's guard to raise briefly. No matter, they wouldn't recognize her because she had not been caught.

In a giant stroke of luck, it was Rick that had found them in those woods once the sun came up, John's withered body limp and still in her arms. His first reaction was shock, which she understood. When her tear-filled eyes met Rick's, his face had softened under the flood of realization and he told her he'd help any way he could. Providing she promised not to knee him in the crotch again.

She had refused to leave John, could not abandon him out there. Then Rick convinced her of two things. First, that he could, and *should* take over for her. She was not abandoning anyone, had done everything John needed her to do already. Rick would stay with John until others arrived, and John would never be alone again. And second, if she was caught, her motives would be impossible for anyone else to understand, and the consequences would be too steep to recover from. He had pleaded with her to consider the charges she would face, and for the first time since this all had started, she did. Because John was legally incapacitated, and his family could not be contacted, he was assigned a caseworker to serve as his legal guardian. That person would surely not consent to his being removed from life support and taken outside the facility by a stranger. This meant Lucy could be charged with kidnapping, and probably manslaughter, too, unless she could somehow prove that he would have died with or without her intervention. Add to that breaking and entering, assault, and likely a few others. This was the best-case scenario, because her own medical knowledge could be held against her. Then it wouldn't be manslaughter they charged her with, but homicide, on the basis that she knew her actions would result in his death. Finally, she would never be granted her license back; could never help anyone else the way she'd helped John.

Still, it took coaxing, but eventually she had left, once Rick had forgiven her for the trouble she caused him. It felt like she was fleeing a sinking ship until she sent a probe back to Rick and saw that, as he'd promised, everything John needed her for was over.

Through Rick's eyes she saw hospital staff wheeling a gurney across the grass near the building's exit. On it was a body bag.

Walking home, she had wept, reflecting on her last moments with John before he passed through and replaying his final words over and over while her chest swelled with warmth, and feeling every bit the hero from Anna's comic book cover.

When she arrived home, she had collapsed on her daughter's bed and slept for sixteen hours.

She had debated fiercely with herself if coming today was a good idea, and deciding that she needed to. She needed to see him one more time, to say goodbye, and to thank him.

They all smiled, these quasi-relatives at John's visitation, a few even laughing. That extra part of her brain told her they were gossiping about him and swapping outdated and embarrassing stories. Lucy wouldn't let herself tune in any closer. She didn't want to "hear" those stories but got a sense these people had no longer known him. They walked outside, surely had seen the anger-colored glance she sent their way.

She was alone with him. For the first time since Rick had found them. Sunlight scattered in through stained glass on both sides of her. The silence was complete.

Before approaching the casket, Lucy decided (stalling tactic) to sift visually through the few small plants that had arrived. One from the hospital—she recognized the card and saw familiar signatures decorating it. *Doctors have such terrible handwriting,* she thought. It was a universal truth of medicine. White lilies, they practically had them on standing order at the florist. So much death surrounding her life, yet it was a helpful notion that it could still affect her. She was not numb. That was good. Very good.

Next to that was a colorful assortment provided by the funeral home. She recognized the verse, had seen it countless times: "Come to Me, all who are weary and heavy-laden, and I will give you rest." She thought it was from Matthew, but was not positive. It wasn't information she had considered useful over the past few years.

He had been weary. And heavy-laden. God had he ever. So had she.

The third arrangement was clearly delivered on the wrong day, the card attached was for a "Dearest Aunt CeCe and Uncle Fred." A large and ostentatious wreath, implying the signature of a relative with far more cash than concern. Lucy almost laughed out loud at that one and was glad to have not disturbed the silence lying around them. John would have thought it funny too.

The last was a single dandelion in a glass Coke bottle. She'd brought that one. It was from Scarlett. Lucy's first stop after waking in Anna's bed had been to the overpass where they had met. Scarlett wasn't there, though. No sign of her except the flower in the bottle on her battered orange recliner and a note that said "keep building the highway" in scrawled and smeared handwriting. Lucy had been doing that, and it was working. Practice gave way to habit and was solidifying into reflex.

She crossed the last few feet between them and cried without sound. No need to mar the silence, it was soothing. His suit was gray, with soft blue checks, hardly noticeable but accented by the yellow and light-blue striped tie. His clothing didn't fit now, though it must have once, before the dozens of months that his body had spent deteriorating.

That body looked unfamiliar, as the dead always do. She saw traces of him, elements recognizable in a basic way, but there was no mistaking the lack of John's presence. This version of his face had been drained of life, of soul. He had left behind this fragile and broken vessel.

Had *Passed through*.

A small sound escaped her, and she extended a hand to touch his cheek. It was helpful to see him at peace; this had not been true in any of her previous experiences. She had seen so many rooms inside of so many funeral homes, but found a deep appreciation now for the ability to view his remains covered in formal attire and the plush interior of his casket. His many frailties and ailments were no more, all evidence of their existence either hidden or completely erased.

She needed to see him this way. Any past attendance at her patients' visitations had done little to soothe her conscience, whereas this one truly helped. She stood for several minutes, grateful for their time together. All of it. Then she sat in the back row for nearly two hours without moving or speaking. No one else came to see him, only the home's ushers who filled in as pallbearers.

She followed to the cemetery, not part of the short procession but close behind. She stood at a distance as oft-repeated and impersonal words were spoken at the site. Watched as he was interred. Waited until the few indifferent relatives and onlookers dispersed, turning away from this minor inconvenience to resume their routines. Waited some time longer, feeling the sun caressing her neck playfully. A mild breeze drifted through and she sighed. Waited a few more minutes still, then approached.

Mags's remains occupied the next plot over, thanks to Lucy. She knew that would please him. After Lucy sent an anonymous tip describing the scene, they found where Mags had been left. A hound had sniffed her remains out in the woods within a half mile of where she was shot. Buried shallow, badly decayed, but identifiable. And full of clues. From the news reports, they were close to making an arrest.

In a dose of fate, they were buried only a few dozen feet from Anna's grave.

Lucy stood at the pair of stones.

On her left:

Margaret Lynn Ivers
1983–2010
Taken too soon

On her right:

Johnathan Robert Camden
1982–2014
Reunited at last

Lucy came close to speaking before settling on the futility of it. She stood offering her presence. A glimmer of light flashed in her periphery. She looked down, briefly saw her right forearm glowing as it had when she and John were together in... the other place. Fleeting though it was, there was proof he had not "passed through" completely. There was a slight flutter, starting in her chest and winding its way outward. Stronger than one other presence. They were with her together now, both of them.

Then it passed. The flutter faded. The light on her arm now was only that cast by the warm early afternoon sun.

Lucy turned to walk away, and something else caught in her view. White, striking soundly enough to cause a brief double take. The bark of the birch tree, one she recognized from her visits to Anna's grave. It symbolized death to her, but now it also meant self-forgiveness.

This particular tree was exactly where it belonged. As though she agreed with the decision (be it nature's or some unknown landscapers, perhaps even a mischievous squirrel) that this spot in this cemetery in this town warranted a singular notation. A unique landmark amidst all the other tales of tragedy, misery, and release.

She returned to her car. As she drove away, she saw the birch tree in her side-view mirror and watched it. Her eyes did not leave it until the horizon swallowed all that mystic white bark. Lucy drove on, passing the ornate cemetery gates and turning toward a new and very different horizon.

That verse, the one she had read on the sympathy card, was floating in her head, and she examined it several times. With that came the renewed intention to finish compiling all of her thoughts on death and on the process of dying.

She even had an idea for the dedication page: "To John, whose death gave me new life."

A smile grew on her face as she drove.

END

stuck: *adjective*

1–confined, trapped or unable to move

2–unable to find a solution or resolve a problem

3–resigned to an unpleasant situation one cannot avoid

4–infatuated with, unable to remove one's attention from

Afterword

I know, I know. These afterwords are usually self-indulgent drivel (no exception here), but there're some things I'd like to say to those of us with big dreams, and this seems the place. I doubt I'll do one of these again, so here goes.

I first decided to write a book in the summer of 2009. At the time, I was newly married and working in what felt like a dead-end job which was also very unfulfilling. Writing seemed like a potential way out (of the job, not the marriage). It had appealed to me as far back as I could remember, but I lacked confidence and I didn't know where to start. One day, I used my lunch break to go to Waldenbooks (this may have been my very last visit to that childhood staple, come to think of it), where I bought a paperback copy of *Carrie* by Stephen King for $8.51. I still have the receipt, though it's a bit hard to read now. I'd considered myself a semi-Constant Reader since grade school, yet had never read his breakout hit book, and in a sort of naive desperation, I was viewing it as a roadmap to living out my new dream of becoming a "Published Writer." This younger version of me thought that if he did a few of the things young Mr. King had done, he might actually get Published, and if he could get Published he may just become a Writer, and then naturally, all would be right with the world.

Idiot.

I recall going back to that crummy job and telling myself over and over (especially when it was *extra* crummy) "it's okay, because I bought my ticket out." That became a mantra over the next few years as I struggled to rise above that job, while little changed.

Today, I can staunchly confirm that this younger me was delusional. Not because of his dream, of course. Because of his unrealistic expectations and absurd plan. But, the writing bug sunk its teeth in and has not left since.

The first version of this book was terrible, and in a further act of naivete, I started blindly querying literary agents with it to see what would happen.

Today, I can staunchly confirm that nothing happened as a result of those queries. (Luckily though, the job wasn't as dead-end as it seemed and life has been very good to me.)

Years passed, during which I pursued more legitimate methods of becoming a writer and getting published. You know, as opposed to picking up a book in a bookstore and thinking I could somehow use it to emulate Stephen King (which I had since realized was wholly unrealistic for a score of reasons, but was also nowhere near as clever or unique a dream as I wanted it to be). Then I threw out my completed manuscript for *Stuck* and rewrote it from scratch. I think it's somewhere less-than terrible now, and hopefully you do, too. Following that, I queried some more, and again failed to get it published through traditional methods. More than once, my wife suggested I self-publish, but I let fear stop me from listening to her or exploring that option.

My desire to be a writer went dormant, and life went on.

Then, last fall, came Books of Horror, a Facebook group my wife kept telling me about. She insisted I join, and I politely declined (a few times) because I have no fondness for social media. As usual, she proved herself wiser and talked me into it.

Today, I can staunchly confirm that Books of Horror has enabled me to achieve my long-held dream of being a Published Writer. It showed me that the indie horror community is thriving and that there is an ocean of support for self-published authors. I found myself aspiring to self-publish, instead of fearing it.

So, here we are, fourteen years *to the day* since that trip to Waldenbooks (yes, I checked the date on that faded receipt and no, I didn't plan to write this on the anniversary, I swear it just happened). My copy of *Carrie* is almost old enough for the prom. I've taken some lumps and learned a few harsh, valuable lessons in that time. But I haven't given up, and we'll see what happens next. I suppose if there's a point I'm trying to make, it's this:

Stay self-aware, listen to trusted advice, and do not give up.

Don't you ever give up.

-Ben Young
August 7th, 2023

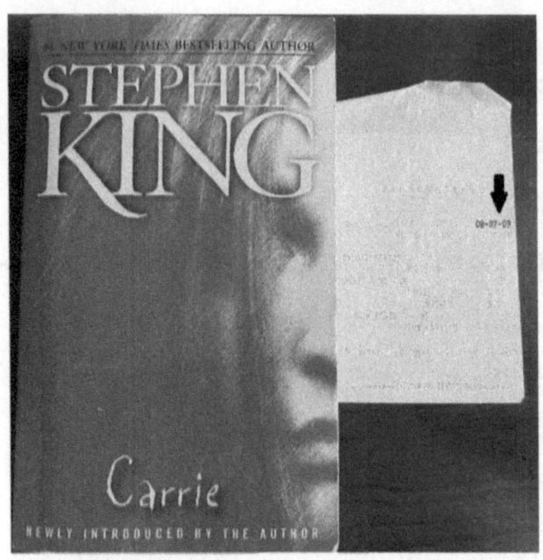

My self-styled $8.51 "ticket" to success, and the faded Waldenbooks receipt, dated 08-07-09

Acknowledgements

It's well-documented that writing is a solo trek, and that's a large reason why it appeals to me. I do well solo. But there's a point on that trek where you decide if you want to keep the story to yourself or share it with others. Doing the latter is the opposite of solo, it takes a lot of people to pull that off. I want to thank everyone who joined me on this trek, but will try to impose some brevity (my way of excusing myself for omissions or oversights, which I'm sure I've made and hereby apologize for).

My wife, Lauren who never left my side (even for the solo parts). My son Welles, who was born toward the trek's end, but has the constant enthusiasm to "help" that you'd expect at his age (and supplies endless creepy artwork). I love you both and strive to make you proud.

My parents, Mike and Tina, who always found money to buy me more books, my siblings Jenni, Mikie, Sarah, Danny, and the other members of the "M Young Mafia," who are each both family and friend. I love you all and should have added you to the trek much sooner.

James, my best friend since high school, who unwittingly joined the trek early on, via bits of several main characters. I love you and I'm proud of you (sorry, but it needed sayin').

Lauren Humphries-Brooks and Danielle Yeager for making the trek far more enjoyable for readers. Ruth Anna Evans for hanging up a creepy sign at the trailhead. Barbara Drake for her medical expertise and input (any mistakes remaining are fully mine). My beta readers for guiding me around a cliff or two, and clearing the brush off the path.

Everyone in Books of Horror (King RJ, the admins, authors, and readers) for dragging me back onto the path when I needed it most. The dozens of authors I've met through BoH who, despite being further down the path, were each quick to turn back and lend a hand. Edmund Stone, my informal mentor and friend. John Durgin, who makes it all look easy and answered questions upon questions. Jason Myers, who took a shot on a story submitted by an unpublished author with a boring name.

And, in no particular order, for your advice, insight, encouragement, and feedback as I stumbled and sought better footing: M Ennenbach, Candace Nola, Alex Ebenstein, Scott Kenemore, James Markert, Laurel Hightower, Todd Keisling, Lyndsey Smith, Jonathan Janz, Ronald Malfi, Andrew Van Wey, Joe X. Young, Debra Castaneda, Justin Boote, Kim Rei, Robert Essig, Ben Farthing, Gage Greenwood, Damien Casey, Paul Lubaczewski, Lucy Leitner, Aron Beauregard, Daniel Volpe, Alexandra Nisneru. Some of our interactions were fleeting, others were indirect, and even if you may not recall helping me, I remember it well, and thank you for it.

Leigh Kenny, Erica Wetzel-Fields, and Bernie Kennedy, my first actual fans. I'm beyond grateful for your support, and thrilled to have you on the path with me.

And to every reader choosing to join me on the trek. I'm glad you're here, and hope you'll hang around for the next leg. It promises to be terrifying for us both, but if we stick together, we just might make it.

Ben lives in the Cincinnati, OH area with his family and dogs, where he is slowly working on another novel or two, along with a prickly smattering of shorter works which may or may not ever see the light of day.

Stuck is his first novel.

He does not like writing about himself, particularly in the third person like this, even if it is considered *de rigueur* (which he just had to Google).

Find him online at *www.benyoungstories.com*

(Oh, and whatever you do, please don't *follow him on social media*. He hates that.)